MA

RAVE REVIEWS
FOR WILLIAM RELLING JR.!

"Relling tells a story well and . . . has a successful career ahead."

—*St. Louis Post-Dispatch*

"Relling is a fine stylist. . . . One of the best writers currently working in this vein, Relling invariably delivers excellent excitement."

—*Locus*

"In an age of splatter and special effects, Bill Relling Jr. is proving himself a true craftsman of the horror story . . . sly, shocking and memorable."

—Graham Masterton, author of *Spirit*

"Relling is a writer of imagination, scope, and dramatic power, and above all a storyteller who's always a pleasure to read."

—Matthew J. Costello

"I was more often touched than horrified, and happily so, for I read fiction to be moved. Relling did not disappoint me."

—Chet Williamson, author of *Second Chance*

ANOTHER ONE

The deputy stepped over next to Rachel, shining his light toward the base of a line of trees. Rachel trained her light on the same spot. They were joined by the other deputy, who did likewise. "That look like anything to either of you?" the first deputy said.

Something was there, all but hidden under a pile of leaves, reflecting the beams from their flashlights back to them. They came forward as a group, letting their lights guide them to the trees. When they were close enough to see what was lying on the ground, Rachel could feel blood pounding in her ears.

She was staring down at the dead face of a small boy. His body was wrapped in thick, clear plastic. The body had been given a cursory burial beneath a pile of wet leaves. . . .

WILLIAM RELLING JR.

THE CRIMINALIST

LEISURE BOOKS NEW YORK CITY

To Jill Relling Knobbe,
one half of another great brother-sister team.

A LEISURE BOOK ®

November 2003

Published by

Dorchester Publishing Co., Inc.
200 Madison Avenue
New York, NY 10016

ISBN 0-8439-5278-4

The name "Leisure Books" and the stylized "L" with design are trademarks of Dorchester Publishing Co., Inc.

Printed in the United States of America.

Visit us on the web at www.dorchesterpub.com.

THE
CRIMINALIST

APRIL

CHAPTER ONE

Jennifer Boyle was thinking, *If I hear one more kid ask me when it's time to eat, I'm going to scream.*

She was taping down the last of the paper table-cloths that she had spread atop the four picnic tables in the open clearing. Aware that her day was not even half over yet, she was already feeling exhausted. She whispered to herself ruefully, "Like George of the Jungle, you knew the job was dangerous when you took it, Jen."

She wondered what she could have been thinking when she had agreed to chaperon the sixth-grade class of St. Matthew's School on an excursion to Sugar Creek State Park. Sister Gina Dinelli, the sixth-grade teacher, had asked her personally—for two reasons Jen could think of. First of all, her son, Teedie (which was how the boy's four-year-old sister, Kristen, had pronounced Theodore when she was a baby), was a member of the class. Second, Sister Gina knew that Jen was a soft touch. Whenever there was any kind of class function—a dance, a field trip, a party—Jen could be counted on to drive the kids or make cakes and cookies for a bake sale or provide refreshments for class socials.

Jennifer sighed. She'd been up since six A.M., when she got out of bed to make breakfast for her husband, Jim. She'd had to awaken him to make sure that he wasn't late for his eight-o'clock meeting. He worked as an attorney for one of the larger law firms in San Jose, fifty miles north of San Patricio via freeway, and if he was going to be on time it meant being on the road by seven. Then she rousted Teedie and Kristen, fed them, and saw to it that they, too, were properly dressed and ready to go.

She loaded the kids into her Ford Explorer, dropped Kristen off at the day-care center, and drove Teedie to school. She waited there until nine-fifteen, when the kids in Sister Gina's class dashed out of the school building into the parking lot to climb aboard the bus that took them on their way.

The group left St. Matthew's for their first stop, the San Patricio Mission. They stayed at the mission for an hour, and it was not particularly a great thrill for Jen, who believed that if you'd seen one old California Spanish-built mission you'd seen them all. Then they'd gone out of the city, north along Highway 9 to Sugar Creek State Park, where following a picnic lunch Sister Gina would lead a hike through the redwoods, while Mrs. Boyle cleaned up the leftover mess.

Jen looked at her watch and saw that it was just eleven o'clock. She sighed again to herself, with mock displeasure.

Then she smiled, because she really didn't mind this at all. She actually enjoyed helping out with Teedie's class, and she liked Sister Gina a lot. Teedie's teacher was in her early thirties, not much younger than Jen herself. Sister Gina was also much more vi-

4

vacious than Teedie's fifth-grade teacher, Sister Monica, who, Jen thought, was a sour old bat. Sister Gina loved to take the kids out into the world—to museums and to the theater (last month to a special matinee performance of *The Wiz* at nearby UC San Patricio). One time she even took them all the way to Monterey—an hour's drive south from San Patricio—to explore the wonderful Monterey Bay Aquarium. Sister Gina did things like that all the time.

Consequently, Jen's bitching about being such a sucker was mostly a sham. *Just my human nature*, she told herself. She could hear the kids running around the trees, shouting at each other, screeching, laughing. It was such a happy-sounding cacophony that, in spite of her fatigue, Jen couldn't help smiling again.

Sister Gina had picked a gorgeous day for the class excursion. The sun was bright and high and the air quite warm. Though here, nestled in the shadow of the tall trees, surrounded by cool dark greens and browns, the air seemed to hold just a hint of crispness. It smelled wonderful: a strong, woodsy, clean scent touched with a hint of decaying leaves and musty earth. The aroma was invigorating.

After she'd finished with the tablecloths, Jen joined Sister Gina, who was tending the fire in the stone barbecue pit in the middle of the picnic grounds. They had gotten the kids to help unload the bus of the three Coleman coolers filled with fruit and vegetables and potato chips and apple juice and soda pop and hot dogs and soy burgers. The latter were for the eight members of Teedie's class who were vegetarians—who, on more than one occasion, had caused Jen to think, *How northern California can you get?* Twelve-year-old vegetarians—did that say San Patricio all over it, or didn't it?

While Jen helped Sister Gina with the fire, several of the girls in the class were arranging paper plates and cups and plastic knives and forks at each of twenty settings—eighteen kids and the two adults. On the tables the girls spread open packages of buns and laid out plastic bottles of ketchup and mustard. They unsealed Tupperware bowls filled with cut pieces of celery and carrots and radishes, piled plates with apples and oranges and bananas, opened bags of Fritos and potato chips and jars of pickles. By the time the girls were finished, Sister Gina was laying meat and soy burgers on the hot grill, filling the air with pungent smoke.

Minutes later she was shouting for the kids to come in and eat. Jen watched the young nun, who was dressed in blue jeans and a Loyola University sweat-shirt and waffle-stomper hiking boots. As Sister Gina called in her brood of sixth graders, Jennifer was smiling broadly. *Those kids just love her*, she thought.

The ravenous horde descended. Soon the picnic area was filled with the sound of children squealing happily. They grabbed their plates and fell into a single-file line, as directed by Sister Gina, so they could march up to the pit and place their orders to Mrs. Boyle: no more than two hot dogs or soy burgers per person.

Once the children were all sitting, Sister Gina stood in the middle of the clearing, crossed herself, and led everyone in saying grace. Presently Jennifer was moving from table to table, pouring from a pitcher of lemonade and listening to a continuous repetition of "Thank you, Mrs. Boyle."

At last she came to a table where there were nothing but boys—Teedie's cadre of friends, the ones he referred to as the "cool dudes." And for the first time, Jennifer noticed that her son was the only kid in the entire class who didn't seem to be around.

She frowned, trying to remember whether she had seen Teedie waiting in line for food, or heading into the outhouse rest room nearby, or anywhere else since Sister Gina had called the kids in to eat. Jen thought that she had—but she couldn't be sure, what with all of the activity swirling around, the kids running and whooping while she was busy with her own duties.

Jennifer knelt at the end of the boys' table, next to Paul Lauber, Teedie's best friend. "Paul," she said, careful to keep any trace of reprobation out of her voice, "where's Teedie?"

The boy looked away for a moment, and Jen thought that she saw him frown. Then he turned back to her and said, "I dunno, Mrs. Boyle."

Jen smiled what she hoped was a don't-worry-he's-not-in-any-trouble smile. "I haven't seen him for a while," she said. "Was he with you guys out in the woods?"

"Yeah."

"So? Did he come back with you or what?"

The other boys had stopped eating and were looking at Jen and Paul. She could read on their faces that something wasn't right, and she could feel her stomach begin to tighten. "C'mon, you guys," she said. "Where's Teedie?"

A voice from over Jen's shoulder said sternly, "What's the matter?"

Sister Gina had come up behind Paul. She was

standing there, hands on hips, looking concerned. Jen stood up and said to the teacher, "I was trying to find out if any of the boys had seen Teedie."

Sister Gina looked from Paul to the rest of the boys. "Where is he, you guys?" Her tone was authoritative but friendly.

One of the boys—John O'Keefe—blurted, "He made us promise, Sister—"

John caught himself when he noticed the other boys glaring at him.

Sister Gina said, "Promise what?"

"We can't, Sister," Paul said. "We promised we wouldn't tell. He said he'd be back before anybody even knew he was gone."

Jen could see Sister Gina switching into serious mode. The teacher moved to the end of the table, leaning on it with both hands. "He's not back yet, boys, is he? So your promise doesn't hold anymore, does it?" She paused. "Now where's Teedie?"

At last, Paul told her.

CHAPTER TWO

Teedie Boyle couldn't believe it. Not one of the cool dudes—not Paul or Greg Miller or Joey Romano or John O'Keefe—had the nerve to come with him. After he'd sworn to them that the last time he'd been to the park—with his dad, less than a month before—Teedie had actually seen some high school guy porking his girlfriend a little ways up from the stream that ran through the middle of the woods. The couple had been on the ground underneath a tree, both of them bare-assed, and the guy was on top of the girl humping away.

Teedie couldn't believe the cool dudes didn't want to go and check out the spot for themselves, just because it was too far away from where Sister Gina and Teedie's mom were setting out lunch. As he made his way alone through the woods toward the creek, he was thinking, *Cool dudes my butt. What a bunch of wimps*.

"Sister's gonna be callin' us back any minute," O'Keefe had said.

Teedie shrugged. "So what?"

"So she told us not to go too far off," said Romano.

9

"What's'a matter with you guys?" Teedie whined. "You don't believe me, is 'at it? You don't believe I saw 'em, is 'at right?"

Paul Lauber was shaking his head. "Nobody's gonna be there today."

Teedie shot back, "Yeah, but they *might* be."

"What about your mom?" Miller said. "Won't she be pissed if we all of a sudden just disappear?"

"Who's gonna know?" Teedie snapped. "I'm not gonna tell her. And none of you guys're gonna tell her. Right?"

Before anyone could answer, they heard Sister Gina calling for them to come in for lunch. O'Keefe and Miller and Romano turned around and started back for the picnic area. Paul hesitated for a moment before turning to follow the other boys.

"Hey, wait a minute!" Teedie shouted to their backs. "Hey!"

Paul called over his shoulder, "C'mon, dude! Time to eat!"

"Forget it!" Teedie shouted back. "I'm goin' down there! The rest of you guys're just chicken. . . ." He began to flap his arms. "Bukkk-bukkk-bukk-bukk-bu-kaawwwwwwwk!"

But none of them turned around to come back. Not even Paul.

Teedie watched them going off toward the picnic area. He scowled, then spun on his heel and headed away in the opposite direction. "Screw 'em," he muttered under his breath as he climbed down an overgrown path through the brush, holding his arms out to either side of him to keep his balance. The path was trampled along the side of a hill that sloped sharply, angling downward toward a gurgling stream less than twenty yards away.

Teedie emerged from the woods into bright sunlight. The cool clamminess that had enveloped his skin when he was in shadow evaporated. The creek lay directly ahead of him. Sunlight shone off the clear water like it was coming off a mirror. He raised one hand to his forehead to shade his eyes from the glare.

Then he saw it, that quickly, much to his genuine surprise. Across the creek on the other side, almost out of sight, hidden in the brush, was a flash of something nearly white, the color of pale flesh.

Teedie broke into a leering grin. For a moment he considered calling out to his friends, then decided against it. *You guys blew it*, he thought. *Don't say I didn't give you a chance.*

He crouched, moving as surreptitiously as possible, all the while keeping his eyes on the flash of white. He couldn't tell yet what it was exactly, whether it was male or female, or how many people, or even if they were moving, because the brush kept blocking his view. But that was good, because it meant they couldn't see him either.

He kept out of sight, going several yards past the spot, until he came to a bend where the water narrowed to shallows and the tops of several rocks lay exposed. He glanced over and saw that he was out of sight of whoever was on the other side.

He slipped out of the brush and scampered across the creek, approaching the spot as silently as he could. In his mind's eye he could visualize the guy and the girl he and his father had caught only a few weeks ago. Remembering that Dad had been just as turned on by the experience as he was, Teedie re-

11

minded himself that he would have to tell his father about this discovery as well.

He pushed aside the brush, and his eyes widened as he saw what lay there. It was a body, all right. But it still had on all its clothes. And it wasn't a grown-up's body, either, but the body of a young boy who was about the same size as Teedie himself.

The boy was not alive.

The body lay partially covered by leaves, as if someone had attempted a perfunctory burial. The boy's exposed flesh was almost translucent. The head lay twisted at an odd angle, and the neck was dark with ugly bruises. The face was turned toward Teedie, who was staring, frozen, from the bushes. Birds had gotten to the face. The flesh had been pecked and torn, and the eye directed toward Teedie was ripped from its socket, leaving a gaping, blood-crusted hole.

Teedie stood there until something in his mind told him what it was he had found, and then he began to scream.

Then he was running, splashing through the water of the stream, scrambling onto the bank on the other side, imagining that the ruined face floated in front of him, seeing the gaping sockets where its eyes had been. Blindly he pushed his way through the brush that tore at his arms and whipped at his legs, all the while screaming.

Because he could hear footsteps.

The footsteps were behind him, pursuing. The sound so stoked the boy's fright that it felt to him as if his heart would burst in his chest. He heard the footsteps, was vaguely aware of a voice that pursued him as well, but could only tell himself to run . . . to run . . . to run. . . .

Until he stumbled and fell.

He tripped over the exposed root of a huge tree and went flying through the air, twisting his right leg awkwardly. He landed hard, hearing a sickening snap, then feeling the sharp pain between his ankle and knee, a fiery agony that, when he tried to push himself back up to his feet, immediately sent him collapsing to the ground.

His leg hurt so badly that it burned. He reached down and could feel the lump beneath his jeans where the broken bone was jutting against the inside of his skin.

In that instant he knew that he would never get away. He knew that whoever it was that had killed the boy whose body he'd found was going to get him, too.

The footsteps were much closer.

Teedie bit his lower lip hard to keep himself from crying out and revealing where he was. But it did no good. He screamed one final time.

Everything began to whirl. Bright spots of dappled sunlight pierced the canopy of trees and kaleidoscoped onto each other. He lay down on the ground, dimly aware of a gray shape that had suddenly materialized above him. He sucked in his breath as the shape bent down and its features became more distinct, forming into the face of someone he knew. He whispered aloud, surprised at the sound of his own voice: "Sister . . ."

"Shhh, Teedie," Sister Gina was saying gently. "It's all right. Everything's all right."

"All right," he parroted, thinking, *Thank God, thank God* as he closed his eyes.

CHAPTER THREE

Rachel Siegel returned home from the supermark[e] little after four P.M. that same afternoon, entering house through the rear door that opened into kitchen. She could hear the sound of the televis[ion] faintly, coming from the family room. She recogni[zed] Will Smith's voice: "Oh, I'm sorry . . . was that y[ou] auntie?"

She thought, *Men in Black*. Again. It was her t[wo] sons' favorite movie—especially Aaron's, younger—ever since she and her husband, Roy, bought the boys a copy of the DVD for Christmas year.

She pushed the door open with a knee, hoist[ing] the two sacks of groceries she was holding in arms. Her keys dangled from the back door's lo[ck.] She moved to a counter next to the kitchen sink, down the sacks, and called over her shoulder tow[ard] the family room, "Aaron! Can you come out h[ere] please, and help me!"

A voice shouted back, "It's not Aaron, Mom! [It's] me!"

"I think you'll do, Denny!" she called. *Teenag[ers,]* she thought with exasperation.

14

She looked up to see the elder of her sons standing in the doorway that led from the kitchen into the family room. The crown of Denny's head was less than a foot from the top of the doorjamb—only fourteen years old and already he was as tall as his father. He was chewing on an apple, looking at Rachel with a disgruntled expression, no doubt unhappy about being interrupted in the middle of Agent J's climactic battle with an interstellar cockroach.

" 'Arn it, Mom," Denny said, his mouth full of apple. "It 'uzz 'ust 'ettin' doo duh 'ood part."

"Good grief," she complained. "How many times have you seen that damn movie . . . ?"

Rachel paused when she saw that he was smirking, and she realized that she'd been had. "Don't you know better than to tease your mother?" she said as Denny moved past her to the kitchen door. Still munching his apple, he grinned disarmingly as he went outside.

Rachel was putting eggs into the refrigerator opposite the counter when Denny came back in, one sack on his left shoulder and two more in his right hand. As Rachel took the sacks from him, Denny said, "Chief Novak called."

"He did? When?"

"About quarter to four." Denny had opened a bag of Chips Ahoy and was holding three cookies in his hand.

"Did he say what he wanted?" Rachel asked.

Denny shook his head. "Huh-uh. 'Ust dat ooh should—"

"Please don't talk to me with your mouth full."

Denny swallowed. "Sorry. He just said that you should call him back right away."

15

"Was he home or at the office?"

"The office."

Rachel moved to the sink to wash her hands as Denny took the bag of cookies with him back into the family room. She stepped to the telephone that hung on the wall beside the kitchen door. She lifted the receiver and punched a number. After three rings a male voice grunted to her, "Detectives' squad."

"It's Rachel. Is the chief there?"

"One second, Rachel," the voice replied.

She heard a click, followed by a flat humming, then another click. Then Earl Novak's high-pitched voice was saying to her, in a tone of challenge, "Rachel, where the hell have you been?"

"I was out grocery shopping, Earl," she said. "Denny just now gave me the message—"

"We just got a call on another victim," Novak interrupted sourly.

Rachel stiffened. "When?"

"This afternoon. A bunch of schoolkids and a nun up at Sugar Creek State Park found a body by the creek."

"Male or female?"

"Male. Ten, maybe twelve years old. Can you get out there right away? I've had 'em close off the area. The coroner's on his way to pick it up. I'd like you to get there before they do, while there's still some daylight left."

"I'm on my way," she said.

She hung up the phone and leaned against the kitchen door, frowning darkly, thinking, *Seven. Goddammit, seven kids in four months.*

As Rachel gathered her purse from the kitchen counter, checking to make sure that her keys and her gun were inside, she called toward the family room, "Denny!"

He shouted back, "Yeah?"

"Come in here for a second, will you, please?"

She was reaching for her keys when Denny returned from the family room. He stood in the doorway, looking at her inquiringly.

"I've got to go to work," she said.

"I thought today was your day off."

"So did I, but something's come up. Tell your father when he comes home that he's gonna have to take care of dinner for you and . . ."

She paused.

Rachel was about to say "Aaron" when her skin began to prickle. A cold sensation of panic clutched at her insides. She thought, *It couldn't be.*

"Denny?" she said, trying to keep an edge of panic out of her voice. "Where's your brother?"

"I don't know, Mom. I haven't seen him since this morning."

Rachel moved back into the kitchen, dropped her purse on the counter, and reached for the telephone once more. The number for Aaron's school was written on a list taped to the wall beside the phone. Rachel ran a finger down the list of numbers. "He didn't have a ball game or band practice or anything like that today, did he?"

"Not that I know of," Denny said.

She was punching the number, made a mistake, and muttered, "Damn it." She jabbed down the hook and punched the number again.

Denny said worriedly, "Mom, what's the matter?"

Rachel held up a hand to quiet him as she heard the school secretary's voice in her ear. She said into

17

the phone, "This is Rachel Siegel, Aaron Rodgers's mother—"

Just then she and Denny both turned to the sound of the front door opening and closing. Denny peered around the corner of the kitchen doorway. He looked back to Rachel and said, "He's home."

A moment later Denny stepped aside to let his ten-year-old brother move past him and into the kitchen. Aaron looked up, saw his mother holding the telephone, and paused. The boy's expression was glum.

Rachel sagged with relief. *Thank God,* she thought.

"You need me anymore, Mom?" Denny asked.

Rachel shook her head, and Denny went back into the family room. She then became aware of a tiny voice saying, "Ms. Siegel, are you there?"

It took a moment for the voice to register. Rachel lifted the phone and stammered into it, "Yes . . . I'm sorry. Everything's all right. I'm sorry to have bothered you."

She hung up, then turned back to Aaron. He was holding a white envelope in one hand, looking away from Rachel, his eyes cast downward.

Rachel said, "How come you're so late?"

"I had to stay after school."

"How come?"

"I got in trouble."

"What kind of trouble?"

He shrugged.

"Is that for me?" Rachel asked, pointing to the envelope.

"You *and* Dad," Aaron said. "You both gotta sign it."

"May I see it, please?"

Aaron shuffled over to her like a condemned pris-

18

oner on his way to execution. He handed Rachel the envelope.

Inside was a letter from Mr. Landsburg, Aaron's teacher. Aaron and a couple of his friends had gotten into an eraser fight during noon recess that day, when they were supposed to be policing their classroom. "You gotta sign it," the boy said. "So Mr. Landsburg knows you read it."

Rachel handed the letter back to him. "You're going to have to show this to your father when he gets home," she said.

He looked up at her, his expression anguished. "I have to go to work, honey," she explained.

Aaron nodded sadly.

"I think you'd better go to your room and wait for him," Rachel said.

"Okay, Mom," Aaron said disconsolately.

As she watched him turn away she could feel her heart aching. "Come here," Rachel said. She knelt and reached out for the boy, pulling him close and hugging him tightly.

He kissed her on the cheek and whispered, "I'm sorry I got in trouble."

She pulled away to look into his face. Aaron's wide brown eyes were glistening with tears. *He looks so pathetic*, she thought. She had to force herself to keep from smiling at him.

"Go on," she said, pushing him away gently.

He ran from the kitchen. She listened to his footsteps going up the stairs to the second floor, heading for his bedroom. Rachel rose, picked up her purse, and moved to the door. "I'm leaving, Denny!" she called.

"Okay, Mom!"

"Don't let your brother watch TV! He's being punished!"

"Okay, Mom!"

Closing the door behind her, Rachel went outside to the carport where her Toyota Sienna XLE was parked. The Sienna's back hatch was still open, Denny having neglected to close it after taking out the last of the groceries.

She pushed the hatch shut, stepped around to the driver's side of the minivan, and climbed in. She buckled the seat-belt harness around her shoulder and waist, pulled her keys from her purse, and started the van.

Rachel paused for a moment, telling herself, *Aaron's okay. Everything's okay. Which means it's time to stop thinking like a mom and start thinking like a cop again.* Then she shifted the Sienna into reverse, backed out of the driveway, and drove away.

CHAPTER FOUR

Per the instructions she received from Chief Novak, Rachel drove around the eastern border of Sugar Creek State Park. She turned left into the main entrance at the park's north end. There she was stopped at the entrance by a uniformed deputy sheriff whose patrol car was blocking the road in such a way as to keep out any unauthorized traffic. Rachel braked the Sienna to a halt and reached into her purse, which lay on the seat beside her, as the deputy climbed out of his car to approach hers.

He walked up to the driver's-side window of the station wagon and bent over to poke his head inside. "Sorry, ma'am," the deputy said, "but the park's closed. Sheriff's Department business."

Rachel displayed the leather wallet that held her badge and identification card. "I'm Detective Siegel. Somebody's expecting me."

The deputy glanced at the badge and ID, then stepped away from the minivan. He turned and trotted to his car. Sliding behind the wheel, he started the engine and rolled the car backward, out of Rachel's way, then gave her a small salute as she drove past.

Following signs that directed her to the park head-quarters, Rachel came to a single-story, wood-frame building. Parked before it were three California Park Service jeeps and another Sheriff's Department patrol car. Standing in front of the building, watching as she wheeled to a stop alongside the jeep that was farthest away, were two men. The older of the two was portlier and shorter than the other. The older man also wore the khaki uniform and cap of a San Patricio deputy sheriff. There were sergeant's stripes on the upper left sleeve of his uniform blouse. The other man was slim, bearded, shaggy-haired, and a good two decades younger; he wore Levi's jeans, hiking boots, and the forest-green uniform shirt of a park ranger. A cell phone was attached to his belt.

As Rachel came out of her car and walked over to join the two men, she recognized the deputy: Sgt. Harold Siefert, one of the department's oldest members, both in terms of age and years of service. Siefert was something of a legend, a sharp-eyed buffalo of an old-school-cop who was famous for taking rookie deputies under his care and breaking them in gently—as he had done with Rachel herself more than a dozen years before.

She noticed that Siefert was not wearing his customary smile of greeting—the expression he usually wore whenever he saw her. She could tell by his grim look that whatever was waiting for her, it was not going to be pleasant.

"Hello, Harold." She extended a hand for him to shake. "I'm sorry it took me so long to get here."

He nodded to the other man. "Rachel, this is Charlie Wilson, chief ranger of the park. Ranger, this is Detective Siegel."

Rachel shook the ranger's hand, then turned back to Siefert. "Is it what I think it is?"

Siefert nodded gravely. "I'm afraid so."

CHAPTER FIVE

"This is called Jimson Trail," Wilson was saying to Rachel and Siefert. "It cuts through these redwood trees here and then slopes down to the creek."

"That's where you found the body?" Rachel asked. "By the creek?"

Wilson nodded. "This way."

She and Siefert followed the ranger through a stand of ancient redwoods, staying behind him on the dirt-packed trail. Once they were past the trees, Rachel could hear the murmur of running water. She looked ahead and could see the creek beyond the trees.

Moments later the three of them had reached the bank of the narrow stream. Wilson pointed to a spot about twenty-five yards away. Rachel squinted, and she could see something that was a dingy, yellowish-brown color, contrasting with the deep green of the vegetation on the creek's other side.

She looked to the ranger questioningly, as if to ask, *Are we going on or not?* Without a word he started across the stream. Rachel turned to Sergeant Siefert, who had made no move to follow. "I'll wait for you here," Siefert said. "I've seen it already. Besides, this old man's done enough hiking for one day."

She nodded and started after the ranger. He was already on the other side and moving downstream, a dozen yards ahead of her. She crossed the stream, stepping gingerly on exposed stones to keep from getting her feet wet.

By the time she reached the other side, Wilson was at the spot. He was crouching beside what Rachel could now see was a dirty canvas tarpaulin. The tarpaulin covered a lumpy shape that lay unmoving on the ground. Rachel came up beside the ranger and crouched next to him. He lifted up one corner of the tarp, exposing the dead boy's head and upper body.

The ruined face startled her. "Birds did that," Wilson said matter-of-factly.

Rachel commanded herself to come forward and take a closer look. She noted the bruises and finger marks on the dead boy's pale throat. Shaking her head, she turned to the ranger and said, "Are you the one who covered him up?"

Wilson nodded.

"You didn't move him at all?"

"None of us laid a hand on him."

She regarded him darkly. "Who else besides you came down here?"

"Just a couple of the other rangers ..." Wilson paused, registering the look of displeasure on Rachel's face. "Did we do something wrong?" he asked.

She had come to her feet and was making a cursory examination of the area near the body. She noticed immediately the dozens of footprints that had trampled the ground near where the dead boy lay, ruining any possible evidence that might have been there.

Rachel shook her head with resignation. "It's not your fault."

Wilson was about to reply when his cell phone tweedled. He unsnapped the device and answered, "Wilson."

The ranger listened for a moment, then turned to Rachel. "The ambulance is here from the coroner's office. You want 'em to go 'head and pick up the body?"

"Yeah." She sighed dejectedly. "They may as well."

CHAPTER SIX

After leaving the park, Rachel drove to San Patricio Community Hospital. There she spoke to Teedie Boyle, his mother, Jennifer, and Sister Gina Dinelli. Teedie was fine. His broken leg had been set and put in a cast, he'd been treated for shock, and his doctor had ordered him hospitalized overnight for observation. His mother and Sister Gina remained at his bedside while he spoke to Rachel, the two women confirming Teedie's story, such as it was.

Disguising her disappointment at learning nothing helpful, Rachel thanked them, promised that she would call on them again if she had more questions, then departed. She drove downtown to Sheriff's Department headquarters. It was after eight o'clock by the time she arrived. She'd stopped at a Chinese carryout place to pick up her dinner: an order of beef with broccoli and two egg rolls.

As she drove from the restaurant, she concentrated on the greasy aroma from the bag on the passenger seat beside her. *How come I like Chinese food so much?* she asked herself, aware that thinking about such an innocuous question kept her from dwelling on the grisly image in her mind's eye: the body of the murdered boy lying beside Sugar Creek, covered by a grimy tarpaulin.

Rachel walked into headquarters, pausing at a soda machine on the first floor to buy a can of diet Pepsi, then carried her dinner with her upstairs to the detectives' squad room on the second floor. There was only one other detective in the room, a young man named Roberto Ornelas. Ornelas was at a computer, typing a report, when Rachel came in.

She stopped at his desk and asked him if he'd like to share her egg rolls. Ornelas accepted, and as Rachel sat down on the corner of his desk to open the bag containing her dinner, he said, "The chief wants you to call him at home as soon as you can."

Rachel popped open the can of soda. "Does he want to talk to me about anything in particular that you're aware of?"

Ornelas's expression became chagrined. She eyed him warily. "What?" she asked.

Ornelas said, "The media knows about your victim."

She grimaced. "Already? How the hell did they find out so fast?"

"The beat guy from the *Press-Telegram* happened to be hanging around the squad room when the call came in."

Rachel grumbled, "Aw, shit."

"Sorry, Rachel," Ornelas said. "It was just an unlucky break he happened to be here."

"Did the chief talk to him, or what?"

Ornelas nodded.

She rolled her eyes. "And?"

"That's what he wants you to call him about."

Rachel sagged. She climbed down from Ornelas's desk and headed for her own, saying to herself, *And to think this day started off so well.*

Ornelas called to her, "Hey, Rachel?"

She turned around. Ornelas was holding up the bag of Chinese food. "Don't you want your dinner?"

She shook her head. "It's all yours, Bobby."

"You sure?"

"I just lost my appetite," she said.

CHAPTER SEVEN

It was after eleven-thirty P.M. by the time Rachel finally arrived home. She was exhausted, having spent close to three hours at her desk. From eight-thirty until a quarter to ten she'd been on the phone, talking first to Earl Novak; then to Jeffrey Webber, the *Press-Telegram*'s crime reporter; then to the Sheriff's Department's head of media relations; then to Sheriff Peter Joyce himself; then to a representative from the county coroner's office.

None of the conversations had gone well, especially the last. The pathologist from the coroner's office reported that the victim was a Caucasian male, approximately ten years of age, who had been dead for about twelve hours. The cause of his death was strangulation—in the exact same manner as that of the six other victims whose murders Rachel was currently investigating.

She spent the remaining hour and a half checking a list of persons reported missing in the past seven days. No one on the missing-persons list matched the description of the boy found in Sugar Creek State Park. By the time Rachel was finished, she was too bleary-eyed with fatigue to do anything more.

She came into the house via the kitchen door. The house was dark. Through the archway that led into the family room she could see the flickering glow of the television. She heard the sound of tinny laughter, then Jay Leno's voice telling a joke. There came more laughter from the TV set, this time accompanied by a low, deep male voice that was chuckling along with the television audience.

She pulled the kitchen door shut quietly and locked it, set her purse on the counter, then passed through the kitchen into the family room. None of the lights in the room were on. The only illumination came from the television set.

Roy Rodgers, Rachel's husband, was sitting on the sofa opposite the television. His long legs were stretched out in front of him, propped onto the coffee table. He was wearing a UC San Patricio T-shirt, sweat-pants, and gym socks. A pair of untied New Balance running shoes lay on the floor beneath the coffee table. He looked as he usually did when he was dressed in his most comfortable clothes: like a lanky, middle-aged, former point guard just returned from basket-ball practice.

Rachel paused in the doorway to look at him, think-ing how glad she was to see him. She couldn't help once again reflecting how, on the surface, he and Rachel appeared to be such opposites. Roy was tall and lean and fair-haired, while she was short and dark and had to work hard to keep from weighing more than she did when they were married seventeen years before. Roy wasn't really a handsome man, but he was certainly attractive in a craggy, ascetic way, while she herself was quite pretty, with soft, creamy skin and huge brown eyes. He was a conservative Republican Methodist born in Orange County, California; she was a liberal Democrat, a Jew, and a life-long resident of San Patricio—except for the years she'd spent at UC Berkeley, where the two of them had met while Rachel was an undergraduate sociology major and Roy was a grad student in computer science. Even their occupations reflected a fundamental difference. Rachel, as a cop, was action-oriented and emotional, while Roy was more cerebral, the president of his own software-design company. They agreed on everything and nothing, and they loved each other very much.

Roy turned away from the television, seemingly aware of her eyes upon him. He smiled sympathetically and patted the sofa beside him. "C'mon over here. Sit."

She crossed the room, kicked off her shoes, and eased onto the sofa. He draped an arm around her, allowing her to snuggle next to him. "Rough day?" he asked.

"Rough *night*." She grunted.

"You want to talk about it?"

"Not particularly."

"You want to talk about it anyway?"

Rachel pulled back slightly so she could see his face. He was looking at her intently, all attention focused on her.

At last she said, "We found another kid. We haven't identified him yet, but we probably will in a day or so. There'll be a story in the paper tomorrow morning."

"So soon?"

"I didn't have any choice. My boss talked to a reporter before I got a chance to prevent him. I had to call the guy myself and give him enough information so the story didn't sound like the usual wild-ass nonsense those bozos print when they have to make most of it up. It turns out that I've also got to be part of a press conference tomorrow morning with the sheriff himself. TV and everything."

Roy raised an eyebrow. "Tomorrow?"

She sighed. "Ten o'clock sharp."

She nestled herself in the crook of his arm once more, laid her head against his chest, and closed her eyes. He reached down and gently stroked her hip.

Within moments Rachel had begun to snore quietly. Roy shook her. "Hey," he said.

"Hm?"

"Why don't you go upstairs and go to bed?"

"Yes, sir," she purred into his chest, nuzzling him. Moments later she was sleeping soundly again.

CHAPTER EIGHT

The following morning, at a cemetery in west St. Louis County, some two thousand miles east of San Patricio, a score of people were gathered at an open grave site. The morning was unseasonably warm, the sun hanging high over the horizon to the east, sparkling so brightly off the bleached-white headstones that the glare was near-blinding.

One of the mourners, a man named Kenneth Bennett, could feel his clothes sticking to him. He wondered, *Why do they always make you wear black?*

He decided it was much better where he was, sitting in the shade. The hot sun didn't beat down on him the way it did on the others who weren't members of his late wife's immediate family, who weren't privileged to sit on folding chairs beneath the canvas tent mounted on aluminum poles that glimmered in the brightness.

Bennett was thinking about the sun, and the clear blue sky, and the smell of the cemetery's freshly mowed grass. Until he looked at the faces surrounding him and remembered why they were here.

He realized how beautiful a day it was, and he

whispered to himself, "This is all wrong."

It should be gray, he decided, not sunny. Slate gray, a lead-colored sky. And cool. Rainy, even. Not warm and clear. Not today.

Bennett glanced at the minister, who was standing at the head of the casket, which rested upon a hoist that would lower it into the rectangular pit beneath. Sunlight glinted off the casket's gunmetal surface, reflecting up into the minister's eyes. He had to turn away to read from the small leather-bound book in his hands.

Bennett thought that the minister looked uncomfortable, though less so from the circumstances that had brought him here than from the heat. The minister was a short, stocky man, dressed in full vestments. Perspiration trickled down his forehead.

His voice was low and deep as he read from the book: "Our sister, Christina, has gone to her rest in the peace of Christ. With faith and hope in eternal life, let us commend her to the loving mercy of our Father, and assist her with our prayers. She became God's daughter through baptism and was often fed at the table of our Lord. May the Lord now welcome her to the table of God's children in heaven, and may she inherit the promise of eternal life."

Bennett could hear someone behind him choking back a sob. He turned around to look over his shoulder. It was Estelle Cooper, Christina's mother, Bennett's mother-in-law. She was leaning on the man sitting beside her, her brother Harvey. Harvey had one hand pressed to Estelle's cheek, holding her face against his chest.

Estelle's body was shaking, as if she were fighting to hold in her grief while at the same time trying to let it out, not really able to do one or the other. Uncle Harvey looked up, saw Bennett looking back at him, then shook his head. Harvey's expression was full of pain.

Bennett turned around again as the minister was pausing to dab his forehead with a handkerchief. The minister slid the handkerchief under the book he was holding, then said, "Let us pray."

The mourners bowed their heads. The minister closed his eyes as he spoke. "We commend our sister Christina to you, Lord. Now that she has passed from this life, may she live in your presence. In your mercy and love, forgive whatever sins she may have committed through human weakness. We ask this through Christ our Lord."

Several voices whispered together, joining the minister's voice in a low chorus. "Amen," they said.

CHAPTER NINE

Except for his driver, Bennett was alone in the rented limousine. He was sitting in the backseat, asking himself for the thousandth time the same question that he had been trying to keep from his mind every day for the past week. Ever since the day Christina died.

The question, *Why?*

"It's just not fair," he whispered to himself. *Only six weeks* . . .

Six short weeks. He and Christina had been married for a month and a half. A lifetime, thirty-eight years of bachelorhood; then a month and a half of marriage; and then, in a flash of fire, a bachelor once more. Or, more accurately, a widower . . .

The word engendered a sour taste in his mouth. *Widower*. A hard word, Bennett realized, hard and ugly, because of what it implied. Because one moment Christina had been beside him, promising him that they would be together for the rest of their lives, and the next moment she was gone.

Bennett tried to bring her face into focus in his mind's eye, then felt frustrated that it wouldn't come. He could hear her voice, could smell the aroma of her, her clean, fresh, woman smell. But he couldn't see her face.

He whispered out loud, "Christina," trying to use the sound of her name to force the image to become clear.

The driver of the limousine, a young black man dressed in a dark suit, glanced over his shoulder at the pale, sad-faced man behind him. "You say something, Mr. Bennett?" the driver asked.

Bennett shook his head. "Nothing," he answered. "Nothing at all."

He was remembering eight months before, at a cocktail party given by the chairman of Washington University's medical school. Bennett had gone to the party with his friend, Dr. Tom Hanson, the two of them representing the school's Department of Neuropsychology. It was Hanson who introduced Bennett to Sam Rosenthal, the sociologist, and to Rosenthal's date.

Christina Cooper.

According to Hanson, Christina was an investment banker, less than a year out of St. Louis University's MBA program, and ten years younger than Bennett. She wore glasses that could not disguise her wide, sea-blue eyes. Her ash-blond hair was cut short, almost mannish, but in a way that framed her face attractively. In the brief time they spoke to each other after they were introduced, Bennett noted that not only was she nice-looking, but she was also smart and witty and charming—much too fine a woman to be dating such an obnoxious snake as Rosenthal. Who, Bennett decided, was a lucky bastard.

It was shortly after eight o'clock when Bennett and Hanson and their host, Dr. Richard Koch, were on the patio watching the sunset. They were talking about the chances that the city might get another NBA franchise anytime soon, when Bennett felt the back of his neck tickling. Someone was watching him.

He turned and saw Christina through the glass double doors that opened into the living room. She was inside with a handful of other people, engaged in conversation, saying something to a woman standing beside her. But Christina was looking at Bennett.

She smiled.

He smiled back at her. Then he lifted the glass he was holding, drained the rest of his scotch on the rocks, and excused himself, telling Hanson and Dr. Koch that he was going for another drink.

He opened the glass door and stepped into the living room, moving past the crowd of people to where a young woman was standing behind a rollaway bar. Bennett was handing the young woman his glass when he heard Christina's voice behind him. "I didn't realize it when we were introduced before," she was saying. "You're *that* Kenneth Bennett."

He turned to her. She was still smiling, but there had been the hint of a challenge in her voice—something that Bennett heard from people all too often. Although from her the challenge was somehow inoffensive. Perhaps the fact that she was the most attractive woman at the party had something to do with it, Bennett told himself.

Restraining a smile of his own, he said, "I didn't know there was more than one of me around." Before she could respond, he turned to the bartender, who had handed him his drink, and said, "Could I also have a gin and tonic for the lady, please?"

He noted the expression of surprise on Christina's

face. Then her eyes narrowed. "Are you reading my mind already, Mr. Bennett?"

"Mmm-hmm," he acknowledged, sipping his drink. "I've been doing exactly that since the moment we were introduced."

She looked uncertain as to whether she should believe him. Bennett handed her the gin and tonic. She took the drink from him hesitantly. He asked, "Would you like me to tell you what you're thinking right now?"

She was frowning uncertainly. "What?"

He couldn't hold back his own smile any longer. "You're wondering whether Ken Bennett, the famous psychic, is for real."

Her look of surprise reappeared. Then: "Lucky guess," she said unconvincingly.

"No guess," he replied. "How else would I know about the gin and tonic?"

She thought for a moment, then said, "I was drinking one when Tom Hanson introduced us."

Bennett said coyly, "Are you sure?"

She was pressing her lips together in a pout, trying to remember. She looked up at him and saw the twinkle in his dark eyes. Slowly she broke into a wary smile of her own. "*Are* you, Mr. Bennett?"

"Am I what?"

"For real?"

"Oh, yes," he said.

CHAPTER TEN

Their first date came the following weekend. He took her to a Humphrey Bogart double-feature of *The Big Sleep* and *The Maltese Falcon* at a revival house in University City. They knew they were in love with each other by Thanksgiving, and a month later, for a Christmas present, he gave her an engagement ring. They'd known each other not quite seven months when they were married in February, on the twenty-eighth, the first marriage for each of them. From the start, Christina had referred to their relationship as "your basic whirlwind courtship."

And six weeks to the day after they were married, she was dead.

Bennett's limousine was now traveling east on Interstate 44, moving with the light late-morning traffic. At first he didn't notice that they had gotten onto the highway, because he was still lost in thought. Then he looked up, and he saw the sign, the white letters on green: *Junction—Interstate 270—1 Mile*.

All at once it registered on him, and he thought, *Here*.

The memory images unreeled in his mind, like

41

frames of film on a Moviola from which Bennett could not turn away.

Here. Interstate 270.

Five nights ago, he and Christina had been on their way back from Estelle's house in St. Peters, across the Missouri River. They'd gone there for dinner, had driven from town separately: Bennett in his BMW, Christina in her Celica. After dinner they'd stayed late to play cards with Estelle.

They left for home at the same time, separately. It was midnight. Bennett followed Christina onto the highway ramp, eastbound on Highway 70. He remembered watching the taillights of the Celica ahead of him, smeared by his windshield wipers because of the rain.

The rain.

The storm had begun around ten o'clock. Bennett remembered hearing the first rumbles of thunder while he and Christina and Estelle were playing cards. By the time they left Estelle's, the rain was coming down in sheets, a Midwestern gully-washer of a type common in the early spring. Both Bennett and Christina had left their umbrellas at home—all day long the weather had been gorgeous—and Estelle had to give each of them sections of the *Post-Dispatch* to hold over their heads as they trotted to their cars.

As they turned south on Highway 270, Bennett was still watching Christina's taillights as he listened to the *slup-slup* of his windshield wipers. He was vaguely aware of his car's radio having been tuned to a late-night call-in show. He eased onto the highway, staying in the outside lane. Christina's Celica moved into the middle lane, accelerating away from him.

Then, gradually, he became aware of another

sound: a low-pitched roar, rising in volume, coming from behind. Bennett glanced into his rearview mirror to see a double set of headlights glaring at him, coming closer: huge white lights, beneath which lay another row of smaller lights that glowed yellow, like luminous teeth. Behind the lights was a shape like some prehistoric monster's, its massive body bearing down on the BMW.

The beast was sliding over into the lane to Bennett's left. As he watched it fly past, he could see into the cab and make out the silhouetted man-shape and the red tip of a glowing cigarette; could see the long silver cylinder mounted on its eighteen-wheel trailer; could glimpse the diamond-shaped sign attached to the long tank and the words, *Caution—Flammable Material.*

Then the rig was past him, its wheels throwing up a fan of water that drenched Bennett's windshield so that he could no longer see the road. He eased on his brakes, slowing down, thinking that the tanker's driver was in a bit too much of a hurry, given the conditions of the road and the weather.

It was the touch of his foot on the BMW's brakes that saved Bennett's life. His windshield cleared, and he saw everything, as if in slow motion:

The taillights of Christina's Celica, now nearly a half mile ahead of him, still visible.

A second set of taillights, those of a white Lincoln Continental that Bennett had observed when he'd first pulled onto I-270. He'd noticed then that the Lincoln was weaving, having trouble staying in its lane. It wasn't until later that Bennett found out that the Lincoln's driver was a sales rep for a plumbing supply company in northern Illinois. The man had been on the road for ten hours, and he was exhausted from his grueling drive, fighting to stay awake behind the wheel of his car.

Then the lights of the tanker truck, sliding from the middle lane to the fast lane inside.

The Lincoln, in the middle lane, a halfdozen car-lengths in front of Christina's Celica.

The tanker, passing the Celica.

The Lincoln unexpectedly edging over toward the inside lane, crossing the white line. Moving directly into the path of the oncoming tanker.

The tanker's brake lights flashing bright red, shimmering in the rain.

The silver cylinder, jackknifing.

Finally there came the frozen moment when Kenneth Bennett *saw*, even as he was pulling his own car to the shoulder of the highway, coming to a stop, tearing away his seat belt, throwing open the door and leaping from the car and running out into the rain. Then stopping.

Bennett saw the Celica hit the tanker cylinder in midsection. Instantly the sky was filled with a fireball that erupted as if from the mouth of a volcano, accompanied by a sound like that of a thousand thunderclaps all at one time. The fireball engulfed both the tanker truck and the vehicle that had smashed into its side.

All the while, Ken Bennett stood on the shoulder of the road, watching.

The rain drenched him. The light from the flames suffused him with a red glow. He stood still at first. Then he was walking toward the fire, then running— until he was halted by an intense wave of heat that hit him like the slap of a giant hand made of fire. He was still hundreds of yards away, but all he could do was stand. And watch.

Here . . .

"We're here, Mr. Bennett," the driver said.

The limousine was no longer moving. The driver had turned around, his arm resting on the seat. Bennett looked at him questioningly. "You're home," the young man said.

The limousine was parked in the driveway of Bennett's house. He was thinking, *Can we possibly have gone all the way to Webster Groves already?*

Bennett looked up. Before him was the split-level brick house, the garage at the end of the concrete drive, his BMW in front of the closed garage doors. The limousine was parked at the end of the drive, just off the street, beneath the shade of a tall, ancient oak tree planted in the middle of the front yard.

Home. The home that he and Christina had bought together just last January, a month before they were married. Where they had lived as man and wife for less than two months.

The driver was saying, "Mr. Bennett?"

Bennett looked back to him. The young man's expression was creased into a frown.

Bennett said, "Is something the matter?"

"I'm sorry, sir," said the driver. "It's just . . ." He paused, frowning again. "It's just the job, that's all. It's not your fault." He shook his head again. "I'm not working any more funerals, that's all. They're gonna have to get somebody else to do this from now on."

CHAPTER ELEVEN

Bennett paused in his living room long enough to strip out of his suit jacket and toss it onto a chair. Then he went down a short hallway that led into the kitchen. From a cabinet above the kitchen sink he pulled out a two-thirds-full bottle of Glenlivet.

Moments later he was back in the living room, sitting on the sofa, his hand wrapped around a cocktail glass that he had filled with scotch and ice. The glass rested on his thigh, leaving a cold, wet ring on his trousers. The cool perspiration on the outside of the glass dampened his fingertips. Already the ice in the glass had begun to melt.

The front doorbell rang. Bennett looked at the door blankly. The bell rang again. He set his glass on the floor, came to his feet, crossed to the front door, and pulled it open. On the doorstep stood Tom Hanson.

It took Bennett a moment for Hanson's identity to register on him. Hanson was a rotund, middle-aged man with shaggy brown hair that was shot through with gray, the identical color as his full beard. He was wearing the same rumpled, dark suit that he'd had on at the cemetery hours earlier. He said to Bennett,

"I think it's time you talked to somebody, don't you?"

Without a word, Bennett stepped away from the door and moved back to the sofa. He sat down, picked up his drink from the floor, and swallowed what was left of it. Hanson stepped into the room, pushing the door shut behind him. He moved to the chair where Bennett had dropped his suit coat, picked up the coat, and draped it over the back of the chair. Still standing, he gestured to the glass in Bennett's hand. "You got any more of that?"

"In the kitchen," Bennett answered.

Hanson moved from the living room into the hallway and out of sight. Bennett could hear Hanson's footsteps, then the sound of the freezer door opening and closing; the cabinet opening and closing. Moments later Hanson reappeared carrying a tray of ice cubes, the bottle of Glenlivet, and another cocktail glass.

He paused in front of Bennett, who held up his glass for fresh ice. Hanson opened the bottle of scotch with one hand and filled Bennett's drink, then took the bottle and the ice back to the chair opposite Bennett, sat down, and poured a drink for himself.

As Hanson sipped his drink, Bennett was looking at him expressionlessly, through eyes that were heavy with fatigue. Hanson said quietly, at last, "Have you been getting any sleep at all, Ken?"

Bennett's eyes narrowed, as if the question were difficult for him to answer. "Not much."

Hanson waited, staying silent.

Bennett continued to speak without looking at the other man. "I was really exhausted last night when I left the funeral home."

"I noticed," Hanson said. He took a swallow of his

drink and bit into a piece of ice that he chewed carefully.

"Up till last night," Bennett said, "I don't think I've slept four hours in four days. Last night, though, I finally fell asleep. Around midnight. I woke up right before dawn." He frowned once more. "I had a dream last night. You know me, Tom. I hardly ever dream. But I had one last night."

Bennett paused, considering how to say what he wanted to say. "It was a dream about Christina," he continued. "One moment she was there, and then the next she wasn't there anymore." He took a deep breath. "I woke up right when she disappeared, and it was like somebody'd punched me hard, right here." He made a fist and tapped it against his chest. "It sucked all the air out of me. I couldn't breathe at all. It was worse than being scared, worse than any kind of ordinary nightmare. Just this kind of hollow pain . . ."

Bennett paused again, aware of the tears dampening his cheeks. He turned away, rubbing at his eyes with the back of his hand. He looked at Hanson. "She's gone, Tom," he said in a sob, unable to control the tremor in his voice. "She's really gone."

Hanson lifted his glass to take another drink. The glass was empty. He reached down for the bottle of scotch he'd set on the floor, poured the scotch over the ice in his glass, and set the bottle back down. He looked to Bennett, who had both hands wrapped around the still-full drink in his lap, head bowed.

Hanson said, "Ken?"

Bennett looked up. His eyes were red.

"I haven't had to be a real shrink for a long time,"

Hanson said. "And what I have to tell you, you've probably already thought about. Maybe not. Maybe it'll help; maybe it won't."

Bennett kept looking at the other man, not speaking.

Hanson continued. "You know how people, when they lose a loved one . . ." He paused, making a face. "God, I hate that phrase. 'Loved one.' What a lame-ass expression."

He looked for a reaction, but Bennett's face remained impassive. "Anyway," Hanson went on. "Something like this, that happens this fast." He snapped his fingers. "It's always the worst. Always. But you, my friend, you've had something happen to you that's a lot more complicated."

He paused, studying Bennett for a reaction. There was none. Bennett's expression had not changed.

"When people fall in love," Hanson continued, "when they first get together, you go through those first few months and everything is white-hot. Everything's very passionate—the good stuff and the bad, but especially the good. That's how relationships work. The highs are very high and the lows are very low, and that's just the way it is. But then after you're together for a while, you grow beyond that. Your relationship becomes more mature; you're more comfortable with each other. It's still love, but it's different."

He paused. "But you and Christina never had the chance to get there. That's why . . . why it . . ."

Hanson shook his head, fighting the clutch in his voice. "You and Christina," he said. "If ever I saw two people who fit together better than you two . . ." He was shaking his head once more. "I never told you

49

this, Ken. I probably shouldn't even say it at all."

Bennett's voice was soft. "What?"

"What hurt me so much about all this was I knew you two would make it. You really would have been together the rest of your lives. You look at a lot of people, a lot of couples, and you say to yourself, 'It'll never last,' and nine times out of ten, five years later you're saying, 'Um-hmm. I knew it all along.' But the two of you were just so damned good together. . . ."

Hanson was scowling unhappily. "I'm sorry. Here I wanted . . . I meant to try to make you feel better."

Neither man spoke for a time. Hanson lifted his glass to sip more of his drink. The tinkling of the ice cubes sounded unnaturally loud in the quiet house. He lowered the glass self-consciously.

"I . . . uh . . . I talked to Dick Koch this afternoon," Hanson said at last. "He agreed to let you have a leave of absence from your university duties, if you want it. Effective immediately. With full pay, of course."

Bennett nodded.

"I think it'd help you to go away for a while," Hanson said.

He lifted his glass and drained the rest of his drink, then set the glass on the table and rose from his chair. He sighed, then crossed the living room to the front door. He pulled the door open and stood in the doorway as he turned to look back at Bennett, who had not moved from the sofa.

"Call me tomorrow, okay?" Hanson asked.

Bennett nodded. Hanson stepped out onto the porch, exiting, and pulled the door shut behind him.

CHAPTER TWELVE

Later that afternoon, the dream came to Bennett once more. He'd been sleeping fitfully, anesthetized by the liquor he'd consumed.

He'd been asleep for only an hour when the dream came, the same dream he'd had the night before. In the dream, he was standing in the middle of a black road that ran through a bank of sparkling white fog—so white that it glowed. The road was spongy, and with each step Bennett's foot sank almost an inch into the black. He had no idea where he was, nor where the road led. All he knew was that he had to keep moving.

From behind him he heard a voice calling his name. Her voice. Christina's.

He turned around. She was standing in the middle of the road, a thousand yards behind him, fog swirling around her. She beckoned to him.

He tried to bring himself to walk toward her, but his body responded sluggishly, as if he were underwater. His feet sank deeper into the soft surface of the black road. He was coming toward her, but his steps were agonizingly slow. He called out her name.

Then he heard a sound.

It came from behind her, from out of the fog—a deep, dull sound at first, a low rumble. Steadily it grew louder, more ominous, more powerful.

Bennett screamed, *Christina!* just as the thing burst from the mist: a demon truck with eyes of fire, bellowing a primordial cry of triumph as it smashed into her, shattering her body like a statue made of crystal.

Then Bennett stood there, frozen in place, watching the beast bearing down upon him. Coming closer . . . closer . . . closer . . .

Bennett screamed aloud, and his eyes snapped open.

He sat bolt upright in his bed, shaking with terror. He remained sitting for some time, waiting for the sensation of fear to subside, to be replaced by a feeling as if his head were wrapped in a thick, wet blanket that smelled of stale perspiration and whiskey.

There was a sharp, angry pain in his forehead above his right eye. The pain radiated outward, wrapping his entire head in steely-strong fingers that squeezed with every pulse of his heartbeat. The sound of rushing blood roared in his ears.

Sound . . . ?

A harsh ringing serrated his nerves. An inner voice spoke to Bennett from somewhere inside his aching skull, a voice that whispered to him, *The phone.*

The drapes that hung over the window opposite the foot of his bed were open. The window faced west, and bright sunlight was streaming into the bedroom, striking him full in the face. He rolled onto his side, shading his eyes with one hand as he reached with the other for the telephone that was on the nightstand beside his bed. He grasped the receiver, only to have it slip from his shaking fingers and drop onto the floor beside the bed. The receiver landed with a thud that sent a coruscating bolt of pain from his temple, around his head, and down his neck.

Bennett groaned out loud as he pushed himself to a sitting position at the side of the bed. His clothes felt tight and restrictive. It was only then that he realized he had fallen asleep while still fully dressed.

From the receiver on the floor, he heard a tiny voice floating up to him. "Kenny?" the voice implored. "Kenny, are you there?"

Recognizing the voice, Bennett said to himself, *Denise?*

His sister, whom he had spoken to twice already in the past four days: first when he called to tell her about Christina, then again the following day when she called him back to apologize for not being able to come in from San Francisco for the funeral. Bennett knew that his sister's aversion to funerals battled fiercely with her affection for him. He had no wish to force her to do something that disturbed her so badly, *had* disturbed her ever since their father had died of cancer when Bennett was nine years old and Denise was six.

He bent down to pick up the receiver and put it to his ear. "Denise?" he croaked hoarsely.

"Kenny?" Her voice seemed slightly distorted by the long-distance connection. "Are you all right?"

"What time is it?" He grunted.

"Almost four-thirty. My time."

He looked at his wristwatch; he had only six-twenty. *Must be slow*, he thought.

She repeated, "Kenny?"

William Relling Jr.

"Sorry," he said. "I'm a little groggy. You woke me up."

"I'm the one who should apologize."

"It's okay," he told her.

Denise was silent for several moments. Bennett could picture her face, twisted into an expression that he knew well: a discomforted look that she wore whenever she had something difficult to say.

At last she asked, "How'd everything go today?"

His head had begun to pound. "As well as could be expected, I suppose."

"I'm really sorry I wasn't there."

"Denise," he said, rubbing his forehead, "I don't mean to be grouchy, but we talked about this already, didn't we? It's okay. I know how you feel. You don't have to apologize to me. For anything."

"I know, but—"

"Then what do you want?"

"What are you being so angry about?" she snapped.

He sighed wearily. "I'm not angry. You just woke me up, that's all."

He waited again for a time, until she went on. "Kenny, I was wondering about something."

"What?"

She hesitated. "You haven't been out here, to California, in an awfully long time. I was thinking if maybe you were considering getting away for a while, you know, getting out of St. Louis . . ."

Bennett had stopped listening to her. He was hunched forward, the pain in his head so severe that he felt nauseated. *Please God*, he begged silently. *Make it go away*.

He heard Denise's voice again. "Ken?"

54

He grunted. "Have you been talking to Tom Hanson?"

"He called me an hour ago. Right after he left you."

"Great," Bennett said bitterly.

"I agree with him," Denise said, her tone firmer now. "It'd do you a world of good to get away. It's been damn near ten years since you've been out here. I think it's a terrific idea."

He considered for a moment, then said, "Look, Denise, right now I'm in no condition to make a decision about this. Let me call you back. Will you be home later tonight?"

"I'll be here. Just promise me you'll think about it, okay?"

"I'll think about it," he said.

MAY

CHAPTER ONE

Ken Bennett was sitting in the reception area of the office of Dr. James Herbert. A week-old copy of *Time* magazine was open on Bennett's lap. Without being aware of it, he had read the opening paragraph of a cover story on capital punishment four times.

Sighing, he closed the magazine and looked up to study his surroundings. The reception room was tastefully appointed. The walls were paneled walnut on which were hung several signed serigraphs. The carpet was a dark blue-gray. In the center of the room was a quartet of wing-backed chairs—one of which Bennett occupied—arranged around a glass-topped coffee table from which he had taken the magazine. Brass floor lamps stood in opposing corners.

There were two doors: one that led from the outer hallway of the medical building where Dr. Herbert's suite was located, and one that led into the doctor's office itself. A receptionist's desk sat near the latter door, but the young woman who usually occupied the desk was absent, having gone into the doctor's office to announce Bennett's arrival.

He looked at his watch. It was three-thirty P.M. She'd been gone for three minutes.

Bennett frowned, aware of a sour feeling in his stomach. He'd had the same feeling several times during the past week, ever since he had given in to Tom Hanson and made the appointment with Dr. Herbert.

Herbert, a psychiatrist like Hanson, was Hanson's friend and former mentor. The older man's name was still on the faculty roster of Washington University's medical school as professor emeritus, but he did not teach classes anymore, having gone into semiretirement. He still maintained a small, exclusive private practice, working no more than twenty hours a week. He was, according to Tom Hanson, the best shrink in the Midwest.

I do not want to be here, Bennett thought.

He was screwing up the courage to walk out of the office and go home when the inner door opened and the receptionist reappeared. She was a petite black woman in her twenties. "Would you come in, please, Mr. Bennett?" She showed him a bland, sympathetic smile.

He came to his feet. She held the door open for him, allowing him to pass by. She stepped back out into the reception room, closing the door behind her.

As he took in Dr. Herbert's office, Bennett had the disconcerting feeling that he was a small boy walking into his father's study, welcome by invitation only. The office was not a typical physician's sanctum— there was no desk, no framed diplomas on the walls, which were paneled in the same wood as the reception room. There were bookshelves, but they weren't filled with medical volumes; what books were there were an eclectic library of contemporary hardbound novels and nonfiction. The rest of the shelves was taken up by various mementos and photographs representing Dr. Herbert's life. It was a room that had obviously been designed to make visitors feel as much at ease as possible. Unfortunately, Bennett found himself too aware of that effort, and the effect that the room had upon him was just the opposite.

Dr. Herbert rose from one of a pair of small settees that were perpendicular to each other, in the corner of the room farthest from the door. The doctor was a tall, thin, white-haired man—Hanson had told Bennett that Herbert had celebrated his sixty-fifth birthday in January. Physically, Herbert was in fine shape—he had the physique of a distance runner, his movements were loose-jointed but graceful, and his eyes were clear and bright, glittering with intelligence.

He was smiling as he came forward, extending a hand to Bennett. "Please," he said genially, "have a seat. I've been looking forward to meeting you."

Bennett shook hands with the doctor and sat down on the settee opposite the one to which Herbert returned. The psychiatrist was picking up a notepad and pen that lay on the cushion beside him. He said, "I wish I knew what I could do to make you feel less reluctant that you're here."

Noting Bennett's expression of surprise, Herbert smiled again. "I'm not stealing your thunder, Mr. Bennett. After thirty-five years of practicing psychiatry, if nothing else, I've become a pretty good judge of body language."

Bennett nodded. "I'm sorry."

"No one should ever apologize for the way they feel," said Herbert. "As I say, I just wish there were something I could do to change that."

Bennett shrugged.

61

Herbert went on. "Maybe you'd simply rather not talk to me at all. I can certainly understand it if you feel that way."

Bennett considered for a moment. "I wouldn't be here if I didn't really want to be."

"Good."

"So what do we talk about?"

"What would you like to talk about?"

"That depends," Bennett answered. "I don't know how much you know about me."

Herbert nodded. "Well, naturally, I know who you are and what you do. And I know that you're a friend of Tom Hanson's." He paused. "I also know that your wife died recently."

"A month ago," Bennett said.

"Tom told me that you hadn't been married for very long. Is that right?"

"Yes."

"How long, may I ask?"

"Six weeks."

Herbert's brow furrowed. "I'm sorry."

Bennett shrugged again.

"Had you known your wife for very long before she died?"

Bennett shook his head. "We'd only met eight months before."

The furrow deepened. "Tom didn't tell me that." Herbert raised his pen, tapping it thoughtfully against pressed lips. "Maybe you should talk to me about what specifically led to your deciding to get in touch with me."

Bennett looked away from the other man for a moment. Then he turned back and asked, "Do you know much about parapsychology, Dr. Herbert?"

The psychiatrist shook his head. "Not as much as I probably should, I'm afraid. I'm not a skeptic, if that's what you're asking. I believe that there may very well be such a thing as extrasensory perception."

Bennett asked, "What do you know about the different categories that psychic powers fall into?"

"I didn't know there were different categories of psychic powers."

"There are," said Bennett. "Myself, for example. I'm a clairvoyant. Which is different from being telepathic or precognitive."

"How so?"

"A telepath is someone who's capable of reading someone else's thoughts or emotions. A precog is someone who can glimpse future events, like a seer. Clairvoyants—like me—can receive information about objects or events that they aren't witnesses to, in a very literal sense. We're different from telepaths in that we tune in to physical realities—locations and such—rather than mental energy or emotion."

"I didn't know that," admitted Dr. Herbert.

"Most people don't. They also don't know that, in spite of what some psychics themselves claim, the categories don't generally overlap. Telepaths can't see the future, and clairvoyants can't read minds. At least that's been the case with me, and I've been a clairvoyant for more than twenty years."

Herbert asked, "You mean you weren't born psychic?"

"Not at all. I had an accident when I was seventeen years old. One day I hit my head and knocked myself unconscious. When I woke up, I . . ." He shrugged. "I was clairvoyant."

"Just like that?" Herbert asked.

"Pretty much," said Bennett. "There's more to it, of course, but that's basically how it happened. Anyway, the point I wanted to make is that I have two jobs in the neuropsych department. Part of the time I'm a guinea pig. I take tests, participate in experiments, that sort of thing. The rest of the time I'm a researcher myself, administering tests and such to other people who come in. . . ."

Herbert had begun to scribble on the notepad. He paused when he became aware that Bennett had stopped speaking. Herbert looked up and noticed that Bennett was eyeing the pad. "You don't mind that I'm jotting this down, do you?" the psychiatrist asked.

Bennett shook his head. "It's all right."

"If it bothers you I'll stop."

"No, no." Bennett forced a smile. "For a moment, I forgot I was in a psychiatrist's office."

"I meant what I said. I can put it away if you like."

Bennett shook his head. He let out a deep breath, then asked, "What were we talking about?"

"Your job," said Herbert.

Bennett nodded thanks. "What I was about to say is that I have kind of a unique status in the department. I'm a full-time employee, but I'm not a faculty member and I'm not really part of the regular lay staff. I'm somewhere in between, kind of an island unto myself. I'm allowed to stick around, though, and do what I do because I'm valuable to the department. For a couple of reasons."

"I assume that one of them is because you've gotten them some favorable publicity over the years?"

"Among other things, but that's the main one. Obviously I draw attention to the department just by being there. But I'm also aware that my value is greatly diminished if I no longer can do what I do that attracts the attention the department and I get."

Dr. Herbert's eyes narrowed, his expression questioning. Bennett took another deep breath. "Last week," he continued, "on the day before I made my appointment with you, I had a meeting with the chairman of the medical school."

Herbert held up a hand. "Dick Koch, right?"

"Do you know him?" Bennett asked.

"Oh, yes."

Bennett nodded knowingly at the tone of Herbert's reply. "Then you know he's not the most diplomatic person in the world."

"To say the least."

"He called me into his office because he wanted to give me what he described as a 'fitness report.' Apparently he'd been observing me ever since Christina . . . since my wife's death. He was as gracious as he could be, but essentially what he said to me was that lately I haven't been cutting it." Bennett shrugged. "He wasn't wrong. That didn't make hearing the news any easier to take, but he wasn't wrong."

"What exactly did he say?"

"He told me he thought I might be pushing myself toward a nervous breakdown. He suggested I take a leave of absence and get away for a while. I asked him if that was an order, and he said, 'If it has to be.' "

Dr. Herbert was tapping his pen against his lips once more, frowning. "Is that the reason you came to see me? Because Dick Koch threatened you about your job?"

Bennett was silent for a time before answering, "No."

Dr. Herbert waited, not speaking.

William Relling Jr.

Bennett said, "I've been drinking quite a bit lately. I'm starting to worry about that."

"How much is 'quite a bit'?"

"Almost every night."

Herbert's expression became one of deep concern. "Have you ever had a drinking problem before?"

Bennett shook his head.

Herbert thought for a moment. "If it's any consolation, the fact that you're aware of it is a good sign that it may not be as serious as you might think. Do you have the feeling that you could stop drinking if you wanted to?"

"I don't know," Bennett answered truthfully.

Herbert nodded. "That's actually a good sign, too. Most alcoholics believe they can quit whenever they want to; they just don't want to." He paused. "Is it because of your wife that you started drinking?"

Bennett nodded. "But not for the reason you think."

"What do you mean?"

"The only way I seem to get drowsy enough to fall asleep is if I drink myself into a stupor," said Bennett. "If I didn't drink, I'd never fall asleep at all."

"Why not?"

Bennett exhaled deeply. "Because I'm afraid."

Herbert's eyes narrowed. "Of what?"

"That I'll dream."

The room fell silent once again. Dr. Herbert sat, patiently watching the man opposite him.

Bennett said, "On the night of my wife's funeral, I had a nightmare. I dreamed I was standing in the middle of a road on a foggy night. I was alone, but I could hear her calling me. I turned around, and I saw her through the fog far away, motioning for me to join her. Before I could move, though, this huge truck, like some kind of monster, came barreling out of the fog to run her down. . . ."

Bennett could feel his heart palpitating. "After the thing killed Christina, it came after me. But right before it could run me down, too, I woke up." He looked at Dr. Herbert. "I had the very same dream every night for a week after that. It got to the point where I was afraid to go to sleep, because I knew it'd happen all over again. That's why I started drinking."

Herbert asked, "Did the booze help? Did you stop having the dream?"

Bennett shook his head.

Herbert said, "I realize that this is painful, but could you tell me exactly how Christina died?"

Bennett recounted to Dr. Herbert the circumstances of his wife's death, from the time they left her mother's house up to the moment that her automobile crashed into the gasoline tanker truck. While he spoke, Bennett gradually became aware of a curious sense of relief. He hadn't told the full story to anyone since that night, when he'd been questioned by the police officers who arrived at the scene of the accident. No one else had asked him to talk about it since then, no doubt believing that reliving the experience would be unbearable for him. It surprised him to realize that telling the story to Dr. Herbert was cathartic. In a way it felt good to try to make someone else understand what he saw and heard and felt at the time.

When he'd concluded his story, Bennett sat back against the settee. He felt drained, as if someone had opened a tap to emotions he'd kept bottled inside him for a long, long time. He turned to Dr. Herbert, feeling a kind of admiration that the psychiatrist had gotten him to open up so easily.

Herbert, however, wore a look of uncertainty. "I have one more thing I'd like to ask. But I'm afraid it might be an even more painful question than the one I just asked you."

Bennett could suddenly feel the hairs tickling the back of his neck. "What is it?"

Herbert said, "It doesn't take a psychiatrist to recognize that you're feeling a great deal of guilt right now, along with the severe pain of loss. But from listening to you, I don't get the impression that you're feeling guilty because you didn't do something to prevent your wife from being killed. You seem to realize, consciously and subconsciously, there wasn't anything you could've done to prevent the accident. Because it was just that—an accident. That's why you told me about your power—that you're a clairvoyant and not . . . what was the word you used? For someone who can see the future?"

"Precognitive."

Herbert nodded. "You clearly understand that you could not have used your power to foresee what would happen and prevent it, because that's not the power you possess. But I also get the sense that you're feeling tremendously guilty because you didn't die along with your wife." He looked pointedly at Bennett. "If you can tell me I'm wrong about that, I'll be glad to hear it."

Bennett said nothing.

Herbert uttered in a voice touched with sincere concern, "You know, Mr. Bennett, grief is a very peculiar emotion. When you lose somebody you love, you go through almost the same sort of stages a terminal patient goes through when he finds out he only has a short time left to live: denial, anger, depression, and so forth. But all of that takes different forms, depending on the individual. It's an intense, personal, private battle, and the people who care about you often aren't much help. Consequently, it's a battle that a lot of people lose."

Bennett asked, "So what do I do?"

"What do you think you should do?"

Bennett reflected for a moment. "As much as I hate to admit it, maybe Dick Koch was right."

Herbert smiled. "Then that makes it unanimous."

CHAPTER TWO

Denise Bennett stood in the American Airlines terminal of San Francisco International Airport, scowling. She was telling herself that she would believe her brother really was coming only when she saw him emerge from the passenger walkway attached to the L-1011 that had just landed from St. Louis. She estimated that three-quarters of the people aboard the flight had already disembarked. There was still no sign of Kenny.

He couldn't have changed his mind at the last minute, she told herself unconvincingly. As of last night—Friday—he was still coming to San Francisco, ostensibly on board this very flight. Denise had called the airlines an hour ago—at six P.M.—and verified that the flight would arrive on time.

Her uncertainty was tinged with worry. Kenny had seemed so depressed the last several times she spoke to him on the phone—even last weekend, when he called to ask if her invitation to visit was still open.

The request had come as a complete surprise. Following their conversation on the day of Christina's funeral, Denise had made up her mind that any further attempts to persuade him to make the trip would be futile. Then, out of the blue, he had telephoned to say he'd like to come to California for a visit, if it was all right with her.

Same old Kenny, Denise thought wistfully. *Asking if it's "all right" if he comes out to see me.*

Then she looked toward the maw of the walkway, and there he was. Denise broke into a wide smile and waved, calling to him, "Kenny! Kenny, over here!"

Bennett saw her, and he broke into a grin of his own. As he approached, Denise was grateful that her joy at encountering him face-to-face superseded her concern. It was obvious that he'd lost weight. His color was pale, his cheeks were noticeably drawn, and his shock of straight, mud-brown hair was streaked with more gray than she remembered there being the last time she saw him. He was well dressed, as always: a fawn-colored Burberry topcoat over a dark cashmere sweater and tailored slacks. But the topcoat seemed to hang from his shoulders as if it should have belonged to a stockier, healthier-looking man.

Still, he was smiling—the same familiar, crooked grin he wore whenever he was happy. Denise could not remember a time when she hadn't been charmed by his grin, as she was right now.

He came up to her, throwing open his arms. She ran to him, and they hugged each other fiercely. Denise could feel tears welling in her eyes. She kissed him on the cheek. "I'm so glad you're here."

Bennett pulled back, held her at arm's length, and smiled at her. "How's my baby sister?"

"Just fine now," she said.

CHAPTER THREE

An hour earlier, as the L-1011 had been gliding west over the Rocky Mountains, pursuing the setting sun, Ken Bennett was staring out the window beside him and thinking about the past.

Aware that he was about to see his sister for the first time since his wedding, Bennett could not help recalling the times they'd had together when they were children. Which, in turn, caused him to think about death. First Dad, when Bennett and his sister were still kids. Then Mom, a decade ago. And now . . .

He frowned, chiding himself. Before he left St. Louis, he had made a vow not to think about the reason behind his trip. This was supposed to be a vacation. He was on his way to San Francisco to relax.

He could hear Dick Koch's voice in his mind: *I don't have to remind you about the effect that stress has been demonstrated to have on people with your ability, do I, Ken? You're as familiar with the data as I am. There is a clearly established correlation between periods of emotional duress and decreased levels of psychic performance. I'm not saying there's anything wrong with you that can't be fixed. All I'm saying is that I think you need to get away for a while to some new environment. Someplace you can unwind.*

Bennett's frown deepened. He was quite unhappy with Koch's having "encouraged" him so vigorously to take this trip. Not so much because the suggestion that Bennett was pushing himself toward a break-down had been so blatant, but because Koch was right. Every test that Bennett had taken since return-ing to work led to the same conclusion: that whatever psychic gift he had possessed before the death of his wife had dissipated. Trying to force the power to man-ifest itself served only to frustrate and discourage him. Bennett told himself that he should have known bet-ter. Even at best, he could coerce and control the power to a small degree, could deliberately induce it only under certain conditions—one of those condi-tions being a relaxed, receptive state of mind. It had always been that way with him, ever since the begin-ning. Ever since . . . *his accident.*

A golden Midwestern fall afternoon. A half dozen teenage boys playing football in the middle of a tree-lined residential street. One of the boys—the quarter-back—fades back to throw a pass to another boy. The defender—seventeen-year-old Kenny Bennett— matches the pass receiver stride for stride.

Backpedaling, Kenny fails to see the curb behind him. He trips. Arms flailing, he pinwheels awkwardly. Falling, he lands hard. The side of his head smacks the concrete curb with a heavy, wet thunk. For him, the world goes black.

An eternity passes, until Kenny feels the touch of a hand on his wrist—the pressure of fingertips. And—
gas tank
An image forms in the center of the blackness. Kenny

opens his eyes and stares into the face of the doctor who is holding his wrist to take his pulse. Kenny's eyes lock onto the doctor's eyes, and he says, "Don't worry. You've got enough gas to make it home. It'll be okay." Startled, the doctor drops the boy's wrist.

Later Kenny discovers that the doctor had been concerned whether there was enough gasoline in his car for him to make it back to his house, as it was well after midnight and most service stations would be closed. . . .

Don't think about that now, Bennett commanded himself. *Don't think about any of that.* He told himself to think about Denise instead, and about how much he was looking forward to seeing her again.

CHAPTER FOUR

"How much time off do you have?" Denise was saying as she guided her Alfa Romeo convertible from the airport parking lot to an access road that would dump them onto the northbound 101 freeway. Bennett's suitcase was crammed in the backseat.

"As much as I want," he answered.

She glanced at him skeptically. "Really?"

He nodded. "I'm on an official leave of absence, with full pay. I don't have to be back till the fall semester starts in September." He smiled. "Don't worry. I promise I'll be gone long before then. I'm aware of the rule about houseguests."

"What rule is that?"

"That we're like fish. Keep us around longer than a couple of days, and we start to stink."

"Very funny," she said dryly. "You know, of course, you're welcome to stay all summer if you like. I've got plenty of room."

"We'll see how you feel about that a week from now."

Denise said, "Is there anything in particular you'd like to do while you're here? A lot's changed in San

75

Francisco since the last time you were here."

"Are you sure you can be taking that much time off to play tour guide for me?"

"That's one of the joys of being self-employed. You get to come and go as you please."

"Your business has been that good lately?"

"Um-hmm."

"Great," said Bennett.

He felt proud of Denise and all that she'd accomplished, entirely on her own. She'd moved to San Francisco when she was twenty-four years old, following the death of their mother. Bennett had visited his sister only once since then, seven years ago. At the time she was working as a $2,500-a-month staff photographer for the *San Francisco Chronicle* and living in a studio apartment in Haight-Ashbury. For the past five years, however, she'd been a freelance photographer. Two years ago Denise had saved enough money to buy a house in the Marina District, near San Francisco Bay. He knew that for her to be able to afford the house—what with real estate prices being as exorbitant as they were in San Francisco—Denise must be doing well for herself.

Bennett eased back in his seat, looking out at the nighttime landscape as they rode by. To his right lay the black water of the bay, reflecting the twinkling lights of the city. In the distance, hanging over the water, he could see the Bay Bridge that connected San Francisco to Oakland. Two broken ribbons of headlights crossed the bridge, one atop the other: westbound traffic above, eastbound below. To his left lay the hills of the city of San Francisco itself, dotted with lights. The tops of the hills were wrapped in a gray mist that was rolling in from the west, creeping down to cover the houses that clung to the hillsides.

"Springtime in the Bay Area," Denise said.

Her voice roused Bennett from his reverie. "Hmm?"

"I noticed you were looking at the fog," she said. "This is nothing. Wait'll we get to my place; you'll really see some fog."

She paused. He'd turned away from her to look outside again. He wore a pensive, not-quite-sad expression on his face. Denise said, "Kenny?"

He turned back to her.

She fixed him with a look of determination. "I'm not going to let you do this. I'm not about to let you just tune out on me. I'm telling you that right up front, just so you know."

After a moment he smiled at her. Denise nodded tersely: *So there.* "I'm glad we got that straight."

"Yes, boss," he replied.

CHAPTER FIVE

Denise exited the freeway at Van Ness and drove north. The fog grew denser as they drove. She came to Lombard Street, where she made a left turn and headed west. She drove several more blocks, then turned right onto Pierce Street. Her house was on Pierce, a block and a half north of Lombard, near Chestnut.

It was a narrow, wood-framed, two-story structure with an octagonal-shaped facade and a turreted roof. The place looked to Bennett like something that might be found along the shores of Cape Cod. It stood between two nearly identical houses, virtually side by side. Bennett recalled how, on his only previous trip to San Francisco, he'd registered that living space in the city was so dear most homeowners had no conception of "yards" as Midwesterners conceived of them. The front door of Denise's house was accessible via a concrete porch that seemed to grow right out of the sidewalk. There was a short driveway that led to a built-in garage that lay a few feet below street level.

Denise pulled the car into the driveway. She leaned

across Bennett to open the glove compartment and activate the remote-control device she kept there. The garage door raised itself slowly. When the door had opened all the way, a light went on in the ceiling of the garage. Bennett saw that there was space enough for the Alfa and little room for anything else. Denise wheeled the car inside, and the garage door closed behind them.

He pulled his bag from the car and followed Denise into the house through a door in the rear of the garage. Climbing up a short flight of steps to another door that opened into the kitchen, Denise pressed a switch inside the doorway, flooding the room with light.

To Bennett, the room was as immaculate as an operating theater: the black-and-white checkerboard floor, the white walls and cabinets, the stainless-steel sink, the chrome-and-glass dinette and chairs all gleamed. Before he could compliment her kitchen, however, Bennett heard the patter of clawed feet racing down from the second story. Then came a skittering on bare wood, followed by a happy bark of greeting. An instant later a black, furry shape burst into the kitchen from the doorway that led to the rest of the house—a male cocker spaniel who dashed up to Denise, cheerfully shaking his rear end.

She knelt down to nuzzle the animal, who smeared her face with dog kisses. The cocker spaniel then turned his attention to Bennett, looking up at the man with a quizzical expression. "That's my brother, Kenny, Clem," Denise said to the dog. "I told you about him."

The dog yapped, and Bennett bent over to scratch his head. Clem's backside shook more vigorously.

"He loves it when you do that," Denise said to her brother. "You just made a friend for life."

Bennett followed his sister through the kitchen and into the living room. The decor there was more of the same: white walls, bleached parquet floors, a coffee table lacquered in glossy black around which stood a sofa and love seat made of soft charcoal-gray parachute material. A fireplace was set into one wall, its bricks also painted white, charred around the edges from use. The only personal decorations were several of Denise's photographs hung around the room. Bennett looked at the pictures his sister had taken and thought, *Wow*.

The subject matter of the black-and-white photographs was the same for each: portions of buildings and other man-made structures, shot from subtle but dramatic angles that would have occurred to few other photographers. Denise clearly had an artist's eye for pattern and composition and chiaroscuro; that much was obvious from even a casual glance at her work. *Now I know why she's doing so well*, Bennett told himself, feeling even more proud of his sister than he had before.

"These are wonderful," he said, indicating the pictures. "Really."

She grinned. "C'mon. I'll give you the grand tour later. Right now let's get you unpacked, and I'll make you a cup of tea."

Denise allowed Clem to lead them up a staircase that went from the living room to the second floor. There were three rooms upstairs: the master bedroom, a guest room, and a third bedroom that Denise had converted into a combination studio and darkroom. They dropped off Bennett's suitcases in the guest room, then went back downstairs.

Denise asked her brother to start a fire in the fireplace while she went into the kitchen to put a pot of water on to boil. Presently they were back in the living room: Bennett on the love seat and Denise on the sofa, her legs curled beneath her, Clem on the floor in front of her. The fire was crackling behind them as they drank mugs of Constant Comment.

For a time neither of them said a word. Bennett could feel a pleasant, numbing fatigue settling over him. He yawned, and Denise raised an eyebrow. "You're bored already? You only just got here."

Bennett sipped his tea. "I'm still on St. Louis time. It's almost midnight for me."

"Just so it's not me," she said. "I don't want to be accused of being a poor host."

Bennett raised his mug in salute. "So far, you're doing a fine job."

"I also want you to get a good night's sleep," she said. "I've got a very busy week planned for you."

He leaned back against the love seat, wrapping both hands around the mug of hot tea, aware of a contentment that he hadn't felt in many weeks. He yawned again, suddenly feeling very tired.

"You pooping out on me already?" she asked.

Bennett nodded. "Jet lag. Then I'd better get to bed soon, if you're going to want me at my most charming from here on out."

He set his mug on the coffee table and came to his feet. He started for the staircase, then paused to look back at his sister. "I really am happy to be here," he said.

She smiled. "I'm glad, Kenny. I really am."

CHAPTER SIX

At two A.M., Denise lay awake in her bed. The Amy Tan novel she was reading was open and resting upside down on her stomach. A lamp on the nightstand next to her bed was on, providing the only light in the room.

She'd read the same passage three times and was about to read it again, until she realized that the reason she couldn't concentrate on the book was the same reason she was still awake. She shifted restlessly, nudging Clem, who was curled up on the foot of the bed. The dog let out a whimper of protest at being disturbed. "Sorry, Clem," Denise whispered.

She lifted her book once more, then closed it in frustration. She could not get her brother out of her mind.

There was something changed about him. On the surface he seemed mostly to be the same old Kenny: her gentle, goofy, crooked-smiling big brother. In spite of the difference in their ages—which was much less of a difference now that they were adults than it was when they were children—they had always been great pals. The same old easy-going, take-everything-in-stride, stay-close-to-home Kenny. It suddenly oc-curred to Denise that never before had she reflected upon her brother's life so seriously—partly because she was busy leading her own life, and partly because to her he was simply Kenny. *He's nothing special—he's just my brother.*

As Denise thought about him now, however, she realized that he was very special indeed. She remem-bered his accident, of course, the one that had made him a celebrity while he was still a teenager. Over the years she'd read about him many times in magazines and newspapers: *Testimony of Kenneth Bennett Helps Acquit Accused Killer. "Psychic Criminalist" Provides Clues to Victim's Whereabouts.* She also remembered seeing him dozens of times on television talk shows—Kenny smiling his winning smile and deflecting all charges that he was a fraud, proving time and again under the most trying conditions that his power was genuine.

Not that he always succeeded. But his successes far outnumbered his failures, and from what Denise knew about others who shared his gift, her brother was a very different sort of individual than they were. He was neither a suspicious loner nor a wild extro-vert. He never retreated into anonymity, but neither did he seek the spotlight. Rarely did he leave St. Louis, simply because he loved the city. Instead he insisted that anyone who wanted to employ his power come to him. That was Kenny—a pleasant, intelligent, oc-casionally stubborn, goodhearted homebody who happened to possess a strange and wonderful talent.

But to Denise, that talent was only a part of what made him special. No one she'd ever known handled the trauma that life dumped on a person as well as

Kenny did. When their father died, Mom had gone to pieces. Here she was, not even thirty years old at the time, with a husband dead of a brain tumor that took his life four months after it had been diagnosed. Mom had suddenly been a widow with a nine-year-old son and a six-year-old daughter to support. And Kenny had been the one to keep her together. After a time she became functional again. She went back to work, she dated new men, she took care of the kids. If she didn't enjoy her life, at least she found it tolerable—all because of her son, who was an emotional rock.

Kenny was always *there*, as he'd been for Denise when Mom herself passed away. Mom's death had hit Denise hard, much to her surprise. She was too young at the time to possess more than a vague memory of her father's death, a memory that was nevertheless unhappy enough to make attending funerals abhorrent to her. But Denise was an adult on the hot summer morning that Mom's heart had stopped beating while she was working in her garden at the back of the house that she shared with her son. When Kenny telephoned Denise to tell her about Mom, Denise had felt a creeping blackness constricting her. The blackness wrapped itself around her, shutting off her breath, causing her heart to pound wildly, making the edges of her vision sparkle as if lit by tiny fireworks. But there was Kenny, once again, saying, *It's okay, Denise. I'll take care of everything*. Which he did.

Denise wondered for how many people—for how many total strangers—he had done the same thing. On how many criminal cases had he consulted over the last twenty years? For how many missing persons had he searched? How many frightened people had he comforted, simply by being there to help?

And how much had all of that taken out of him?

He's really changed, Denise realized. There was an aura of sadness about him that hadn't existed before. She frowned. *It doesn't take a genius to figure out why that is*, she told herself.

Not that Christina had been the first woman with whom Kenny had been in love. He wasn't a hound, but he went out with women all the time. Though he rarely became seriously involved with anyone, especially while Mom was alive.

But, Denise now said to herself, there was also something special about Christina and Kenny—an indefinable rightness, a feeling that they belonged together. Denise had met Christina only one time, at their wedding, but she knew immediately why her brother and his bride seemed so taken with each other. It was that they just seemed to fit. They were meant to be.

Now it was painfully clear that, for the first time in his life, Kenny wasn't able to cope. The emotional blow was too awful. He could help other people, but he couldn't help himself.

Which just means it's my turn to take care of him, Denise told herself with determination.

She leaned over to place the book on the nightstand, then reached up to switch off the lamp. She shifted into a more comfortable position, pulling the bedcovers up to her chin.

Clem whimpered softly, unhappy at being disturbed again. "Oh, shut up, you old grouch." Denise grunted, and within minutes the two of them were deeply asleep.

CHAPTER SEVEN

On Sunday morning Denise drove them across the Golden Gate Bridge to Mill Valley. They had breakfast at a small café, then drove to the Muir Woods, where they spent the afternoon hiking through the forest. They returned to the city at dusk and ate dinner that night in Chinatown.

On Monday they took the BART to Berkeley, where they spent the day wandering the neighborhoods surrounding the University of California. That evening they went to a Giants–Rockies game at PacBell Park. They sat in box seats belonging to the owner of an art gallery that frequently displayed Denise's work.

On Tuesday it rained. Denise spent the day in her studio while Bennett sat by the fireplace with Clem, reading an Ed McBain 87th Precinct novel he had brought with him from St. Louis. The rain continued all day Wednesday, but stopped by Thursday morning. Denise declined to go with her brother to Ghirardelli Square and Fisherman's Wharf; nor did she wish to ride on a cable car.

On Friday afternoon they took a boat to Alcatraz, where Denise shot photographs. That night they went to an Eric Clapton concert at the Cow Palace. On Saturday they went to Golden Gate Park for a picnic brunch. By late afternoon another storm was blowing through the Bay Area, but they had already decided to stay home that night. Bennett prepared dinner— coq au vin for two—and they sat up until one in the morning watching a Judy Holliday film festival on the Turner Classic Movies channel, on cable: *Born Yesterday*, *The Solid Gold Cadillac*, *Adam's Rib*.

And each night Bennett slept soundly, and he dreamed no dreams.

CHAPTER EIGHT

On his second Sunday morning in San Francisco, while he and his sister were drinking coffee at the kitchen table, Bennett said to Denise, "Last night before I fell asleep, I thought of something I'd really like to do."

"I'm all ears," she said.

"I'm thinking about taking a trip down the coast. You know, along Highway One? A driving trip."

She raised an eyebrow. "Oh?"

"That's not a good idea?"

"I don't know," she said. "Have I heard all of it?"

"Pretty much. It occurred to me that this is only the second time in my life I've even been in California, and both times I never got out of San Francisco. I figured that since I've got the time, it might be fun to drive down the coast. Maybe not all the way down to Mexico, but Los Angeles at least."

Denise made a face. "I'm not real crazy about L.A."

After a moment he said, "I was thinking about going alone."

Denise was taken aback. "Excuse me?"

He apologized quickly: "Don't get me wrong. I'd

love it if you could come along with me—"

"Then why did you just say you wanted to go alone?"

"I don't really. I just . . . I know you said you could take all the time off you wanted to—"

"I wasn't kidding about that."

"I know, but—"

"You just want to be left alone? Is that it?"

"No, no, not at all."

"Then what do you want?"

Bennett sighed. "I'm afraid I'm imposing on you here."

"For God's sake, Kenny, you're not an imposition."

"I realize that," he said. He shook his head, lifted his cup of coffee halfway to his lips, then set it down again.

"While we're on the subject of impositions," she said, "just how were you planning on getting down the coast? In my car?"

He frowned. "Not necessarily."

"How, then?"

"I thought maybe I could rent a car and drive down to wherever I end up. Then I could just turn it in there and fly back up here. Or I might go ahead and drive back. I haven't thought it all the way through yet."

"I see." Denise sipped her coffee, set down the cup, and looked across the table. "When were you thinking of leaving?"

"In a couple of days," he answered. "If I rent a car tomorrow afternoon, I can leave Tuesday morning."

"For how long?" she asked.

"A week," he said. "Two at the most."

Denise leaned back in her chair. She looked to Bennett to be thinking very hard.

Then she said at last, "A very curious thing happened to me a few weeks ago. Right before you called and said you wanted to come out for a visit. I was having dinner with a friend of mine. She's a publisher here in town—mostly calendars and posters, that sort of thing. I've done a little freelance work for her in the past. Anyway, while we were having dinner, she told me she had an idea for a photography book— one of those big coffee-table things. She wants to call it *U.S. One.* What it would be is a sort of black-and-white photo-and-essay collection of a trip down the coast. Not Ansel Adams, nature-type stuff, but man-made architectural structures. She thinks I'm ready for a big project like that, that it'd be right up my alley. I told her I'd consider it seriously. I'd just about made up my mind to call her back and agree to do it—in fact, the day I was going to call her back was the day you called."

Denise looked at her brother. Her expression was still odd. "I never realized this before," she said. "But you truly are amazing. Coincidences like this happen to you all the time. Don't they?" The corners of her lips turned up in a wistful smile. "My car's too small for the two of us for that long of a trip. But if we rent a bigger car in my name, it's a write-off. I'll let you pay for it up front, though, since it sounds like you were planning on paying for it anyway."

"I was," he agreed.

"We'll have to leave Clem at the kennel. He actually likes it there. It's like going to a doggy motel for him. They'll take him on short notice, too. They're used to that." She looked at her brother pointedly. "Tuesday, huh?"

He nodded. "Tuesday."

Denise shrugged. "What the hell? Why not?"

CHAPTER NINE

They left San Francisco at one P.M. on Tuesday, the twenty-fourth of May. They were driving a gold Lexus sedan that Bennett had leased. His choice of automobile had been against Denise's wishes—she believed that a Lexus was too embarrassing, the kind of car that had "rich tourists" written all over it. Bennett insisted that he didn't want to feel cramped on a long trip. Denise accused him of having turned into a crabby old man. Bennett countered by asking her what was the use in being a grown-up if you couldn't enjoy a few adult comforts now and then? Besides, he was paying for it.

Denise was behind the wheel as they drove south, out of the city. As soon as they had passed through Pacifica, San Francisco's southernmost bedroom community, U.S. 1 narrowed to two lanes that paralleled the coastline, following its curves.

It was a gorgeous spring day. To their right lay the ocean, sparkling so brightly with reflected sunlight that the western horizon seemed lit with golden fire. To Bennett it was as if they had fallen into an oil-painted landscape come to life: the scrub brush and rocky beaches and blue water to one side of them, the sheer face of a mountain dotted with trees to the other. He smiled to himself, thinking it unlikely that he was the first person ever to conjure such an impression. Not even the first person to think of it today.

The highway wound and twisted like a serpent made of asphalt. Denise drove carefully—more because she wanted her brother to enjoy the view, she said, than because she was intimidated by the road. Consequently the thirty-mile drive to Half Moon Bay took them nearly an hour. There they stopped for a late-afternoon lunch at a Mexican restaurant called El Perico, then walked down to the harbor, where they watched a fleet of fishing boats straggle in for the day.

It was five o'clock by the time they left, wrapping their arms around themselves as they walked back to the car because the brisk waterfront air had become uncomfortably chilly. Instead of continuing south, Denise drove north through the town to the junction of Highway 1 and Highway 92. She turned right on 92, heading along a narrow road that coiled into the trees, before turning south again on Highway 35.

They drove for an hour through thick mountain woods wrapped in shadow. The woods were so dark and green that, in spite of Denise's having turned on the Lexus's heater, Bennett felt chilly. At last they came to Highway 9 and turned west, passing a sign that read, *Big Basin Redwoods State Park—ten miles.* A half hour after that, they were in the town of Boulder Creek.

It was sunset by the time Denise swung off Highway 9 onto Big Basin Highway. They arrived at Merrybrook Lodge, where Bennett had made reservations for them to share a one-bedroom cottage with a pair of twin beds. The lodge was a postcard-rustic collection of structures that lay in the middle of a grove of mountain redwoods. Their cottage stood alongside a freshwater stream. Bennett could imagine how lovely it would all be in the daylight, and he realized that it had been some time since he had actually looked forward to the coming day.

That night, as he lay in his bed listening to the whisper of the creek just outside his window, Bennett told himself that he was more relaxed and happy than he had been in some time. He looked over at the bed opposite his. His sister lay wrapped in a down comforter, snoring softly. The sound made Bennett smile.

He told himself, *I really am having a good time.*

Though he was aware that he was ignoring a still, small voice in the recesses of his mind—a voice whispering to him that the good times could not last, would not last.

CHAPTER TEN

"I don't mind driving to San Patricio," said Denise. "Besides, I was thinking you'd want to see the sights along the way."

It was nine-thirty A.M. on Wednesday, May twenty-fifth. She and her brother were loading their suitcases into the Lexus's trunk. A misty, drizzling rain that had begun at dawn was still falling, though the change in weather had done nothing to dampen their mood. They had decided to drive into San Patricio for break-fast, rather than hunt for someplace to eat in Boulder Creek. Denise suggested a restaurant she had been to before, a place on the San Patricio boardwalk near the city's beachfront amusement park.

"What am I going to see between here and there that I haven't already seen?" Bennett asked.

She shrugged. "More trees?"

"I'll drive," he said. "You navigate."

Soon they were heading south on Highway 9. Once they were clear of Boulder Creek, Bennett acceler-ated, bringing the car's speed up to fifty miles per hour. The highway seemed to be sloping gradually downward, and he drove carefully, mindful of Denise's warning that some of the turns on this particular stretch could be tricky, especially when it was wet.

Denise had tuned the car's radio to a classic-rock station broadcasting from Monterey, and she was singing along to Elton John's "Crocodile Rock." To Bennett, the song seemed to keep time with the periodic *whup-whup, whup-whup* of the car's windshield wipers. He was concentrating on his driving, guiding the car around a blind turn that broke sharply to the left.

As he rounded the turn, Bennett saw off the shoulder of the road to his right a wide sign set in a patch of bare ground that had been cleared recently of its trees. The sign read, *Glen Arbor Estates. New Homes Under Construction. Single-family Units Priced from $500,000.* Bennett glanced at the sign for only a moment, its information registering on him subconsciously. Then he turned back to look through the rain-smeared windshield at the road ahead of him. The wipers swept up and down a final time: *whup-whup*.

Bennett peered through the windshield, and his eyes widened with surprise. Because the road was no longer there . . .

and Bennett is no longer there behind the wheel of the car and no longer is even Bennett but is someone else, someone much, much smaller, and he is running, running, running, trying to see ahead of him through eyes blurred with tears, trying to see where he is running to, trying not to fall over the pieces of board, trying not to slip on the muddy earth, aware of his heart racing, aware of the blood roaring in his ears, and another sound, a terrifying sound, the sound of footsteps coming closer, closer, and he is wanting to scream, want-

ing very badly to scream but not having enough air in his small lungs, and then feeling the hand, the strong hand, clutching him by the back of the neck and lifting him up and . . .

Denise screamed, "Kenny!"

Bennett blinked. Suddenly he saw the huge tree *right there*, directly ahead of the car. His sister was reaching over to wrench the steering wheel from his hands. She jerked the wheel in an effort to veer the Lexus away from the tree. But the car was traveling too fast, and Denise had reacted a fraction of a second too late.

Bennett could feel the car pitching onto its right side. Denise was screaming his name once more, her voice cutting through the screeching sound of sheared metal and the explosive burst of blown tires and the shattering of glass. Bennett felt a sharp pain at the side of his head as he was tossed forward, then snapped back hard against the driver's-side window. He glimpsed a faint spiderweb crackling in the glass where he'd struck his head.

Then numbness washed over him, radiating outward from the place where an instant before there had been only the fierce pain. Bennett could hear, dimly, the Elton John song playing from the radio, playing softly, then growing fainter.

Then there was nothing: no sound, no sight, no feeling. Nothing but darkness that swallowed him whole.

CHAPTER ELEVEN

The darkness receded gradually, by degrees. One by one Bennett's senses returned.

First there came a sound, vague and faraway: a human voice that was mumbling words he could barely understand. "Temperature . . . second storm front in the ocean west of San Francisco . . . no rain tomorrow . . ." The voice had an unreal, electronic quality. Bennett wondered, *Television?*

Then an aroma: antiseptic, medicinal. Clean, but unpleasantly so. *Too clean*, he thought.

Then a taste in his mouth: sour and stale, like morning breath.

Then tactile sensations: He was lying prone, his head on a pillow. Crisp, laundered cloth against his bare flesh. A dull, throbbing pain in his left temple. Another dull pain in his right shoulder, which, when he tried to move it, stayed immobilized, held in place, strapped to his body.

Finally Bennett opened his eyes.

Rather, he opened his right eye, because his left eye was swollen shut. He turned his head to the right, and the pain in his temple and his shoulder snarled at him, warning him not to move so quickly.

He found himself, as he'd guessed, in a hospital bed. Sitting in a chair beside the bed was Denise. She was watching the television that hung suspended from the top of the wall opposite the foot of the bed, listening to the muted voice of a local news show's weathercaster. There was no one else in the room with them, the space having been designed to accommodate a single patient.

The door to the hallway lay to the left of the bed and was closed. There was another door behind Denise that, Bennett supposed, led to the bathroom. Fixing his good eye on his sister, he grunted to draw her attention. She turned to him, and the corners of his mouth lifted up in a weak smile. "Hi," he croaked in a voice rubbed with sandpaper.

Denise sighed with relief. "Kenny, thank God!"

She rose from the chair and came to his side, bending to hug him gently and brush her lips against his cheek. She pulled back to look at him, her face etched with worry. Then she reached for a button on the intercom in the wall above his head, at the same time saying to him, "I have to let them know you're awake."

"Where am I?" he rasped.

"San Patricio Community Hospital."

Denise returned to her chair after pressing the intercom's call button, and she was looking at him carefully. Without waiting for him to ask the next, obvious question, she went on, "You've got a separated right shoulder and a bad bruise on the left side of your face." She paused. "You've also got a concussion. You were knocked cold."

Bennett frowned. "I was?"

"For nearly eight hours. God, I was so worried that it was the same thing happening, like it did way back then. You looked terrible—"

The hallway door opened, interrupting her. In the doorway stood a young Filipino woman dressed in the uniform of a nurse's aide. Before the woman could say a word, Denise was telling her, "My brother's come to. Can you please go tell his nurse? And see if the doctor is still here also? He'll want to know."

"Right away, ma'am," the aide replied. She disappeared back into the hall.

Bennett asked his sister, "Are you all right?"

Denise's expression became sheepish, almost apologetic. "I'm fine. Not a scratch." The lines of concern reappeared on her face, and Bennett guessed what she was going to say before the words passed her lips: "What the hell happened out there?"

But he was no longer looking at Denise. He'd turned away from her to peer at the television. On the screen now was a shot of a news anchorman sitting behind a desk. Over the anchorman's shoulder was the silhouetted figure of a child with a huge red question mark drawn in the middle of the figure.

Bennett sat up in bed, his attention riveted. He was straining to hear what the anchorman was saying.

Puzzled, Denise said, "Kenny?"

He snapped at her: "Shh!" He pointed to the floor beside her chair, at the television's remote-control device lying there. He commanded, "Turn up the sound, will you?"

She did as she was told. The voice from the television set grew louder. ". . . Craig Tanaka McWilliams, missing since Saturday afternoon. The San Patricio

County Sheriff's Department has put out a call for information concerning . . ."

Bennett said sharply to his sister, "Call them! Now!"

Her eyes grew wide.

He barked, "Goddammit, Denise, *call that number!*"

"Kenny, what—"

"I know where that boy is!"

The pain in his head flared white-hot. He collapsed back onto his pillow, moaning. Denise was by his side in an instant. His open eye was moist and red. Frightened, she breathed his name: "Kenny . . ."

"Call them," he whispered urgently. "Please."

Denise dashed around the bed to the nightstand that stood on the opposite side, pushing past the hallway door that was being opened from without. The door slammed into the nurse's aide, who was returning at that moment with Bennett's nurse. Both of them stared, mouths gaping, at the madwoman who was ignoring them as she grasped for the telephone that rested on the nightstand. The aide was about to cry out in protest, until both she and the nurse turned their attention to the man on the bed.

He lay there unconscious, limp as a rag doll, his head lolling onto his bandaged right shoulder. If it weren't for the rapid rise and fall of the sheet covering his chest, he could easily have been assumed to be dead.

CHAPTER TWELVE

The last time Det. Rachel Siegel had been to Community Hospital was one month before, when she interviewed Teedie Boyle. Tonight—a little over an hour ago—had come a suppertime telephone call from Earl Novak ordering her to go over there right away and talk to a woman named Denise Bennett. The woman reportedly had information about a missing nine-year-old boy whose case file had been dropped into Rachel's lap that morning by an unhappy-looking deputy who spoke the words, "I hope to God this isn't another dead kid, Rachel, but I'm afraid it probably is."

As Rachel drove to the hospital, she was thinking dourly, *Another dead kid. Goddammit.* It was raining, as it had been since early in the afternoon. The rain made her think dark thoughts about the possibility of victim number eight turning up sometime this evening.

Craig McWilliams had been missing for four days. But up till now, Rachel had been telling herself that his disappearance might be unrelated to the seven other homicides, the investigation of which had not budged an inch virtually since day one, in spite of her best efforts. It was possible that the McWilliams boy might not be another victim of Rachel's invisible killer. But she could not shake the sick feeling that he was.

Rachel didn't have to remind herself that this case was easily the biggest she'd undertaken since making detective and becoming the only female member of the squad. The Sheriff's Department's jurisdiction extended across the entire San Patricio County, along U.S. 1 from Monterey to Big Sur. But because the population of the entire county was relatively small—compared to that of a city like San Jose or San Francisco—the twenty members of the county detectives' squad did not divide their work into specialized areas like Robbery, Homicide, Bunko, Juvenile, Narcotics, and so on. Instead each detective did a little of everything, taking turns accepting whatever cases they were assigned by Chief of Detectives Earl Novak.

During her tenure with the squad, Rachel had handled hundreds of investigations of all types. She would work on anything that came along. But none of the cases she'd had since making detective was as frustrating and infuriating as the one she was working on right now.

It started in January, four months earlier. A trio of surfers—college students from UC San Patricio—had gone out at dawn one chilly Sunday to a secluded spot near the western end of the city. The beach was deserted except for the four of them and one other: the fully clothed body of an eight-year-old girl, whom they found half-buried in the sand. Whoever had put her there the night before hadn't reckoned on the tide's going out and uncovering enough of her to make her visible so quickly.

The little girl's name was Emma Lyons. Her mother and father had reported her missing to the Sheriff's Department the previous Thursday. An autopsy performed by the county coroner's office indicated that Emma had been strangled to death. There were dark bruises on her throat, her trachea had been crushed, and the size and shape of the finger marks found on the skin of her neck indicated that the fingers had belonged to an adult male who had been wearing latex gloves.

Much to the surprise of the pathologist who examined Emma, and also to that of the Sheriff's Department to whom he delivered his report, there were no other marks of violence on her body. Of particular interest was evidence that she hadn't been sexually molested, which was not what they'd expected. The other curious fact they discovered had to do with traces of what the little girl had had for dinner not long before she was murdered: the remnants of a Whopper and french fries and a Cherry Coke. As far as the pathologist could determine, on Saturday night Emma had been fed, strangled, and buried on the beach.

Earl Novak assigned the investigation of the murder to Rachel Siegel. She attacked the case vigorously, for a couple of reasons. First of all, it was only the third homicide investigation she'd been assigned since making detective, and she was anxious to do a good job. Second, the heinous crime horrified her. That the victim was a child struck way too close to home.

Rachel worked systematically: interviewing the three students who'd found the body, interviewing

Emma's parents and teachers and classmates to learn exactly when she last had been seen alive, interviewing each member of each crew at each of the Burger King restaurants in the San Patricio County area to learn if any of them who'd worked on Saturday night recognized the little girl in the photograph Rachel showed them. All of the interviews proved fruitless. Consequently there was nothing for Rachel to do but wait and hope for a break and pray that the death of Emma Lyons wasn't the beginning of something dark and horrible.

Two weeks after the discovery of the body of Emma Lyons, a pair of hikers found the body of nine-year-old Terry Donelly alongside a mountain trail. Like Emma, the boy had been missing for a few days, and he also had been strangled by a man wearing latex gloves. Terry, too, had not been sexually molested. There was, however, one new clue: traces of morphine were found in the dead boy's system. There were still no witnesses.

In February there were three more bodies: Mark Krenning, age eleven; Cristy Burgess, also age eleven; and Janice Scheller, age nine. In March there was only one: Brian Hodge, age ten, whose body had been found in the woods at the northern edge of the county. Then, three weeks ago, came eleven-year-old Michael Baker, who'd been discovered near Sugar Creek. Both Brian and Michael had been injected with morphine before being strangled. The others had not.

However, these past weeks had gone by without a new victim being discovered. For the last seven days Rachel had been working on other cases, hoping that the killer had died or left town or just decided to stop strangling children. This afternoon's call from Novak had turned her hopes to ashes.

Rachel parked her Sienna in the hospital's visitors' lot, got out, and trotted across the driveway to the hospital's main entrance, pausing for a moment to shake herself dry. A pair of glass double doors whooshed open to admit her, and she moved to a desk marked *Information*. Behind the desk sat a blue-haired, middle-aged woman in a salmon-colored smock.

Rachel opened her purse to pull out the wallet that held her ID and badge. "I'm Detective Siegel, County Sheriff's Department," she said to the woman in the smock. "I'm supposed to talk to someone named Bennett."

A female voice from behind Rachel's shoulder said, "That's me."

Rachel turned. The woman she found herself facing looked to be a few years younger than herself; also two or three inches taller, though close to the same weight, which made her, to Rachel's thinking, on the thin side. The woman had long, straight light brown hair tied in a ponytail. She was dressed casually: Nike sneakers, black jeans, a white oxford-cloth button-down shirt beneath a red, vee-necked wool sweater. Her eyes were dark and bright, the eyes of someone who observed and remembered what she saw with precision. At the moment the woman's eyes were narrowed slightly, an expression of controlled agitation.

"I'm Denise Bennett," the woman said. "My brother needs to talk to you right away."

Without waiting for a reply, Denise started off toward a bank of three elevators. Rachel jogged to catch up with her. "Ms. Bennett," Rachel said as she fell into step with Denise, "I was told it was you who was going to give me some information. About a missing boy?"

They'd reached the elevators, and Denise was pressing the button to summon a car. She looked back to Rachel and frowned, pursing her lips. "I'm sorry if you misunderstood. Things got a little hectic around here all of a sudden. I guess maybe I wasn't exactly clear to whoever I talked to on the phone."

A bell dinged, and the doors of the middle elevator opened. As the two women stepped inside, Rachel said, "Your brother's the one I'm supposed to see?"

Denise nodded. "He's conscious now."

Rachel's eyes widened. "Conscious?"

The elevator doors slid closed.

CHAPTER THIRTEEN

Rachel was asking herself, *Don't I know him?*

There was something awfully familiar about Kenneth Bennett, the man propped up in the hospital bed. His back was pressed against a stack of pillows. Rachel had seen him before, and it annoyed her that she could not recall where it might have been.

Her memory was not helped by the fact that he could not have looked then the way he looked right now. His face was gaunt and pale, except for the left side, which was purple, with an ugly bruise that extended from his temple to his cheekbone. His left eye was puffy and discolored and swollen shut. His lank brown hair was damp and had been brushed straight back and slicked to his skull. He was dressed in a hospital gown, and his right arm was wrapped in a sling that kept the arm pressed tight against his body.

There was another man in the room with Bennett, standing at his bedside: a short, middle-aged, sandy-haired, bespectacled man who was wearing a lab coat over dress slacks and a shirt and bow tie. The man looked up at Rachel and said, "I'm Dr. Small. Mr. Bennett is my patient."

Rachel introduced herself. Dr. Small said to her solemnly, "I hope I don't have to remind you that Mr. Bennett has some rather serious injuries. I don't really approve of your questioning him at this time—"

The man in the bed grumbled, "Get out of here, Doc."

The man turned to Bennett, his forehead furrowing with displeasure. Then he stepped away from the bed, squeezing past Rachel and Denise to leave the room.

After the doctor had gone, Denise pulled the hallway door closed, shutting the three of them in. Bennett turned to gaze at Rachel with his good eye. "Have a seat," he said. "Please."

She moved to a chair on the man's right. Settling herself, Rachel slid the chair closer to him. She regarded him expressionlessly, waiting. Finally Bennett asked her, "Do you know who I am?"

"It's funny you should bring that up," Rachel answered. "As soon as I walked in the door I couldn't help thinking that you looked familiar to me."

"Denise didn't tell you?"

"All she said was that you'd been in a car accident this morning on Highway Nine and you were a little banged-up. She wasn't kidding about the banged-up part."

Bennett nodded. "I just . . . I want you to listen to what I have to tell you, listen to it all the way through. Try not to make any judgments until after I'm finished. All right?"

"Whatever you say."

He took a deep breath. "I heard on the news about an hour ago that the police were looking for a missing boy—"

"Sheriff's Department," Rachel corrected him.

"I beg your pardon?"

"I'm with the Sheriff's Department. In San Patricio, the county Sheriff's Department is the primary law-enforcement agency. The city police . . ." She paused, then made a wave of dismissal. "Never mind. It's not important. I didn't mean to interrupt you."

"I'm talking to the right person, aren't I?" he asked.

Rachel nodded. "I'm the right person. Go on with what you were saying."

Bennett continued. "The reason I had my sister call you is because I know where that boy is. There's a place, some kind of housing development or subdivision that's not far from the highway . . . Highway Nine. It's called Glen Arbor Estates. You'll know it's the right place because they haven't started to build anything yet—it's just cleared land and they've laid out . . . I don't know what to call them. Planks, I guess. Pieces of wood that mark the shape of the houses, where they'll go. Anyway, that's where you'll find that boy. Somewhere up there."

Rachel asked him carefully, "Mr. Bennett, how do you know this?"

Bennett's expression became pained. He had to have been expecting the question, Rachel told herself, but clearly he did not relish having to answer it. She urged him, "Mr. Bennett—"

"I'm a psychic," he admitted.

Rachel thought, *Spare me, please.*

And then, in the next instant, it came to her where she had seen him before. *I remember now*, she thought. *Last fall, sometime. Good God, I saw him on* Oprah.

Then Bennett was speaking to her again, slowly,

calmly, rationally. As if trying to assure her by the very quality of his voice that what he was saying—however fantastic it might sound—was absolutely true. "This morning, while I was driving, I happened to see a sign. 'Glen Arbor Estates.' It triggered . . . you'd have to call it a vision, for lack of a better word. I saw the little boy. He was running away from something . . . I don't know who or what it was." Bennett drew another deep breath. "He's still there. That's where you'll find him."

Rachel sat watching the man in the bed, not speaking. Denise was standing in front of the door. "He's not making this up," she said to Rachel. "I swear."

Rachel turned to her. "Did I say I didn't believe him?"

"You just don't look very convinced—"

"Denise," Bennett cut in, his tone chiding her. Both women turned to him. "I don't necessarily expect you to believe me, Detective Siegel," he continued to Rachel. "But couldn't you at least check it out?"

She studied him for a moment, making up her mind. "I suppose I could do that."

"Thank you," he uttered gratefully.

"Like you said," she told him, "it's the least I can do."

CHAPTER FOURTEEN

The beams from the Maglites held by Rachel and the two deputies who had met her at the construction site wavered ahead of them. Raindrops lit by the flashlights' glow glistened like falling gems. Rachel and the deputies were walking along a slight uphill grade on a wide road made of packed earth. Rachel was at the point, a deputy to either side of her.

Eventually, she supposed, the road would be paved over, becoming the new subdivision's main street, but right now it was nothing more than a slick, muddy trail. The footing was treacherous, and they made their way cautiously, taking care not to lose their balance.

The rain and the night air and the breeze that had kicked up chilled Rachel to her core. She assumed that the deputies were feeling the same about the weather as she was, but none of them complained. "Let's just take a look around and get it over with," she'd told them as they climbed out of their patrol cars to join her at the bottom of the road. No point in bitching about the job. It had to be done.

As she shone her light ahead of her, Rachel noted

111

that Bennett's thumbnail description of the site was accurate. *Score one for you, Mr. Bennett*, she thought. Whoever was building on the site was just beginning to lay down two-by-fours on either side of the trail, arranged in a kind of three-dimensional, full-size floor plan of the houses. The entire area was little more than a large man-made clearing carved from the surrounding woods.

Rachel was trying to imagine what it would all look like once the houses were built, when the deputy to her left called out, "Detective? I think I see something over here!"

He stepped over next to her, shining his light toward the base of a line of trees. Rachel trained her light on the same spot. They were joined by the other deputy, who did likewise. "That look like anything to either of you?" the first deputy asked.

Something was there, all but hidden under a pile of leaves, reflecting the beams from their flashlights back to them. They came forward as a group, letting their lights guide them to the trees. When they were close enough to see what was lying on the ground, Rachel could feel blood pounding in her ears.

She was staring down at the dead face of a small boy. His body was wrapped in thick, clear plastic. The body had been given a cursory burial beneath a pile of wet leaves. The wind had blown some of the leaves away, exposing enough of the body to allow Rachel and the deputies to find it.

She turned to the deputy who had spotted the body first and said, "Go call the coroner."

While he trotted back to his patrol car, Rachel and the second deputy knelt beside the dead boy and shone their flashlights around the immediate area.

Rachel was certain they would find nothing. The boy had to have been left here today, this very morning, while the rain had kept the construction workers at home, and there would have been nobody around to witness anything. Any evidence that the killer might have left behind—footprints, blood, anything—would have been washed away by the rain hours before Rachel and the deputies arrived.

She and the deputy brought their lights to play on the body once more. Rachel could hear the deputy sucking in his breath. "Damn this son of a bitch, anyway," he said in a hiss. His exhalation made a spout of vapor in the chilly, damp air.

"I hear you." Rachel grunted. "I hear you."

CHAPTER FIFTEEN

Later that evening, Rachel made four telephone calls from her desk in the detectives' squad room. The first was to her husband, Roy, to tell him that she wouldn't be home until very late and that he shouldn't wait up for her. The second was to Earl Novak at his home. Novak was not pleased to hear about another murdered child. The third call was to Kenneth Bennett at Community Hospital, who told her that yes, he would be there all day tomorrow and Friday as well, and that Rachel could visit him whenever she found the time. The fourth and most difficult call was to Craig McWilliams's mother and father.

While Rachel was working on her report, she received three calls. The first was from an evidence technician who told her that the plastic sheeting in which the boy's body had been wrapped was an ordinary shower curtain that could be bought at a dozen different stores, and that it was clean of fingerprints or any other incriminating evidence. The second call was from the pathologist who performed the autopsy on the dead boy. The postmortem confirmed what Rachel already knew about who had killed the boy. The pathologist also told Rachel that Mr. and Mrs. McWilliams had come to the morgue and identified their son.

The last call was from Novak. He told Rachel that he'd spoken to Mayor Barbara Underwood and Sheriff Peter Joyce, both of whom had agreed to an emergency meeting with him at the mayor's office at nine-thirty tomorrow morning. Novak then added that he wanted to invite Rachel to be in his office at noon sharp. It was not a request.

She got home at twelve-thirty A.M. The house was dark and quiet, her husband and sons asleep. She went into the bathroom that was connected to the master bedroom upstairs, closed the door, switched on the light, undressed, and prepared herself for bed.

Switching off the light, she made her way in the dark to the king-size bed that she and Roy shared. "Love you, babe." He grunted sleepily as she kissed him on the cheek and crawled under the bedcovers. He rolled onto his stomach as she settled herself on her side of the bed.

Rachel folded her arms behind her head, staring up at the ceiling in the darkness. Though she was exhausted, she lay awake for some time, unable to shut off her mental motor. She was thinking about several people: Roy and Denny and Aaron; Earl Novak; Mr. and Mrs. McWilliams. But mostly she thought about Kenneth Bennett, until at last she dozed off shortly after three A.M.

She was roused a few hours later by the aroma of coffee and the sensation of something heavy settling beside her on the bed. She opened her eyes, and there was Roy, sitting beside her, dressed in jeans and a faded Polo shirt. The room was filled with morning sunlight.

"Time to wake up and smell the you-know-what," he said, holding out to her the mug he was carrying. Rachel pushed herself up, sliding back against the headboard, and accepted the mug with a nod and a grateful smile.

She sipped the coffee carefully so as not to sear her tongue. "What time is it?"

"Nine-thirty."

"How come you're not at work?"

"I'm the boss, remember?" said Roy. "I get to come and go as I please."

She grunted. "Did the boys get off to school okay?"

Roy nodded. Then his eyebrows rose up in a leer as he edged closer to her. "You and I are all alone."

Rachel eyed him suspiciously and warned, "I don't have time to fool around with you this morning. If I'm not in Earl Novak's office at noon, he'll skin me alive."

Roy was sliding his hands under the covers. He touched the bare flesh of Rachel's right thigh and pinched her gently. She squealed. He pulled one hand out and took the coffee mug from her, setting it on the nightstand beside the bed. He was coming toward her again.

"I'm not kidding, Roy," Rachel said sternly.

Without warning she shot forward, grabbing him on either side of his rib cage and tickling him hard. Roy whooped, and the two of them tumbled onto the bed, tussling with each other, twisting themselves up in the covers. Soon he was on top of her, kneeling so that his legs straddled her waist, pinning her shoulders to the bed with his hands. She was gazing up at him, her eyes half-closed suggestively.

Roy looked down at her, his expression feigning reproach. "I thought you didn't have time to fool around with me."

"I think I can squeeze you in," she told him.

CHAPTER SIXTEEN

Rachel left the house at a quarter to eleven. She drove west on the freeway, skirting San Patricio's downtown area, and exited at Mission Street. Three blocks from the freeway she pulled into a parking lot beside a squat, adobe-style building. A sign hanging above the entrance to the building read, *The Third Eye Metaphysical Bookstore*.

She climbed out of her car and walked to the front entrance. The building was two stories tall. Going in, Rachel crossed to the front counter, behind which sat an attractive, smooth-faced young woman with curly brown hair. She was eighteen or nineteen years old, Rachel decided, wearing a long, floral-print dress and Birkenstocks. The girl smelled faintly of patchouli.

"Excuse me?" Rachel said politely.

The young woman smiled. "Hi."

Rachel returned the smile. "Hi. Listen, I know you carry a lot of stuff on parapsychology and ESP and all, but I'm kind of in a hurry, and I'm looking for something specific. Is there anybody who works here who is your, I don't know, your resident expert or anything like that? Somebody who could point me in the right direction pretty quickly?"

The woman nodded. "As a matter of fact . . ." She leaned forward, looking past Rachel's shoulder as she called out, "Rick? Can you come over here for a minute, please?"

Rachel turned around and saw that the woman had summoned a man who was sorting through a stack of new books that were lying atop a table behind where Rachel was standing. He was not much older than the woman behind the counter—at most in his mid-twenties, Rachel guessed. He had frizzy, shoulder-length, reddish-brown hair the same color as his droopy Fu Manchu moustache. He wore Levi's, a chambray shirt, and Doc Marten boots.

He approached the counter with an expression of curiosity on his face. "What's up?" he asked pleasantly.

"This lady needs some help," answered the woman behind the counter, gesturing to Rachel.

The man smiled at Rachel, extending a hand. "I'm Rick Plummer."

She shook hands. "Rachel Siegel."

"What can I do for you?"

"I'm looking for some material on a certain person, and I was wondering if you had anything on him here."

"Who's the person?"

"Kenneth Bennett."

"Kenneth Bennett, the psychic?"

Rachel thought, *Bingo*. "Obviously you've heard of him."

Plummer shrugged. "He's not as famous as some, but I'm sure he's made the pages of the *National Enquirer* once or twice."

"Have there been any books written about him? Or by him?"

Plummer frowned. "I don't think so. What I mean to say is, I know he hasn't written any books himself, and I don't think there've been any books that are just about him. . . ."

His voice trailed off as he thought for a moment. Then he snapped his fingers. "Wait right here."

Rachel watched Plummer move away toward the rear of the store. He disappeared behind a high bookshelf, then reappeared less than a minute later. He was coming back toward the counter, carrying a paperback book with him. He was looking at Rachel, wearing a smile of triumph.

Plummer handed her the book. She scanned the cover: *Psychic Criminalists: Heroes or Hoaxers?* The author's name, Matthew Pallamary, was underneath the title.

Rachel looked up at Plummer, her expression querying. "There's a whole chapter on Bennett," he explained. "I read this when it came out in hardback a couple years ago, and I remembered that it had a pretty good account of him. The paperback's a new edition."

Rachel opened the back of the book to the first page of the index. There, between *Bell, E. T.* and *Berdyaev, Nikolas* was *Bennett, Kenneth.*

"I hope it's what you're looking for," Plummer said. "If you give me a little more time, I might be able to find something else."

Rachel smiled gratefully. "It's perfect. I'll take it."

CHAPTER SEVENTEEN

She was at her desk in the squad room at eleven-fifty, a cup of coffee on the blotter in front of her. *Psychic Criminalists* was open in her hands. She was reading closely, oblivious to the activity in the room that swirled around her:

The life of American-born psychic Kenneth Bennett parallels the lives of his Dutch counterparts Hurkos and Croiset in several ways, but differs in others. Like Hurkos, Bennett displayed no particular talent until after he had sustained an injury. One afternoon, when he was seventeen years old, Bennett was playing football with friends in the street outside his house, and during the game he hit the back of his head on a concrete curb. He was knocked unconscious and lay in a near-comatose state for several hours. He awakened abruptly, just as the doctor who had been called to treat him—and who was about to order him taken to a local hospital for care—was

121

holding his hand to take his pulse. Bennett surprised the doctor by telling him that his automobile had more than enough gasoline than he would need to return home that night. It turned out that the doctor had been concerned over that very thing as he drove to Bennett's house to respond to the emergency call.

Bennett's career as a psychic criminalist did not commence, however, until a few years later, when he was attending college. Early one morning, while he was a sophomore at the University of Missouri, a young female student named Deborah Walsh disappeared while jogging in the area near her dormitory. For weeks the local police were stymied in their efforts to uncover any evidence that might lead them to discover her whereabouts, until they received a telephone call from Bennett, who identified himself as a fellow college student and told them that he knew where her body could be found. He was ordered to report to police headquarters for questioning, and there he described "a place like a barn, a big, open structure, with a kind of silo." According to Bennett, no one lived there. Three days later a dog belonging to a hunter who was crossing through the woods north of the city was attracted by a foul smell emanating from one of several buildings of a run-down, abandoned farm. It turned out to be the decomposed body of Deborah Walsh, hidden in an empty grain silo. She had been raped and then stabbed to death, and her body callously dumped at the abandoned farm.

Bennett was called in again by the police, this

time as a suspect. It was not long, however, before he was able to convince them of his innocence, that he had seen the girl's photograph in the newspapers, and that the image of the place "just came to him" in a vision. He was taken by detectives to Deborah's dormitory room, where he examined several items belonging to the girl, including some textbooks. He announced that Deborah's killer was someone that she knew, definitely a man, probably another student. Within the week the police had arrested James Ross, a twenty-year-old University of Missouri student who had dated Deborah occasionally, but had grown frustrated with his inability to establish a serious, permanent relationship with her. Ross subsequently confessed to the crime, and was eventually found guilty of second-degree murder.

An awareness of his burgeoning talent led Bennett to transfer from the University of Missouri in his senior year to Duke University in North Carolina, where he served as both a student and a subject for study at the Foundation for Research on the Nature of Man. While there, he demonstrated his remarkable faculty again and again. He demonstrated that power most dramatically in the early 1990s, when he assisted in the search for a serial killer in his hometown of St. Louis, Missouri. Bennett had moved back to St. Louis after living only a year in North Carolina, preferring instead to live with his widowed mother and work out of Washington University's Department of Neuropsychiatry.

One summer, a series of five murders occurred

in the central part of the city. All of the victims had been young men between the ages of eighteen and twenty-two, and all of them were homosexuals. An investigation of and interviews with dozens of members of the city's homosexual community had provided little information, at which time a detective in the Homicide bureau took it upon himself to contact Kenneth Bennett. Bennett knew about the murders, and was able to provide help almost immediately, describing the killer's vehicle as a "gray van with silver wheels." He was also able to give a description of the killer as a stocky, middle-aged man with a dark mustache. Descriptions of the killer and the van went out over the radio and television airwaves as well as in the newspapers, and six days after Bennett was consulted, one of the neighbors of a man named Vincent Stein telephoned the police to say that she suspected Stein of the murders. The suspect fit Bennett's basic description, and he owned a gray van with silver wheels—which had formerly belonged to his son, who had died earlier in the year from complications that developed as a consequence of his having AIDS. Stein was a widower, and he blamed the death of his only son on the homosexual lifestyle the younger Stein pursued. Upon being shown a photograph of Vincent Stein, Bennett promptly identified him as the killer, though when police arrived at Stein's house to arrest him, they found that he had taken his own life by hanging himself. A search of the house provided evidence to link Stein to the serial killings.

The case was officially closed, and Bennett became a national celebrity.

Though, like other psychic criminalists, Bennett has had his share of failures—

Rachel's attention was pulled away by the ringing of her telephone. She looked at it curiously, forgetting for a moment where she was. Finally she picked up the receiver. "Detective Siegel."

"Why aren't you in here, Rachel?" Earl Novak snapped.

She glanced at her watch. It was two minutes past twelve. *Cut me some slack*, she pleaded silently. "I'll be right there, Chief," she said into the phone.

Rachel hung up, then closed the book, marking the page she was reading by folding down the top corner. She opened a desk drawer and dropped the book inside. *Just as it was getting interesting*, she was thinking as she shut the drawer and came to her feet.

Novak's office was at the opposite end of the squad room. The office was a twelve-by-twelve-foot cubicle, the upper portion of its pressboard walls made of glass. There was a single door on which was hung a plastic nameplate that read, *Chief of Detectives*.

Rachel entered without knocking. Novak was sitting behind his desk, scowling at her. He was a big man, an inch over six feet tall and weighing slightly more than two hundred pounds. Though he was in his early fifties, most of his weight was still muscle. Novak's size and the close-cropped crew cut he wore gave him a gruff, intimidating appearance, like that of a Marine Corps drill sergeant. But any fear of him would vanish as soon as he opened his mouth and spoke in his high-pitched, squeaky voice that always forced the detectives who were new to the squad to stifle amused smiles. They would snicker, though, only until they had worked for him long enough to learn that he was a brownnoser par excellence and an officious, buck-passing prick. After that, he didn't seem quite so funny.

As she sat down in one of the two hard wooden chairs on the side of the desk opposite where Novak was sitting, he said to her sharply, "Let's have it."

"Have what?"

"The poop on that victim you found last night. And what you've been doing since then."

"Didn't you read my report?"

Novak's scowl deepened. *Don't fight with him*, Rachel cautioned herself. "Where do you want me to start?" she asked.

"How 'bout with what you did after I called you at home?"

Rachel summarized her activities of the night before: going to the hospital, as ordered, and speaking to the Bennetts; leading the deputies on the search that uncovered the body of Craig McWilliams; returning to the squad room and contacting the dead boy's parents, whom she had also arranged to interview later today; receiving confirmation from the coroner that Craig was killed by the same man who had killed the seven other children. She concluded by asking Novak, "Didn't I tell you all this on the phone last night?"

He scowled again. "What about this guy Bennett? How'd he know where to find the kid?"

Rachel had been dreading the question. *Here we go*, she thought uneasily. "He's a psychic."

Novak's eyes widened. "I beg your pardon?"

"A psychic. He had a vision, and in it he saw the kid up at that housing project."

"You're shitting me."

Rachel shook her head.

"Jesus Christ," Novak muttered. He looked at Rachel pointedly. "I hope to Christ you checked him out."

"That's what I was just doing," she replied. "It turns out he's legit. He's a genuine psychic."

"Jesus Christ," Novak repeated, rubbing his jaw with a beefy hand.

Rachel said, "Look, Earl, I'm not any happier about this than you are—"

"Let me tell you how I spent my morning, Rachel," Novak snapped, cutting her off. "The sheriff and the mayor both took turns chewing on my ass about this fucking case. 'What the hell is wrong with your investigation, Earl? When are we gonna see some results?' I tell 'em the same thing I've been telling them for months now. I got one of my best people on it, but we're just not turning up any clues because there aren't any clues. Except they're tired of hearing that. This morning they tell me, 'Eight dead kids, that's enough. We want you to call in the state bureau to take over the investigation, and we want you to do it today.' "

Rachel's mouth fell open. "They can't do that—"

"What the hell would you like me to do? Call the sheriff back and say, 'Forget the CBI, Pete. Rachel's bringing in a psychic who's gonna help us catch this guy'?"

"Goddammit, Earl, this is my case—"

"And you are getting nowhere with it, aren't you?"

She could feel her face flushing. "That's not my fault."

"I don't give a shit whose fault it is. I've got my orders, and now I'm giving you yours. I don't want to hear the word 'psychic' pass your lips again, all right? It's still your case, at least until the CBI shows up. At which time you'll be the department's liaison, working with whoever the fucking state sends us."

For a moment neither of them said anything, until Rachel asked, "How soon before they get somebody here?"

"As soon as possible," Novak answered. "I'm calling them right after you leave, and I'm gonna tell them this is an A-one priority situation."

Rachel frowned unhappily. "And that's it?"

Novak nodded. "That's it."

CHAPTER EIGHTEEN

As Rachel was leaving Novak's office, the news that the state's bureau of investigation would be taking over her case hung above her head like a black cloud. She was wondering if the day could get any worse, until she remembered her scheduled meeting with Craig McWilliams' parents. It was not going to be a pleasant interview, Rachel told herself, and she considered canceling the appointment. *Not a good idea*, she decided. Even if it meant just going through the motions, the case was still hers. At least until the CBI arrived.

Edward and Yoshiko McWilliams lived in a large ranch-style house near the UC San Patricio campus. Both of them were on the faculty at the university. Edward McWilliams, Ph.D., was a professor of English literature, and his wife, also a Ph.D., was an associate professor of biology. Craig was their only child. They were home when Rachel arrived, as they had promised to be. As Rachel feared, the meeting did not go well.

Her interview with them lasted an hour and a half, but it yielded nothing that she did not already know.

Last Saturday morning, in the company of three friends, Craig had ridden his bicycle down to the San Patricio Boardwalk to spend the day at the city's beachfront amusement park. It was well after dark when Yoshiko McWilliams received a telephone call from the mother of one of Craig's friends. At some time during the day Craig had become separated from the other boys and disappeared. The woman was calling to see if he made it home all right.

Following the instructions he'd been given by a deputy sheriff to whom he'd spoken on Saturday night, Edward McWilliams reported his missing son to the Sheriff's Department on Monday. While Rachel questioned Craig's parents, it became obvious to her that Dr. Edward McWilliams was a bitter man. The focus of his bitterness was the Sheriff's Department in general and Rachel Siegel, its representative, in particular. He blamed the department for two things: their—in his opinion—stupid rule that "We can't take a missing-person's report until the person has been missing for forty-eight hours," and their inability to catch the killer before last weekend.

That Rachel could sympathize with the way he was feeling did not assuage her anger at being the target of McWilliams's tirade against the law-enforcement powers-that-be. He went too far, she thought, deciding that McWilliams was probably a miserable human being under the best of circumstances. She bore his verbal attacks with equanimity, restraining herself from responding in kind, allowing him to vent his fury while maintaining her best professional demeanor.

Rachel felt more sorry for Dr. Yoshiko McWilliams, who sat stoically beside her husband while he ranted, never once interrupting him, answering only those questions that Rachel placed to her directly. In spite of her reticence—or perhaps because of it—she seemed desperately sad to Rachel. So delicate and fragile, like a figurine made of porcelain.

Rachel had to caution herself not to think of Dr. McWilliams as a stereotypical demure and subservient Japanese wife, if for no other reason than that stereotyping people was a dangerous habit for a police officer to embrace. Though she could not have explained how she knew this, Rachel could tell that the loss of their child hurt Yoshiko McWilliams much more severely than it did her husband.

Rachel gratefully left the McWilliamses' house at four-thirty and drove to Community Hospital. There she found Kenneth Bennett in his room, sitting up in bed as he had been the evening before. A pile of newspapers lay spread atop the bedclothes covering his legs. Bennett looked much better than he did the last time Rachel had seen him. He'd had a bath since then, and he was wearing new pajamas. His color was rosier as well, though his left eye was still badly swollen. The bruise surrounding it was turning yellow around the edges. He greeted Rachel with a smile that, while it wasn't full of cheer, was nevertheless warmer than the greeting she had received from Mr. and Mrs. McWilliams.

As Rachel sat down in the same seat she'd taken yesterday, she said to Bennett, "Is your sister here?"

He shook his head. "She's had a lot to do today: talking with the doctor, settling up about the car. . . ." His expression became sheepish. "It was a rental. I bought insurance for it, but it's still turning into a royal pain in the ass, trying to straighten everything out. Not to mention they're not real keen about renting me another one."

"I can imagine."

"I think Denise got bored just hanging around here," Bennett said. "Especially once she found out for sure they're going to let me check out tomorrow instead of Saturday."

"I guess that means you're okay?"

He shrugged. "My head still hurts, and my shoulder aches. Other than that, I'm fine."

"I'm glad to hear it."

"Yeah." He took in a deep breath and sighed. "So. Detective Siegel. How's everything with you?"

"You really want to know?"

He regarded her seriously. "As a matter of fact, I do."

Instead of answering him, Rachel gestured to the newspapers. "I see you've been catching up on your current events?"

"Uh-huh."

"Did you find anything in particular that interested you?"

"Uh-huh."

"What?"

"I found out that since January there've been eight kids from San Patricio murdered by the same person, and you don't have a clue who's doing it."

Rachel said, "Did you also happen to find out who's in charge of the case?"

Bennett nodded.

She leaned back in her chair, considering. Then she came forward again, resting her elbows on her knees, folding her hands. She propped her chin atop her hands and said, "I don't want you to think that I don't appreciate the help you gave me last night."

Bennett swallowed. "But . . . ?"

"But . . ." Rachel scratched an ear. "How do I say this politely? 'Thanks, but no, thanks'?"

Bennett's eyes narrowed.

"I know you're legit," she continued. "The boy's body was right where you said it would be." She paused. "I also did a little homework myself today. I found a copy of this book called *Psychic Criminalists*."

Bennett sat watching her, saying nothing. Rachel asked, "What do you know about San Patricio, Mr. Bennett?"

The question seemed to catch him off guard. "What do you mean?"

"It's a simple question."

Bennett thought for a moment; then he shrugged again. "Not much. But then, I've only been here for a day, and for most of that time I was unconscious."

"It's kind of a funny place," Rachel explained. "We've got a very interesting mix of people, and everybody's view of what it's like to live around here is a little bit different from everybody else's. The best assessment I've ever heard is that San Patricio is really what everybody in the country who doesn't live here thinks of when they think of California. You know what I'm saying? San Patricio is sort of California in microcosm, with all the good and bad that implies. Very laid-back, very mellow, very much do-your-own-thing. But also sometimes very weird. We've got lots of leftover hippies, nice weather, the beach right off our back porch."

She paused, trying to read his expression. Then: "I'm not saying it isn't like that, because it is. But that's only part of what makes San Patricio unique. For example, in all of California, this is the county where it's easiest to qualify for welfare. As a consequence we've got a real problem with some of the transients who pass through and then stick around to settle down. But to turn them away would go against the very nature of San Patricio. We've also got a city council that includes among the usual businessman types in its membership one lesbian feminist, one Rastafarian, and two card-carrying members of the American Communist Party. Basically the city has a clean reputation—it's a college town and a resort community and kind of a haven for all sorts of artist types. But at the same time it's one of the biggest illegal-drug distribution centers on the west coast. We've got yuppies and bikers and dot-com zillionaires living side by side with surfers and sculptors and real estate speculators. Up in the mountains there are people who still live in cabins—I swear, it looks like Appalachia. They've got no electricity, no running water, their kids don't go to school, and that's the way they like it. We've got other residents whose families have been around for more than a century, and they own some of the most valuable land in the whole country. To tell you the truth, we've got a little bit of everything. Which makes it just about the most schizophrenic place you'd ever want to see."

Rachel paused again. Bennett said, "I have the feeling you've got a point you're trying to make."

"That's right, I do," she said. "I just don't want you to get the wrong idea, that's all. The reason I'm telling you about the way things are around here is because I really don't want you to think I'm not grateful."

"You said that already."

"I know. But I also know that you're thinking seriously about staying around for a while so you can help me with this case."

He eyed her warily. "Now who's reading whose mind?"

"I'm not joking. In the past four months we've had a dozen 'psychics' of our own crawl out of the wood-work and offer to help us find this guy. We listened to all of them, too, just on the chance that they might actually know something, though not a one of them did. Unfortunately, some reporters found out about it, and the Sheriff's Department got lambasted in the media as a result. We were made to look very foolish, and that's something our sheriff doesn't like very much."

"Only I did know something," Bennett insisted.

"I'm aware of that," said Rachel.

"And you still don't want me to help?"

She looked away for a moment. "I'd like you to leave town as soon as the hospital releases you."

She turned back to him. Bennett drew in a breath and exhaled slowly. He studied Rachel's face. "I guess I can't ask you to make it any plainer than that."

Rachel came to her feet. He frowned at her, but the frown faded quickly, replaced by a look of resigna-tion. He reached across his body, extending his left hand for her to shake.

Rachel let go of his hand and moved toward the door. She paused there to look back at him, showing a small smile. "I hope the rest of your trip goes better than it's gone up till now. I really do."

He managed a smile of his own in return. "Me, too."

She waved good-bye and stepped out into the hall-way, closing the door behind her.

CHAPTER NINETEEN

Rachel encountered Denise Bennett in the hospital's parking lot. Denise was coming back from having rented another car—in her name this time. She told Rachel that she and her brother had reservations at a bed-and-breakfast in Carmel the following night.

Rachel noticed the cameras in the backseat of Denise's car. Denise said that she had spent much of the day wandering around the San Patricio waterfront taking pictures. Until then Rachel hadn't known that Denise was a photographer.

As they parted, Rachel repeated to Denise her desire for the Bennetts to have a better trip than they'd had so far. With that, Denise headed for the hospital's entrance, and Rachel climbed into her minivan. While she drove home she was telling herself that she hoped Roy had dinner on the table by the time she got there. If he didn't, the Siegel-Rodgers family was going to McDonald's tonight or someplace like it, or else they weren't going to eat.

CHAPTER TWENTY

Denise was awakened at eight A.M. on Friday morning by a phone call. She knew who was on the other end of the line, having spoken to him the night before after she had left the hospital and checked into a motel. She mumbled into the phone sleepily, "Hi, Tom."

Tom Hanson said to her from two thousand miles away, "Didn't I tell you last night that if I called this early I'd wake you up?"

She yawned. "Uh-huh."

"Do you want to go get a cup of coffee or something first?" he asked. "I can wait for you to call me back."

"No." She yawned again. "It's okay."

A brief pause, then: "I just got off the phone with Jim Herbert," Hanson said. "He was pretty upset when I told him about what happened to Ken."

Denise said, "And?"

"He said just what I thought he'd say."

"He did?"

"Uh-huh."

Denise sat up in bed. "Did he say anything else?"

"That's it," said Hanson.

"Okay," she told him. "Thanks, Tom. I appreciate your getting in touch with him for me."

"Anytime," he said. "Listen, if you get a chance, maybe you can call me later and let me know how everything goes."

"I'll do that," Denise said. "I promise."

CHAPTER TWENTY-ONE

When Denise walked into her brother's hospital room an hour and a half later, she found him up and dressed. He was sitting in the chair beside the bed, waiting for her. His packed suitcase rested on the floor.

Bennett said to her as she came through the door, "I want you to cancel our reservation in Carmel."

"Why?" she asked.

His lips were pressed together in a thin slash. "I'm not leaving San Patricio. I know last night I said maybe we'd just go. This morning, though, I changed my mind. I have to stay and help, if I can."

"Even though nobody wants your help?"

He nodded.

Denise took a deep breath and exhaled slowly. "I talked to Tom Hanson this morning. I had a feeling you might decide to stay. I asked Tom to call your psychiatrist and see if he thought it was a good idea. Would you like to know what he told Tom to tell me to tell you?"

Bennett watched her closely, saying nothing.

Denise went on. "Dr. Herbert says your emotional state is very fragile right now. To get involved with something like this, before you've completely dealt with your feelings about Christina . . . it's just too risky. He's afraid you might have a nervous breakdown."

She brushed tears from her eyes with the back of her hand. Her voice became choked with emotion. "Dammit, Kenny, the police think you should go, your doctor thinks you should go, Tom Hanson thinks you should go, I think you should go. . . ." She shook her head. "What happens around here is not your responsibility, no matter how much you believe it is. Your only responsibility is to take care of yourself."

Denise was sobbing now. Bennett came to his feet and reached for her, wrapping his arms around her, pulling her close to him.

She hugged him, burying her face in his chest. "I just want you to be happy," she whispered. "I'm so scared of what might happen to you. . . ."

He was stroking her hair gently. "I know."

She pulled back to look up at him with red-rimmed eyes. "If you want to stay, I can't stop you. But after I check you out of here, I'm driving to Carmel. I'd like it if you came with me."

Bennett looked away for a moment, then turned back to her. He nodded. "Okay."

"Are you sure?" she asked. "You're not just giving in?"

He nodded again. "I'm sure."

CHAPTER TWENTY-TWO

By noon they were in Carmel. Denise had driven the entire way, having agreed to the stipulation of the rental company that leased her the car that her brother would not spend any time behind the wheel. Bennett told Denise that he didn't particularly mind, since the car was a compact Toyota. He didn't much care to be driving so scrunched up as she seemed to be.

They checked into the Sea View, a wood-shingled bed-and-breakfast painted pale blue. The place stood a block from the beach. After they had settled in, Bennett asked his sister if she would mind if he took a walk along the shore by himself. At first she was hesitant to let him go, but he smiled his crooked smile at her, and that was that.

She lay down for a nap, exhausted from the drive and a restless night's sleep. When she awoke a little after four that afternoon, she found that her brother hadn't yet returned. A spark of panic fizzled along her spine. She was up quickly and she trotted out of the house, not at all sure that hunting for him by herself was the right thing to do. He could be anywhere.

But she found him right away. He was sitting at the edge of a rock jetty that thrust out into the bay, looking out over the water. She spotted him as soon as she reached the beach: a solitary figure perched virtually statue-still. Wrapping her arms around herself for warmth against the chilly late-afternoon breeze, she walked to the jetty and called his name. He turned around, and she saw that his cheeks were flushed from the cold. She knew from looking at him that he had been sitting there for some time.

He acknowledged her with a wan smile, came to his feet, and accompanied her back to the house. That night, during dinner, they talked about the remainder of their trip. On Sunday they would leave for San Simeon; they had tickets to tour the Hearst Castle on Monday morning. On Tuesday they would be in Morro Bay; on Wednesday, Santa Barbara. They would spend the weekend in Los Angeles, and the first few days of the following week in San Diego. After which they would fly back to San Francisco on Wednesday, June eighth. It turned out that the accident in San Patricio had upset their schedule very little. Fortunately they'd programmed ahead of time a few extra days scattered here and there.

At midnight, as Denise lay in bed waiting for sleep to take her, she was thinking dark thoughts about all that had happened over the past few days. It was obvious that Kenny had reverted to the way he'd been when he got off the plane from St. Louis two weeks ago: sad and quiet and introspective. Just when it seemed he was starting to snap out of it.

THE CRIMINALIST

I guess it's back to square one, Denise told herself, thinking that it would suit her just fine if no one mentioned the words "San Patricio" to her for a long, long time.

JUNE

CHAPTER ONE

The man drove carefully, as he always did at night. It was late—nearly midnight—and he was traveling north along U.S. 1. He'd crossed the city limits of San Patricio, and his car seemed to be the only one on the highway. He was pleased about that. He preferred solitude whenever he could have it. Solitude allowed him to think, to remember. There was nothing wrong with wanting to be alone, he told himself. Nothing at all.

Except he was not alone.

He glanced at the small figure curled up on the passenger seat. The girl was sleeping, her head resting against the glass of the side window. She was inhaling and exhaling rhythmically, a series of small sighs. She looked so young—she'd told him that she'd turned eleven years old just two days before. So young, so delicate, so innocent. So sweet.

The girls were much more delicate than the boys, he decided. But the boys had their own attraction— their roughness and their energy. The man liked boys and girls equally well. He had no favorites. None was better than any other. They were just different.

He drove, thinking about the girl.

There had been so many children to choose from today. He knew why, of course. Today, June eleventh, was the first Saturday following the last day of school for the year for many of them. Today was the day that the children celebrated their freedom. For them it was the true first day of summer, and it didn't matter that the calendar might insist that summer was still officially a week and a half away.

Hundreds of children were there for him today. So merry, so full of life. So many happy children that his heart ached. *Which one?* he asked himself over and over, unable to choose from among them. *Which one?*

He looked at the girl.

Her name was Amanda. She'd come up to him a little after nine-thirty P.M. *Excuse me, but did you see my friends? The ones who were with me when we were here before? We were supposed to meet up right here so we could ride home together, but I forgot if we said nine o'clock or ten o'clock, and now I'm afraid they've left without me. . . .*

Trusting the big, hairy, friendly teddy bear of a man whom all the children knew. Trusting him because he was nice, and he was always smiling, and he seemed to enjoy their company so very much. Trusting him to know what to do.

He asked Amanda if she knew her telephone number. She did. She lived in Boulder Creek, she said. He asked if she had any money left so she could call her mother and father, but she'd spent all the money she'd brought with her. He told her to give him the number and to stay right where she was, while he went to contact her parents and let them know she was all right. He went away for a few minutes, pretending to make the call, then came back and told her that he'd gotten permission from her mother to take her home himself just as soon as he got off work. He asked if she was hungry, if she wouldn't like a hot dog and a soda pop while she waited.

He turned his attention from the highway to glance at her once again. He smiled to himself, whispering a silent prayer of thanks to God for providing him with another little one who this night would be sent to her Father in heaven.

The man's name was Joshua Wright, and he was quite insane.

CHAPTER TWO

There were few lights along the twelve-mile stretch of U.S. 1 between San Patricio and Davenport. Wright's vision was not helped by the fog that had begun to roll in from the bay. Night fog was not uncommon this time of year—huge paws of mist that slowly clawed their way inland. The bay was a sheet of rippling black glass that lay to one side of the highway, beyond a narrow stretch of beach. On the other side were miles and miles of wooded hills wrapped in shadow. The beams from the headlights of Wright's car—the Pontiac station wagon that he and his father had bought new more than twenty years ago— caused the mist to sparkle.

Wright drove, no longer thinking of the girl beside him. Instead he was thinking about Daddy.

Images flashed upon the projection screen of his mind, as if he were watching a slide show. In each of the transparencies was one or the other or both of two prominent figures: himself, Joshua Wright, and his daddy, Judson Wright.

Daddy . . .

The first slide was of a boy: Josh, age seven. Taken

150

fifty years ago at a faraway place called Arkansas. Wright could not remember the exact name of the town: Swifton? Amity? Fisher? Bradley? In his mind, Wright could see Josh's face—*his* face—lit by the glow of lanterns, perspiring from the humid heat of an Arkansas midsummer night and the closeness of hundreds of squirming, sweating bodies packed together beneath the tattered canvas of the chautauqua tent. The boy's face was crossed by the shadows of the tent posts. His eyes were riveted on the man at the front of the tent, standing on a makeshift stage. Over the stage hung a huge banner, *Hear Brother Jud Wright! The light to light the darkness!*

Daddy . . .

He could hear Daddy's voice in his mind: dry and soft, the thick east Texas drawl. As he heard it every day of his life, even on the days since Daddy had . . .

. . . passed away.

Daddy's voice spellbinding the crowd packed into the tent: "I hear you people askin' me, 'Brother Jud, how do we light a candle in the darkness? How do we fight the good fight of faith?' And I say to you, you fight the good fight by laying hold of eternal life! Now you have to understand, this is something that came as a drastic shock to me when I learned this myself. I used to not realize that eternity is now. You don't get into eternity after you die. You're in it now. When you die, all that happens is you just change places. That's all. I used to believe that when you accepted Jesus and you got saved, you'd live forever. But that's not so. I know now that ever'body, whether they know Jesus as their savior or not, will live forever. Ever'body. See, what happens when you choose Jesus is that you *choose* where you'll live forever. All of us, already we're livin' forever. Ever' human being, whether they've been saved or not. It's just that when you die after you've been saved, and you go to heaven, that's where you are goin' to be a child of God."

Then another slide, of him and Daddy, jouncing along in the cab of Daddy's battered old Ford pickup along some dusty, nameless road in the middle of nowhere, on their way to another prayer meeting. The back of the truck filled with everything they owned, covered over by a dirty canvas tarpaulin and tied down with lengths of rope. Listening to the radio: Hank Williams singing "Old Rugged Cross." He and Daddy are singing along, smiling at each other.

Another slide. Himself, asleep. Dreaming about Mama, a slight, quiet, plain woman who was much younger than Daddy, hardly more than a child herself. Who had gone away a long time ago. *Run off*, Daddy said. *She's not "Mama" anymore. Don't you say the word "Mama" to me ever again. She run off with some other man, and that makes her a whore. Don't you even think "Mama" anymore, Joshua. If you think of that woman at all, you think "whore," and you pray to God to punish her. That's what you do.*

Another slide. Himself, older now, in his twenties. Behind the wheel of another pickup—not the same one as before, that one having given up the ghost years ago. Heading west to California on Route 66 to get away from the dwindling crowds. The people who were turning away from Daddy—and from God. As the crowds got smaller and smaller, Daddy grew more sour and sullen, and he drank more and more often. Then he woke up one morning and announced that he was going to retire, and they were moving to California. Showing his son all of the money he'd saved over the years: stacks of bills he'd accumulated and kept in a locked strongbox, the only key to which he wore on a strip of leather around his neck, and never took off. More money than Joshua Wright could have imagined. *Let 'em all be damned*, said Daddy. *I've done my share of the Lord's work. It's time to rest.*

Another slide. The two of them moving into a small, single-story, two-bedroom, wood-frame house in Davenport, a quarter of a mile from the nearest neighbors. Their house that Daddy had paid for entirely, in cash.

Another slide. Himself, working at the job he'd taken in San Patricio, not long after he and Daddy had settled in. The job he'd had ever since, for more than twenty years.

Another slide, from one year ago. Himself, in the doctor's office, hearing the doctor say, "What's wrong with your father, Mr. Wright, is a cancer that started in his pancreas but has spread much too quickly and too far. I'm sorry to have to tell you that his prognosis is not good. He'll have moments of lucidity when he'll be free of pain for the rest of the time he's got left, but those moments will become fewer and farther between. What I'd recommend is either that you place him into a convalescent home that has hospice facilities, where they can keep an eye on him 'round the clock, or else hire somebody to stay with him while you're out of the house. I'm thinking of your own well-being, Mr. Wright, because, to tell you the truth, there just isn't a lot that we can do for him. . . ."

Another slide. Himself, preparing the injection of morphine. Going into Daddy's bedroom, to the bedside of the shrunken, misshapen figure that writhed beneath the sheets, whimpering in agony. Lifting the sheet, exposing the bare hip, slipping the needle into the purplish-black bruise that discolored the slack, wrinkled skin.

Another slide. Himself, on his knees beside his own bed. Praying: *Dear God, please help my Daddy to get better again. Please.*

Another slide. Himself, driving home from work on Saturday evening, the weekend after New Year's Day this year. Thinking dark, uncharitable thoughts. Thinking about Daddy. Thinking about how perhaps it would be better if Daddy were simply to die after all . . .

Another slide. Himself, coming home that same day. Coming into Daddy's bedroom. And seeing the Daddy shape on the bed—Daddy no longer moving, his mouth sagging open, his eyes wide and staring. Wright himself, seeing the expression of sheer terror carved on Daddy's shriveled features, as if death had not taken away the pain, not at all, but had merely locked it into place for all eternity.

Another slide. Of Daddy's casket, being lowered into an open hole in the earth.

Another slide. Himself, on the sofa in the living room. Alone. Sobbing. His head buried in his hands.

Another slide. Himself. Sitting alone in the darkened living room. And listening to Daddy's voice in his mind, urging him, *Suffer the little children to come unto Me, and forbid them not; for of such is the kingdom of God.*

Then listening to another part of his mind that was saying to him, *The Book of Luke, chapter ten, verse forty.*

Then listening to Daddy again: *Suffer the children to come unto Me . . .*

To come unto Him. Unto their Father. In heaven.

Another slide. Of himself, Joshua Wright. Holding the hand of a little girl named Emma Lyons . . .

It was nearly one A.M. by the time Wright guided the station wagon into the gravel driveway that led to a cement-slab carport at the rear of his property. The house was at the end of a lonely cul-de-sac off San Vicente Street, one of the two main thoroughfares of the town of Davenport, on the wooded side of the town, north of the highway, nestled at the edge of a grove of trees. The crunch of the Pontiac's tires upon the gravel sounded very loud to him, even though he had the car's windows rolled up to keep out the chilly night air. The sound made Wright's heart beat faster, and he had to command himself to relax. He assured himself that there was no one around who could hear him, no one who was watching him, no one who had a clue in the world what he was about to do.

He switched off the car's ignition and paused for a moment to look once more at the little girl sleeping in the passenger seat. He showed her a blissful smile. Then he climbed out of the car, shut his door as quietly as he could, crossed to her side, opened her door, and lifted her gently. He stepped back and eased her door shut with his foot. She reached up to circle her arms around his neck, mumbling something that he could not understand. He smiled again.

As he carried her into the house, he was recalling a favorite song. Keeping his voice low, not wanting to awaken the sleeping burden in his arms, he sang the words to himself: " 'Jesus loves the little children. All the children of the world. Red or yellow, black or white, they are precious in his sight. Jesus loves the little children of the world. . . .'"

He carried Amanda through the back door into the kitchen, where he switched on a light. From there he went into the dark living room, where he set her down on the threadbare sofa that was the only remaining piece of furniture of all that he and Daddy had brought with them when they first moved in. Everything else in the house—tables, chairs, beds, television, stove, refrigerator, and so on—had been picked up over the years, as they needed them. But the sofa had been Daddy's favorite place to sit and watch television or listen to the radio or tell stories about his preaching days or quote from the scriptures. Wright kept the old sofa because it seemed as if it had soaked up a part of Daddy, his having rested on it for so long all those years.

He laid the girl down, then took a tattered afghan that was draped over the back of the sofa and covered her with it. He stood above the sofa for a moment, watching her. The light from the kitchen fell across the middle of the sofa. Her face was in shadow. She was deeply asleep—exhausted, no doubt, from her long, happy day, he told himself.

Wright moved from the living room down a short hallway. The first door he came to was on the left-hand side of the hall, opening into a bathroom. He went through the door, switched on the bathroom light, and found himself looking at his own reflection in the mirror that fronted the medicine cabinet opposite the door. The harsh light made him flinch momentarily.

He blinked, adjusting his eyes to the brightness. Then he opened the cabinet, pausing to examine what lay inside. On the upper shelf was a pack of disposable hypodermic syringes. Beside them were ampules of morphine. Wright frowned, thinking about how much he disliked having to use the drug, but the frown quickly faded when he realized that tonight he didn't have to, because Amanda was already asleep. A warm sensation of gratitude washed over him.

On the shelf beneath the syringes and the morphine was a box that dispensed surgical gloves. Wright had bought several boxes of the gloves last summer—right after Daddy had started to get so bad. He wore them whenever he had to deal with the more unpleasant tasks that went along with caring for a gravely ill individual: changing Daddy's bed linens and his pajamas and his soiled diapers. Now, even though Daddy was gone, the gloves still came in handy.

Wright slipped on a pair of gloves and went back into the living room. The little girl lay on her right side, curled into a ball on the sofa. Wright looked down at her, and he felt such an aching of love in his heart that he had to bite his tongue to keep from crying out in joy. He whispered to himself, "Jesus loves the little children."

He knelt on the floor beside the sofa. Tenderly he used a forefinger to brush aside a stray lock of hair that had fallen from her temple and across her left eye. She stirred, grumbling again something that he did not understand. Carefully he rolled her onto her back. She resisted at first, her face crinkling into a frown.

Then he wrapped his thick hands around her neck, thumbs pressing against her windpipe. The pressure caused her eyes to open. She looked at him with terror in her eyes.

He smiled and whispered, "Please give Daddy my love when you see him."

Then he squeezed.

CHAPTER THREE

"When did your nightmare start coming back?" Dr. Herbert asked.

" 'Nightmares,' you mean," Ken Bennett replied. "Lately I've been having a couple of different dreams. The old one still comes and goes. But there's a new one, too."

They were in Herbert's office on Monday afternoon, the twenty-seventh of June. Inside the office it was cool and comfortable, the air-conditioning turned up high. Outside, the city of St. Louis was sweltering. By noon, two hours ago, the temperature downtown had risen to ninety-six degrees.

The sky was sunny and clear, but the air was thick with humidity—typical weather for the first week of summer. In the short time it had taken Bennett to walk from the parking lot of the medical building into the lobby, his armpits and chest had become damp with perspiration. He was grateful to be indoors, though the heat made him look wearier and more haggard than he had the last time he'd visited the psychiatrist in early May.

"Nightmares, then," said Herbert. "You said you'd

stopped having them while you were in San Francisco. When did they resume?"

"About three days after the accident," said Bennett. Already he'd told Herbert about the time he'd spent with Denise, about the drive from San Francisco to San Patricio, and about the vision he'd had of Craig McWilliams. "They started again right after my sister and I got to Carmel."

"How long ago was that?"

Bennett hesitated. "A month ago."

Herbert was taken aback. "You've had the same nightmares every day for the past month?"

Bennett nodded.

The doctor's expression became stern. "How long have you been back in St. Louis?"

"Twelve days," Bennett answered.

"And you only got around to calling me this morning?"

Bennett sighed. "I didn't want anybody to know I was back."

The answer drew a look of surprise from Herbert. "You haven't talked to anyone in twelve days? No friends, no relatives?"

"No one."

"Why not?"

"I didn't want to."

"But you finally decided you needed to talk to me?"

Bennett nodded.

"How come?" asked Herbert.

Bennett pressed his lips together. "Because I think I'm starting to lose my mind."

They sat in silence for a time. Then Herbert said, "Have you been drinking?"

Bennett shook his head. "Not really."

"What have you been doing?"

Bennett took a deep breath and exhaled slowly. "Just . . . dreaming. Sometimes it's that same dream I was having before. The one I told you about last time . . . with Christina and the monster and the mist, that one. When Denise and I were in California, though, after the accident, I started having another dream."

Herbert asked, "What about?"

Bennett shook his head unhappily. "It's so odd. In the dream I seem to be a little boy. Very small, maybe ten years old. But I'm thinking like an adult. And I'm standing before this huge, black shape, like a big hill or something. I can't quite make out what it is. And there's this awful sound, like a loud clacking and rattling. It's familiar to me, somehow. I recognize the sound, but I can't put my finger on what it is, exactly. And I can hear screams. Very high-pitched. Like children's screams."

Herbert tented his fingers, studying Bennett, not speaking.

"Then I watch this figure detach itself from the black shape," Bennett went on. "It's a man—or, rather, it's the figure of a man. Except that he has wings made of silver, so he looks sort of like an angel. His whole body is silver, very bright and shining. And he flies. He literally lifts himself off the ground and starts coming after me. I try to run away, but it's like it always is when you run in a dream. I pump my legs as hard as I can, but I can't get anywhere. I can hear his wings beating the air behind me; he's getting closer and closer. Then I feel his hand clamp on my shoulder like a claw, and I'm being lifted up off the ground. Then I start to scream myself. . . ." He paused. "That's when I wake up."

Herbert was regarding Bennett with compassion. "My God."

"Needless to say, I haven't slept very much in the last month," Bennett said. "But I've kind of gotten used to it. I doze off in the afternoons for an hour or so at a time. If I'm lucky, I'll get maybe two or three full hours of sleep at a stretch."

Herbert said, "And it's been going on like this for a month?"

"Every night."

Herbert pressed his lips together in a tight frown. "I don't know what to tell you, Ken. Honest to God, in all the years I've been a psychiatrist, I've never worked with a problem quite like this one." He scratched his head thoughtfully. "The first thing we need to do is see that you start getting some good sleep. If you don't, it's only a matter of time before you break down completely. Generally I don't like to prescribe sedatives, but I don't think in your case I've got a lot of choice."

"If you think it'll help," Bennett said, "I'm willing to try anything."

"I'll start you on something fairly mild," said Herbert, "and then we'll take it from there. As for the rest of it . . . ." He paused briefly, considering. "Doesn't Tom Hanson do sleep research? I seem to recall he published a paper one time . . . ?"

"That was four or five years ago," said Bennett. "He hasn't been interested in the subject for a long time."

"Is there anybody else in your department right now who's doing work with sleep problems?"

"Not at the moment," Bennett said. "At least, not that I know of."

"Then I think it'd be worth your while to talk to

Tom," said Herbert. "If nothing else, maybe he'll have a little different insight. I tend to believe that a lot of times dream interpretation is a crock, but I'm aware of situations where it's been helpful, so we can see what he thinks about it. It'd probably be a good idea for you to give him a call."

Bennett said warily, "Because he's a shrink who's going to have some clue as to what's wrong with me, or because he's my friend, and I could use a shoulder to cry on?"

"What's wrong with having a shoulder to cry on now and again?" Dr. Herbert asked.

After a moment Bennett said, "You really think I should call Tom?"

"Yes, I do."

Bennett sighed. "You're the doctor."

CHAPTER FOUR

On his way home Bennett stopped at a pharmacy on Big Bend Boulevard, where he had filled the prescription for Seconal that Dr. Herbert had given him. It was three-thirty P.M. by the time Bennett got back to his house. He was exhausted. Talking to Herbert for an hour, opening up as he'd done, had drained him physically as well as emotionally. Bennett went directly into his bedroom, stripped to his under-shorts and T-shirt, and sat down on the edge of the bed.

He held the bottle of pills in his hand, debating with himself whether he should take one. He decided that it was too early in the day for a long sleep. He set the bottle on the nightstand next to his bed and lay down. Listening to the low hum of the house's central air conditioning, feeling the gentle wafting of cool air over his exposed skin, he closed his eyes. Almost instantly he was asleep.

An hour and a half later he awoke with a start. The room was bright with late-afternoon sunshine. He thought for a moment that he had slept for an entire day, until he sat up and looked at the clock on the nightstand. He sighed.

Bennett eyed the telephone resting next to the clock. He shrugged, lifted the receiver from the hook, and pressed Tom Hanson's number. The other end rang four times before there came an electronic click, followed by a recorded voice: "You've reached the home of Dr. Thomas Hanson. Please wait for the tone; then leave as long a message as you'd like."

The recorder beeped at Bennett, and he said into the phone, "Tom? It's Ken. I'm back from California. It's about quarter after five in the afternoon on Monday, June twenty-seventh, and I was wondering if maybe you might be free for dinner this evening. I thought I'd barbeque some hamburgers at my place. If you get this message anytime soon, give me a call back."

Bennett got up from the bed and crossed to a chest of drawers on the opposite side of the room. In the bottom drawer he found a pair of faded Dockers. He slipped on the trousers, then crossed barefoot to a closet beside the chest. From there he pulled out a pair of huarache sandals that he laid on the floor and stepped into.

As he walked out of his bedroom, he was suddenly aware of a comfortable if vague sense of relief. Bennett realized that he was feeling less fatigued than he had in many weeks. It was, he decided, a consequence of having finally done something about what was bothering him, instead of just sitting around the house as he'd been doing. Sitting around, and suffering, and quietly going mad.

Bennett went into the kitchen and filled a glass with bottled water from the refrigerator. From there he went into the den that was off the living room, and he switched on the wide-screen television that sat in one corner of the room. He settled down in an easy chair opposite the TV. On a magazine table in front of the chair was the TV's remote control. Bennett picked up the device and switched the TV set to CNN.

The television screen was lit with a medium-close shot of the cable network's evening news anchorperson. Just as the anchor was beginning his introduction to the show, Bennett heard his phone ringing. There were two extensions in the house: one in the bedroom and another in the kitchen. He set his glass on a coaster on the magazine table, got up, and walked back into the kitchen.

The phone was mounted on a wall near the refrigerator. Bennett picked up the receiver in mid-ring. "Hello?"

"So when did you get back?" Tom Hanson asked in a tone of mock castigation. "I was starting to think you fell into the ocean out there, I hadn't heard from you in so long."

Bennett said, "I got back about two weeks ago. I'm sorry I haven't called you till now, but—"

"Two weeks?" Hanson's incredulity was edged with a discernible note of hurt.

"I said I was sorry."

"Hell, the last time I heard from you was when you and Denise got back to Frisco from San Diego. You mean to say you came home right after that, and you're only just now getting around to calling me?"

"Tom, I—"

"Hmph." Hanson snorted. "Some pal you are."

The good humor was back in Hanson's voice. Bennett smiled. "Do you want to come over for dinner tonight or not?"

"I'll have to check my social calendar. . . ." Hanson

paused, and Bennett could hear him riffling through the pages of something for effect. "It looks like I'm free. Do I have to bring anything?"

"Just yourself."

"You've got beer?"

"I've got beer."

"You've got chips?"

"I will after I go to the store."

"You've got TV? The Cardinals are on tonight."

"I got TV."

"How's seven o'clock sound?"

"Perfect."

Grinning, Bennett hung up the phone. He went back into the bedroom to retrieve his wallet and car keys. His car was parked in the driveway, twenty paces from the front door of the house.

He was heading out the door, making a mental list of the items he wanted to pick up at the supermarket, when he remembered that he'd left the television on in the den. After wondering whether it was worth the bother to turn off the TV when the entire trip to the supermarket would take no more than fifteen minutes, he chided himself for being lazy.

Bennett went back into the den. As he was reaching for the remote control to switch off the set, he happened to glance at the screen just as CNN's anchor was saying in a somber tone, ". . . serial killer in an idyllic, northern California resort city."

Bennett froze. His attention was riveted to the television set. He whispered to himself, "Sweet Jesus in heaven." And he watched.

CHAPTER FIVE

A short time later, Bennett was in his bedroom packing a suitcase when the front doorbell rang. It was only then that he remembered his invitation to Tom Hanson. Bennett muttered under his breath, "Oh, shit."

He stalked unhappily to the front door and found Hanson standing on the porch, dressed in loud Bermuda shorts, knee socks, sneakers, and a shapeless Izod golf shirt that had been washed too many times. Hanson grinned hello. But the grin quickly fell away as he read the expression of grim determination on Bennett's face. Hanson said with concern, "Ken? What's the matter?"

Bennett shook his head. "Nothing. I was just packing, that's all. I forgot you were coming over—"

Hanson cut in, "Whoa, whoa, slow down. What do you mean, you were packing?"

Bennett frowned. "I've decided to go back to California."

"What?"

"I'm going back. I've got a reservation for a red-eye flight to San Jose tonight. I can catch a shuttle bus or a cab or something from there to San Patricio."

"Wait a minute," Hanson said impatiently. "You're going way too fast for me." He paused, looking past Bennett's shoulder into the house behind him. "Is it all right if I come in?"

"Sorry." Bennett held the door open, allowing the other man to enter, then closed the door behind them. They stood in the living room, looking at each other with uncertainty, until Hanson said, "Don't let me interrupt whatever you're doing."

Bennett nodded. He turned away and started for the rear of the house. Hanson followed. Neither man spoke to the other until they reached the bedroom. Bennett went on with what he had been doing when the doorbell rang, laying a stack of laundered and folded shirts atop a pile of underclothing in a suitcase that lay open on top of his bed.

Hanson stood in the bedroom doorway, watching. He said, "Even if you don't think you owe me an explanation about how come it took you two weeks to call me once you got home, don't you think you at least owe me one as to why the hell you're going back there?"

Bennett was arranging his shirts in the suitcase. "I saw Dr. Herbert today. It was his idea that I give you a call."

"Otherwise you wouldn't have bothered?"

"I'm sure that sooner or later I'd have gotten around to it."

"That's considerate of you."

"I really am sorry about that, Tom. I just didn't want to talk to anybody about what I've been feeling. I knew if I saw you you'd find a way to squeeze it out, and I just didn't feel like opening up. Until today, when I went to see Herbert."

"What made him suggest you call me?" Hanson asked.

Bennett hesitated. "He thought I could use a friend. He figured maybe you could help me with these nightmares I've been having."

"What nightmares?"

Bennett described the dreams that had been haunting his sleep for the past month. While he spoke, he tried to read Hanson's expression. He couldn't tell how much damage he had done to their friendship, how much he had wounded Hanson by failing to contact him until this afternoon. Hanson observed him dispassionately, assuming a demeanor of interested but clinically reserved concern. Bennett decided that he had badly injured his friend's feelings.

But as Bennett opened up, recounting the awful dreams in detail, Hanson's look of professional concern softened, becoming a look of genuine sympathy. When Bennett had finished, Hanson said to him, "Ken, for God's sake, why didn't you tell me this before?"

Bennett shook his head. "I didn't think I could. I didn't think it was my place to do that."

"Not your *place*—"

Bennett held up a hand to cut him off. "Look, Tom, it's water under the bridge. I figured out what the dreams were trying to tell me. I know what I have to do."

Hanson gestured toward the suitcase. "Is going back to California what you have to do?"

Bennett nodded. He crossed to the chest of drawers, opened one, and was choosing from among a stack of pullover sweaters. "I saw something on TV tonight. A news report." He returned to the suitcase and dropped two sweaters beside the shirts. "I was watching CNN. They did a story on the serial killings out in San Patricio. Two days ago they found another dead kid. The third one they've found this month. Eleven kids altogether, since January. They even interviewed this woman I met while I was out there, the detective in charge of the investigation. I could tell by the way she talked that she was trying to make the best of a really bad situation. They still don't have any real clue who's killing those kids. Everybody's just about reached the boil-over point out there. I'm talking about the whole city, not just her."

Outside, the sun was sinking in the western sky, turning the horizon into a lipstick smear of reddish orange. Though the bedroom was still bright, the gradually approaching dusk had begun to fill the room with slanted shadows. Bennett said to Hanson, "Do you remember that night you came over here? After Christina's funeral? I told you about the dream I'd had the night before. Remember?"

Hanson nodded. "I remember."

"That night I started to tell you something else that I couldn't bring myself to say. Herbert guessed what it was, though, the very first time I went to see him. He knew that I wasn't feeling guilty because I thought I could have done something to save Christina. I was feeling guilty because I didn't die with her."

Hanson said, "Ken—"

"Let me finish, all right? Don't you see? It was tonight that I finally figured it all out. I honestly believe that something or someone—call it God or fate or whatever you want—something had a reason to keep me alive. There's something that I'm supposed to do, and now I know what it is. And I don't want you to start rationalizing to me, 'There's no proof that there's such a thing as fate': don't even start in on me with that. You and I both know there's too much out there in the universe that's inexplicable. That's why we do what we do."

Hanson was shaking his head. "I can't believe this."

"Tom," Bennett said determinedly, "I've never been more certain of anything in my life."

"And that's what you have to do? Go back to San Patricio and find out who's killing those kids?"

"That's what I have to do," said Bennett.

"What if you don't? Go back there, I mean?"

"There's no question about whether or not I'm going," Bennett said.

"But what if you can't find him? This killer?"

Bennett swallowed. "I still have to try."

Hanson took a step forward to bring himself out of the shadows. He looked pointedly at Bennett. "So what can I do to help you?"

Bennett considered, then asked, "Drive me to the airport?"

"I guess I can do that," Hanson said.

CHAPTER SIX

Shortly after one-thirty P.M. on Wednesday afternoon, June twenty-ninth, Rachel Siegel left Sheriff's Department headquarters and headed for home. While she was driving, she found herself fighting back tears. She felt old and tired and angry.

Old, because today was her forty-first birthday. She tried not to think about that, because she hated perpetuating the stereotype of people—especially those of her gender—who worried about their age. *Who gives a shit?* she asked herself anytime she encountered anyone who was vain enough to be coy about it. What difference could it make? You were what you were. If there was something about yourself you couldn't change, you learned to live with it.

But all day today Rachel could not help reminding herself that she was one year past forty, and there was no going back. Which caused her to recall other milestones in her life. That even though she could remember events that had happened during her teens as clearly as if they'd occurred last week, she'd still graduated from high school more than twenty years ago. That come September she would be married for fifteen years. That she had been a deputy sheriff—and a mom—for nearly as long.

Where the Christ did the time go? she wondered. *How did I ever get here from there?*

Rachel also felt tired, because the futile hunt for the killer of eleven children in the past half year was badly wearing her down. Three more bodies had been discovered in June: Amanda Schreiber on the twelfth, Jaime Gonzalez on the twentieth, and Sean Patrick Callahan five days ago, on the twenty-fourth. In the past two weeks a greater amount of media attention had been brought to bear upon the investigation. News reports had boosted the number of confessions and leads that the Sheriff's Department received. Each confession and lead, no matter how phony-seeming on its face, had to be checked on the odd chance that some valuable piece of information might turn up. The checking required a great deal of time and energy. So far all of it had proved fruitless.

And Rachel was also angry, which was partly the news media's fault as well. Last Saturday morning a family of tourists from Utah had discovered the body of Sean Callahan in the woods not far from the entrance to a state park just west of the San Patricio city limits. That afternoon, while Rachel was at headquarters interrogating the family, she was interrupted by a call from Lt. Daniel Sloane, the department's media-relations officer. Sloane informed Rachel that a reporter named Gillian Friendly, from CNN, had come down from San Francisco that morning with a video crew, anxious to do a report on the serial killings. Already Ms. Friendly had Mayor Barbara Underwood, Sheriff Peter Joyce, and Chief of Detectives

Earl Novak. Now she wanted to speak to the investigator in charge of the case.

"How come she wants to talk to me?" Rachel asked bitterly. She knew that Sloane was aware that the case had been taken out of her hands a month ago, on the day that Special Agent Frank Killoran of the California Bureau of Investigation and his underlings had arrived from Sacramento. Since then Rachel had been reduced to being just another "member of the team," as Killoran liked to put it. Officially she was the liaison between the CBI and the Sheriff's Department. Unofficially she'd assumed a new role that she did not care for one bit.

"Killoran left for the state capital this morning," Sloane told her. "His kid's first communion is this weekend, and he's got meetings up there on Monday and Tuesday. He won't be back till Wednesday afternoon. You're the only one available." Sloane paused. "Besides, Rachel, you're a woman. I think CNN will like that."

Rachel gave in reluctantly. She was later surprised and pleased that Ms. Friendly turned out to be a charming, intelligent human being. The woman also proved to be a capable and conscientious interviewer. Her questions were polite but incisive—quite different from those of the local reporters who lately had taken to acting pushy and indignant and impatient with the lack of progress on the case.

When the CNN report was broadcast on Monday evening, Rachel had to admit that it was a fair if not particularly flattering assessment of the investigation so far. There were only two things in the report that really made her wince. The first was Ms. Friendly's referring to the killer as the Pied Piper, a name coined around Memorial Day by Jeffrey Webber of the San Jose *Press-Telegram*. The second was Ms. Friendly's comparison of the killings in San Patricio to the Atlanta child murders of the late 1970s. It was a comparison that Rachel now thought wasn't so inaccurate as she might have thought it was a few months before. Which, unfortunately for her, was a statement that she made for the record, on camera, as part of the report that was aired.

Why that was unfortunate for Rachel became clear almost immediately. Novak called her at home, twenty minutes after the conclusion of the news broadcast, to chew her out. He'd already spoken to the sheriff and the mayor, both of whom, Novak told her, had to be argued out of being presented Rachel's head on a platter first thing Tuesday morning.

The problem was that what she said appeared to contradict the official line proffered by the Sheriff's Department and the mayor's office. During their interviews, the mayor, the sheriff, and Novak all performed variations on the same theme: the killings were heinous crimes to be sure, but they were not—repeat, *not*—symptomatic of a homicidal epidemic such as the one that had terrorized Atlanta. They took turns assuring Gillian Friendly and her audience that the capture of the Pied Piper was imminent. While Rachel did not say flatly that Mayor Underwood and Sheriff Joyce and Chief Novak were lying, she implied it. It was possible, she allowed, that the Pied Piper would be caught soon. But she did not think that likely.

I should have known that if I went on TV, the shit rain was going to fall, Rachel told herself sourly as she turned the Sienna onto the freeway.

176

Novak's call had been only the first of two unpleasant reactions to her television appearance. The second came later that same night. She'd let Roy answer the phone, with instructions that he deflect anyone to whom she didn't want to speak. He handled the task admirably. "I'm sorry, but Rachel's taken the boys out shopping and I'm not sure when they'll be back," Roy had said into the phone. She was standing beside him as he listened to the caller's message. She looked a question at him, and he mouthed the word *Killoran.*

Rachel rolled her eyes, glad that she had asked Roy to intercept the call. After he hung up, Roy said to her, "He wants you to meet with him at one o'clock sharp on Wednesday afternoon."

"How'd he sound?" she asked.

"Not happy," Roy said.

From Monday night onward, Rachel's impending meeting with Killoran was the proverbial sword dangling over her head. Not that she was worrying about any trouble he might create for her. It was that she disliked having any contact with him. She despised Killoran, and had since the moment they met three and a half weeks before.

Frank Killoran had arrived in San Patricio on Friday, the third of June. Rachel's first impression of the man had been bad, and her opinion declined from there. They were introduced to one another by Earl Novak, and Rachel noticed that as she shook Killoran's hand in greeting that he eyed her appraisingly, almost leering, as if judging her potential for sexual conquest. She found herself cringing inwardly. It was difficult for her not to pull her hand from his and look around for something on which to wipe the unclean sensation from her fingertips.

Not that Killoran was unattractive. He was in his midthirties, and he was handsome, in a slick, beach-boy sort of way. He had straight blond hair and a narrow, neatly trimmed mustache. His body appeared to be hard and fit, and his skin was the deep tan of someone who spent a great deal of free time in the sun. His clothes were nicely tailored and expensive-looking.

But he also wore too much gold: a pinkie ring on his right hand, a thin, ebony-faced Movado watch on his left wrist, a serpentine chain around his neck that was visible whenever he opened his shirt collar and loosened his tie. If Rachel had seen him on the street and tried to guess his profession without having known it beforehand, she would have thought him to be an actor, a gigolo, or a casino employee from Las Vegas. But "cop" might have been her fourth choice. She knew many of them whose personal affectations weren't dissimilar from Killoran's.

He'd brought with him from the state capital three CBI agents named Santos, Seelig, and McEvilly—whom Rachel had come to think of as Moe, Larry, and Curly. Killoran was their fearless leader, and they were his toadies. By the end of the first workday she'd spent with Killoran and his men, she concluded that he very much enjoyed having toadies. She also learned that he enjoyed seeing his face on television, and hearing his voice on the radio, and reading his name in the papers.

Killoran also liked to give orders, and he became surly when those orders were not executed to his satisfaction. He did not have much use for law-enforcement officers who toiled at the municipal or county level; nor did he care for officers who happened to be women. Rachel suspected that Killoran was a bigot as well as a sexist, because he seemed to take delight in regaling his men—and anybody else who happened to be around—with vulgar and occasionally racist jokes. Not that telling off-color stories made him unique, for a cop. It was that Rachel sensed that, for Killoran, the ubiquitous insults in his "humor" were actually heartfelt, whether his jokes were directed against blacks, Orientals, Jews, Latinos, or anyone who was not a white, Anglo-Saxon male. Killoran was, she decided, a big-time jerk-off.

But he was also her boss, as of June third. Novak ordered Rachel to turn over to Killoran every piece of information she had on the Pied Piper murders, then assigned her to work under the CBI agents as they took charge of the investigation. For the past three weeks Rachel had been reduced to doing grunt work. Lately she had begun to think of herself as a glorified secretary who spent her days collating files and transcribing interviews and making sure that Frank Killoran didn't arrive late for any of his appointments with politicians or members of the media. Killoran's men were the ones now conducting field investigations. Rachel spent most of her time at headquarters, in the suite of offices that the Sheriff's Department had donated to the CBI agents for use as a "nerve center." The place where today, one half hour ago, Killoran had let her have it.

Tuesday and Wednesday were supposed to have been Rachel's days off. Were it not for her appointment with Killoran, she wouldn't have gone anywhere near headquarters on either day. She knew that this indicated a big change in her attitude over the past months. Until recently Rachel loved to go to work.

She arrived promptly at one o'clock, as ordered. Killoran was waiting for her in the glass-enclosed cubicle that he had appropriated for his personal sanctum. He was sitting on the edge of his desk, watching her as she came into the cubicle. He motioned for her to close the door behind her. There was no seat in the office for a visitor, so Rachel stood just inside the door.

Killoran was looking at her with an expression that on someone else could have been interpreted as a look of hurt. Rachel couldn't help feeling that the expression looked rehearsed. At last he said to her, "You really stabbed me in the back, you know that?"

Her mouth dropped open. "I did what?"

"Stabbed me in the back. You really did."

"What the hell are you talking about, Frank?"

Killoran set his jaw firmly. "On the first day I got here, I laid down some ground rules. Remember? Rule number one: None of my people talk to the media without first okaying it with me. Nobody."

"*Your* people?"

"You're part of my team," he said. "Aren't you?"

Rachel frowned. "Putting aside for the moment who's part of whose team, you happened to be out of town when this whole thing came up."

"You couldn't get to a phone?" Killoran said petulantly. "You couldn't take the time to track down my home number up there?"

"For Christ's sake, I didn't even want to do the goddamn interview! Ask Dan Sloane! He's the one who told me I should, because you weren't around!"

Killoran was shaking his head. "You still should've called me."

Rachel was exasperated. "I'm sorry, but it just wasn't convenient for me to do that at the time. . . ."

She paused, because an epiphany had emerged in her mind and spread open like the bloom of a flower. She said to Killoran, "You rotten bastard."

"Excuse me?"

"You're not mad at me for the same reason that everybody else is mad at me," Rachel went on. "Because what I said on TV contradicted the party line. You don't give a damn about that. You're mad because you didn't get to be the one interviewed on national television."

"That's a bullshit accusation, Detective," Killoran said. "Total bullshit. The issue is that you violated the rules. You compromised the integrity of this team."

She was stunned. " 'Compromised the integrity'?"

Killoran nodded smugly.

"Where do you get this shit, Frank? Do you just make it up out of thin air, or what?"

"I'm serious, Rachel—"

She shook her head tersely, cutting him off. "I'm just now beginning to understand you fully. I really am." She regarded him coldly. "You couldn't care less about the fact that kids in this town are dying. Your interest only goes so far as what good it'll do you and your reputation if you happen to be the one to catch the killer."

Killoran growled. "You're way out of line here—"

"And you're an asshole," Rachel snapped. "A twenty-four-karat, prima-donna asshole."

"Wait just a damn minute—"

But he was too late, because Rachel had spun

around, pulled open the door to the cubicle, and departed. She stalked out of the office, ignoring Killoran, who was shouting for her to come back. Telling herself, *Dammit, Rachel, don't you start crying. Not here.*

As she drove home, it was hard for her to believe that all of this had happened only twenty minutes before. Thinking about her confrontation with Killoran was causing her eyes to fill with tears. She was approaching the freeway off-ramp, and the tears were making it difficult for her to see. She pulled off at the exit and turned left, rolling beneath the freeway, crossing to the side of the road. Then she eased to the shoulder, where she sat behind the wheel of her car and sobbed.

CHAPTER SEVEN

As she approached her driveway, Rachel saw Roy's two-seater Mercedes parked outside the garage attached to their house. *I warned them*, she said to herself. There could be only one reason why he was home so early in the afternoon on this particular day. Since Roy knew about her meeting with Killoran, undoubtedly he'd been waiting for her to leave the house before returning from his office. The boys had to be in on it, too, one of them probably calling Roy to let him know when the coast was clear. But none of them would be expecting her to come home so soon, supposing that she would be away for hours.

As Rachel eased her minivan to a stop at the foot of the driveway, she was telling herself that somebody was going to be surprised today, all right, but it sure the hell wasn't going to be her. She climbed out of the Sienna, easing shut the driver's-side door, making as little noise as possible. The front yard sloped downward from the house, and she hiked up the slight incline, staying close to the hedges that surrounded the property. She took care to stay out of sight of anyone inside who might have been looking out from the house toward the street.

Reaching the house, Rachel edged around a corner that allowed her a glance through the wide picture window that dominated one wall of the family room. Roy was visible inside the room, as were the boys. Roy and Denny were hanging a homemade, hand-lettered banner on the wall above the sofa. The banner had been made from an old bedsheet, and it read, in letters of red and green and yellow and blue, *Happy Birthday, Mom!* Aaron was sitting on the floor in front of the television set, blowing up a balloon. Several others that he'd already finished lay around him.

Rachel tiptoed away from the window, moving toward the rear of the house. When she reached the kitchen door she tested the doorknob gingerly, hoping that the door was unlocked. It was. She gently pushed it open and stepped into the kitchen. She sniffed the air, taking in the aroma that filled the room. A cake was baking in the oven. The rest of the evidence lay piled in the sink: a ceramic bowl from which batter had been scraped, several spoons, a rubber spatula, a measuring cup, the beaters from Rachel's Sunbeam Mixmaster that stood on the counter near the sink.

She crept across the kitchen to the entryway of the family room. The three of them had their backs to her as she said in a stern voice, "I thought I made it clear I'd better not be having any damn surprise parties."

Aaron screeched, startled. Roy and Denny spun around, losing hold of the bedsheet. Denny stared at Rachel with widening eyes, then turned to his father and shook his head. "I wasn't kidding about her not wanting us to do this."

Rachel was glaring at her husband. "Well?"

She could tell that he was trying to read her expression. Her eyes were still red, she knew, and it wouldn't be hard for Roy to guess that she'd been crying. At last he said to her, "It's not a *party* party. There wasn't going to be anybody invited but us."

"You don't think I believe that, do you?"

Roy shrugged. "It's the truth."

She looked from her husband to Denny. "Just us, Mom," the boy affirmed. "Dad's got it all worked out."

Rachel turned to Aaron. He was nodding vigorously, watching her with an expression of guarded hope.

Roy said to her, "Honey, if you want us to go ahead and treat this day like it was any other day, you just say the word and we'll stop what we're doing right now."

Rachel scowled. She'd been genuinely angry when she saw Roy's car in the driveway. Angrier still when she'd peeked through the window and seen her husband and the boys at work. She'd meant what she'd said about no birthday parties.

But now, as she looked from Roy to Denny to Aaron, it was the expression on Aaron's face, finally, that caused all of the bad feelings inside her to evaporate. The scowl faded. She sighed, then broke into a smile, giving in. "You can go ahead with this only if you promise that you'll all sing 'Happy Birthday' to me," she said. "Loud. Otherwise it's no deal."

Roy turned from Rachel to Denny. Denny shrugged. He and Roy looked to Aaron, who was beaming happily. Roy looked back to Rachel. "We promise," he said.

CHAPTER EIGHT

They had dinner that night at a restaurant on the beach. It was there that Roy gave Rachel her birthday present: a long, flat manila envelope. Puzzled, Rachel opened the envelope and pulled out two round-trip airline tickets from San Jose to Lake Tahoe.

Roy was beaming. "I talked one of my clients into letting us borrow his cabin from July first through the fourth. I thought you could use a little getaway."

"How come there're only two tickets?" Rachel asked.

Roy turned to the boys. "See that, you guys? That's why your mom's such a good detective. She's quick." He explained to Rachel that the tickets were for the two of them. He had already made arrangements for the boys to stay with Rachel's parents for the holiday weekend. The only hitch, Roy said, was whether Rachel could take the time off from work on such short notice.

"I think they can spare me for a few days," Rachel replied sardonically.

When the family came home, shortly after nine P.M., Roy put on a pot of coffee while Denny placed

186

a single candle in the center of the cake that he himself had baked and frosted—yellow cake with fudge icing, Rachel's favorite. Roy lit the candle, Denny dimmed the lights in the kitchen, and Aaron led his father and brother in singing "Happy Birthday." Loudly.

The boys had taken their slices of cake into the family room, where they could watch television. Rachel and Roy sat at the kitchen table. Over coffee Rachel told her husband about what had happened with Frank Killoran that afternoon. Because the evening had gone so well and because Roy was already aware of her less-than-charitable feelings toward Killoran, she was able to recount her meeting with dispassion. Roy listened sympathetically, until his eyes widened with surprise when she told him what she'd called Killoran just before stalking out of his office.

Roy said, "You didn't really call him an asshole to his face, did you?"

Rachel's expression became chagrined. "I think I might have been a little out of line there."

Roy nodded. "I think that's an understatement."

"But he *is* an asshole," she protested. "Isn't he?"

"Maybe so," Roy said. "But he's still your boss."

Rachel sighed. "I know. . . ."

"So what happens now?" asked Roy.

"Tomorrow I go in and face the music, I guess. I'm going to have to apologize to him." She grimaced.

"What do you think he's gonna do to you?"

She shook her head. "I honestly don't know—"

She was interrupted by the sound of the front doorbell's chiming. She and Roy exchanged puzzled looks. A moment later Denny shouted from the front of the house, "Mom! There's somebody here to see you!"

Roy's look questioned Rachel. She shrugged. "I have no idea who it could be."

Roy asked, "Don't you think maybe we should go find out?"

He followed her out of the kitchen, through the family room, into the foyer at the front of the house. Two men were standing there with Denny. The men were dressed in lightweight jackets, summer nights in San Patricio tending to be chilly, regardless how warm the weather got during the day. At first both men were strangers to Rachel, until she recognized the one who was standing slightly forward of the other.

When the man in the lead saw her, he smiled with friendly familiarity. "I realize it's kind of rude of us to drop by unannounced," Kenneth Bennett said. He nodded toward the other man. "This is my friend Wil Krieger. We've been going 'round and 'round all evening about whether I should've called first. I hope you don't mind."

Rachel was astonished. Roy was looking at her with a bemused smile; then he turned to Bennett, extending a hand. "I'm Rachel's husband, Roy Rodgers," he greeted. "And you're . . . ?"

"Ken Bennett." He shook Roy's hand. "From St. Louis."

"We were just having some birthday cake and coffee, Mr. Bennett," said Roy. "Would you and your friend care to join us?"

Rachel turned her expression of astonishment to her husband. Bennett looked to the man with him. The man shrugged: *Why not?* Bennett turned back to Roy and said, "We'd be delighted."

CHAPTER NINE

Rachel was saying to Bennett, "How'd you find out where we live? We're not listed in the phone book."

The four of them—Rachel, Roy, Bennett, and Wil Krieger—were seated at the kitchen table. Dessert plates scattered with cake crumbs lay before each of them. They were drinking coffee. "I thought that might be the case," Bennett answered, "since you're a law-enforcement officer. I've got a close friend who's with the St. Louis Police Department. I had him track down your address and phone number for me before I left town." He looked to Roy. "I was a little surprised when I found out what your last name was. I imagine you took a lot of ribbing about it when you were a kid."

Roy said, "You mean like, 'Hey, Roy Rodgers, where's Trigger?' 'Hey, Roy, how's Dale?' Like that?"

Bennett nodded.

"That never happened," Roy deadpanned.

Bennett and Krieger chuckled. "Ken," said Rachel. He turned back to her. "What I told you a month ago, about San Patricio—"

Bennett held up a hand. "You're not going to talk

me out of staying this time, so don't even try. Whether I work with the authorities in some official capacity, or work on my own, I'm not leaving till this killer gets caught."

"Things have changed around here," she said. "I'm not in charge of the case anymore."

Bennett looked puzzled. "You're not?"

She shook her head. "The state bureau of investigation took over three weeks ago. There's somebody else in charge now, one of their guys. I'm just part of a bigger team, now, no longer solo. The Sheriff's Department's token representative."

"But didn't I see you on TV?"

She made a face. "I'd rather not talk about that, if you don't mind."

Bennett said, "You are still working on the case, aren't you?"

She nodded. "Technically, yes."

"Then could you introduce me to whoever's in charge now?" he asked. "Maybe ask them to—"

"Him," Rachel said. "His name is Killoran."

"So couldn't you and I go to Killoran and get his permission for me to work with the investigation?"

Roy snorted. Bennett and Krieger turned to look at him. Rachel glared at her husband. Roy smiled sheepishly. "Sorry."

Bennett turned back to Rachel. She said, "I don't think that's a good idea. I'm not exactly on the best of terms with these state people."

Bennett looked away, turning his eyes downward, frowning. He pressed a finger to his lips, thinking. Rachel watched him, and all at once several things came into her mind unbidden: the image of Killoran's face, his expression smug and condescending; a memory of her confrontation that afternoon; a recollection of what she had read about Bennett more than a month before: *Kenneth Bennett is as genuine a person as his power is genuine.*

Rachel thought: *Fuck you, Frank Killoran.*

"Ken?" she said. Bennett looked to her. "Roy and I are going out of town for the holiday weekend, so I won't be at work for a while. Can you meet me at my office, say, a week from today? Next Wednesday morning?" She made a mental calculation. "That'll be July the sixth. At ten o'clock?"

Bennett nodded. "I can if you tell me how to get there."

She gave him the directions. Bennett made notes on the back of a napkin. When she'd finished, he said to her, "Ten A.M. on July sixth. I'll be there."

"I'll be waiting," Rachel replied.

CHAPTER TEN

Wil Krieger's automobile was a green 1973 SAAB that looked to Bennett like a kind of mechanical turtle made of metal and rubber and glass. Krieger took excellent care of the car, however, and it was in near-mint condition, humming contentedly as it was driven. They were traveling from the home of Rachel Siegel and Roy Rodgers, heading in the direction of the freeway junction. Bennett was thinking about the car in order to keep from thinking about anything else.

That everything had fallen into place so expediently, once he'd made the decision to return to San Patricio, did not surprise him. It was further evidence to him that he was meant to be here. At Tom Hanson's urging—Hanson having requested that he sleep on his decision to go—Bennett had postponed his flight to San Jose for a day. Correcting for the alteration in plans—exchanging his reservation on a red-eye flight leaving at midnight on Monday for one that departed early Tuesday afternoon—had been simple. The plane left St. Louis on time and arrived in San Jose two and a half hours later, twenty minutes ahead of schedule. A commuter bus was waiting for him as had been promised. And waiting at the drop-off point in San Patricio, when Bennett disembarked at six-thirty P.M., was Wil Krieger.

Krieger was a professor of English on the faculty of UC San Patricio. He was also a longtime friend of Tom Hanson, the two of them having been roommates as undergraduates at the University of Chicago. Bennett had met Krieger twice before: both times when Krieger was visiting Hanson in St. Louis. Bennett and Krieger had gotten along well, their mutual fondness for Tom Hanson providing a basis for their friendship. On the surface, Krieger was the antithesis of Hanson. Where Hanson was short, portly, and shaggy, Krieger was tall and slender, clean-shaven and sharp-featured. His gray hair was straight and neatly trimmed. Where Hanson tended to be rumpled, Krieger was as fastidious about his personal appearance as he was about his automobile. And where Hanson was something of a hound when it came to his relationships with members of the opposite sex—he had been married and divorced three times—Krieger was staunchly monogamous, having lived with the same gay lover for the past decade and a half. Shortly after he'd met Krieger, Bennett had asked him how he and Hanson could have managed to live with each other for four years, during college. Krieger replied that they were the quintessential odd couple. The differences between him and Hanson were superficial; philosophically and intellectually they might as well have been twins.

While Bennett was staying with his sister in San Francisco a month earlier, he'd tried to call Krieger to arrange a stopover during his trip down the coast with Denise. Unfortunately, Krieger had been out of town during the last week of May, gone to Phoenix to attend a symposium. It was Hanson who had called Krieger this past Monday night to ask if it would be all right for Bennett to stay at Krieger's house for a time. Krieger was pleased to have Bennett as his guest. The house was deserted except for himself, Krieger said, his lover having flown to Europe for a monthlong business trip. Bennett then got on the phone himself, and he apologized for giving Krieger such short notice. Krieger pooh-poohed the apology.

His home was a two-story, three-bedroom structure near the edge of the city limits. The house was a mile south of the UC San Patricio campus, and it sat high on a bluff so that the deck off its back porch provided a splendid view of the ocean. When they arrived earlier that evening the sun was just resting on the horizon, causing the water to shimmer and glow red, reflecting the light of the dying day.

Krieger's lover had converted the smaller of the house's two spare bedrooms into an office; the other spare bedroom was available for guests. After Bennett unpacked, he went downstairs to join Krieger on the deck. Krieger had opened a bottle of Donne Vineyards chardonnay. They sat on redwood chairs, sipping the wine and enjoying the sunset.

Bennett explained to Krieger why he was here. Krieger, of course, knew about the Pied Piper murders. The entire town was on edge, he told Bennett, and more than a few people in the area were close to panic. Krieger spoke about the current of fear and suspicion that ran through San Patricio. Bennett listened, and as he did his resolve strengthened. He was doing absolutely the right thing by being here, he told himself. There was no doubt in his mind.

"This Pied Piper business has affected a lot of people personally," Krieger had been saying as the upper rim of the sun dipped into the ocean. "San Patricio isn't really a very big place, if you think about it. It seems like almost everybody knows somebody who . . ." He paused, frowning, then took a swallow of wine. "Even me."

Bennett's look questioned him.

"A colleague of mine in the English department at school," Krieger said. "His son was one of the victims. About a month ago."

Bennett could feel the hairs tickling on the back of his neck. "The McWilliams boy?"

Krieger was taken aback. "How did you know that?"

Bennett waved a hand to dismiss the question. "It's not what you're thinking, Wil. I didn't read your mind."

"Then I gather you've been following this situation very closely?"

Bennett shook his head. "It's not that, either."

He went on to tell Krieger about his accident on May twenty-fifth; about his vision; about his subsequent revelation to the police of the whereabouts of Craig McWilliams's body. While he was describing what had happened, Bennett became aware of a voice speaking to him from the recesses of his mind. The voice was saying, *This is more than a coincidence.* That Krieger was acquainted with the family of the very same boy whose consciousness had touched Bennett's own. *Here is where you start*, the voice whispered to him. *Here.*

Krieger sat quietly, his attention focused. When Bennett had finished recounting the story of the accident, Krieger remained silent. He sipped his wine.

Bennett asked, "Do you think you could introduce me to Craig McWilliams's parents?"

"When?" asked Krieger.

"As soon as possible."

Bennett outlined a plan. They would leave immediately, first to call upon Rachel Siegel so that Bennett could let her know that he was in town again. Then they would visit Edward and Yoshiko McWilliams. Both of the visits would be unannounced.

Krieger was not receptive to that idea. Not only would dropping in on people unexpectedly be inconsiderate, he argued, but there was no guarantee that Rachel or the McWilliamses would be home. Bennett was adamant, however. Catching people off guard was often a good way for him to get a read on them. "And don't worry," Bennett assured Krieger. "I'm certain they'll be home."

In the end, Krieger had given in. Having visited Rachel, they were now heading west on the freeway, in the direction from which they'd come an hour earlier. Krieger explained that the McWilliamses lived near him, a few blocks closer to the UC campus. They rode in a silence that was disturbed only by the soft sound of jazz music emanating from the SAAB's FM radio. But as they exited the freeway, heading in the direction of the university, Krieger said, "I should probably warn you about Ed and Yoshiko."

"Warn me?" asked Bennett.

Krieger chewed his lip. "They aren't the happiest couple I know. Don't get me wrong. They're nice enough people, in their way. It's just that . . ."

Krieger's voice trailed off. Bennett said, "You're stalling, Wil."

"So I am," said Krieger. He sighed. "I know Ed a

little better than I know his wife, because I work with him. He's one of those men who . . ."

Another sigh, then: "He's kind of a show-off. The two of them came to UC in a package deal from where they'd been before. From Iowa, I think. But Ed was the one the university really wanted. There was a lot of pressure on the Board of Regents to bring him here. He's the type a lot of English departments like to have around. He's a Ph.D., but he's also published a couple of novels. In a way, he's a sort of lowercase John Irving. He's not a best-selling author, but he's well enough known so that it's a feather in the department's cap to have him on the faculty. That's not to say that Ed isn't valuable. He helps promote our department just by being here. He's a recognizable commodity, and we can use his name to recruit students who want to study with him or publicize our creative-writing program, that sort of thing."

"What's the problem with him?" Bennett asked.

Krieger considered for a moment. "There are any number of people who just aren't as smart or as talented as they seem to think they are. Unfortunately, you seem to run into a great many of them among academics. I'm sure you've met a few in your time."

Bennett smiled ruefully. "A few."

"Ed's one of them, I'm afraid," said Krieger. "He gets off on playing the artist. Most of the time he's a pleasant person, but sometimes I think he's a little too arrogant for his own good." He shook his head. "I hope that doesn't sound like I'm jealous of him. Honest to God, I'm not."

"I didn't think you were," said Bennett.

Krieger nodded gratefully. "Anyway, that's Ed. As I say, I don't really know Yoshiko that well. The few times I've spoken to her, she's always been rather shy. Especially when he's around. When he's not, she's just a wonderful person. Very bright, very charming. Frankly, to tell you the truth, I think she's much too good for him."

Bennett waited quietly, aware of the dark tone that had crept into Krieger's voice. At last Krieger said, "They've had some serious fights. Mostly Ed's fault, too. I know I risk sounding like a gossipy old biddy telling you this, but they've been here about five years, and he's had at least three affairs that I know of." He paused, making a face. "I hate that term. 'Affairs.' It's such a cheap-sounding word." Krieger shrugged resignedly. "Ordinarily I couldn't care less about anybody's sexual indiscretions—"

Bennett cut in. "Otherwise you'd never be Tom Hanson's friend."

"Exactly. But Tom's only gotten involved with women who could take care of themselves, and never while he was married to somebody else. Ed seems to like to get involved with students." Krieger shook his head again. "I don't mean to sound like a prude, either, but I just don't believe that's something teachers should do."

He sighed once more. "I suppose that's neither here nor there. The point I'm trying to make is that their marriage has never been particularly solid. A lot of us who know them believe that the only reason they've stayed together—and I don't think there's any good reason to hold on to a bad marriage—was for the sake of that poor little boy."

Krieger had pulled the SAAB to the curb in front of the McWilliamses' house. Bennett could see a light burning inside, behind the closed curtains that covered a picture window near the front door. A shadowy shape was moving behind the curtain. Krieger switched off the car's ignition, turned to Bennett, and said earnestly, "Are you sure you want to go through with this?"

Bennett nodded. "I'm sure."

Krieger shook his head doubtfully. Then he reached to open the driver's-side door and climbed out of the car. Bennett opened his own door, stepped out, closed the door gently, and followed Krieger up the walk to the house.

CHAPTER ELEVEN

Edward McWilliams was holding open the front door, blinking with surprise at the man who had rung his doorbell. "Wil?" he uttered. "What are you doing here?"

McWilliams was not as tall as Krieger or Bennett, but he was heavier than either of them—thicker in the arms and upper body, more muscular all around. *He must work out*, Bennett said to himself as he studied the man. McWilliams had a ruddy complexion and rugged good looks. He had the crooked nose of an ex-boxer, blue eyes, a heavy mustache, and thick, curly reddish-brown hair. He was barefoot, wearing a white T-shirt and faded button-fly Levi's. A tuft of chest hair peeked out from the collar of his T-shirt.

"I apologize, Ed," said Krieger. "We probably should've called first, but we decided to just take a chance on catching you at home."

McWilliams said, " 'We'?"

Kreiger gestured to the man with him. "This is Ken Bennett. He's a friend of mine from Washington U in St. Louis. He wanted to meet you and Yoshiko."

Bennett stepped around Krieger to extend a hand.

McWilliams shook Bennett's hand tentatively as he said, "Why'd you want to meet me?"

"You *and* your wife, Dr. McWilliams," said Bennett.

Krieger asked McWilliams, "Is Yoshiko here?"

McWilliams nodded. He looked to Bennett. "You didn't answer my question."

Before Bennett could reply, Krieger was saying, "Ed, we'd really like to come in, if that's all right."

To Bennett it seemed as if McWilliams was unsure what to do. At last, with some reluctance, he stepped aside and ushered them into the house.

The door opened into the living room. Except for a small circle of light thrown from a brass floor lamp, the room was dark. Near the lamp was a wing-backed chair and an ottoman whose upholstery matched that of the chair. Inverted like a pup tent, upside down in the chair was a paperback novel. McWilliams closed the front door and reached for a switch on the wall beside the door. A pair of lamps came on that were at either end of a sofa that stood against the wall to the far right of the front door. The lamps rested on matching end tables.

Bennett and Krieger were standing in the middle of the room, facing McWilliams. He eyed them guardedly. "Now," he said. "Do you mind telling me what it is you two want?"

Krieger opened his mouth to speak, but Bennett held up a hand to quiet him. Bennett said to McWilliams, "I'd like to talk to you and your wife about Craig."

McWilliams's brows drew close together. "Why?"

"I'm helping the police look for the man who killed him."

William Relling Jr.

McWilliams's expression became puzzled. "You're not a cop, are you?"

Bennett shook his head. "I'm from Washington University in St. Louis, just like Wil said."

McWilliams looked away for a moment, his brow furrowed with uncertainty. Then he turned back to Bennett. "She's . . . uh . . ." He nodded toward a darkened hallway that led to the back of the house. "She's in the study. I think she's grading papers."

He started off down the corridor, then paused to turn around once again. "Make yourselves comfortable." He gestured to the sofa.

McWilliams disappeared down the hallway, his bare feet slapping on the hardwood floor. The sound of his footsteps diminished as he moved away. Krieger motioned Bennett toward the sofa. "Shall we?"

They sat down. As they settled themselves, Bennett said to Krieger in a low voice, "He seems like a nice enough guy. A little on the macho side, maybe. He also didn't seem overly upset about our showing up out of the blue like we did."

Krieger scratched his head. "I'm a bit surprised about that. We aren't what you'd call close friends—"

He was interrupted by the sound of footsteps approaching from the darkened hallway. Bennett turned from Krieger to look in that direction. Walking ahead of McWilliams into the living room was his wife, Yoshiko.

Bennett thought, *She's lovely.*

Yoshiko McWilliams was quite petite, no more than an inch or two over five feet tall. She had glossy, straight black hair that hung loosely to the middle of her back. Her eyebrows were dark and thick, crescenting over almond-shaped eyes the color of rich loam. She wore no makeup, nothing to disguise or accentuate her aristocratic cheekbones or color her full lips. She was dressed in denim cutoffs that exposed shapely, slightly bowed legs, and a lightweight vee-necked pullover sweater the color of smoke. The sweater outlined her small, firm breasts. The sleeves were pushed up casually, revealing slender arms. Like her husband, she was barefoot.

She came forward, and Bennett rose politely. She shook her head. "Please," she said, "sit down."

Bennett did as she instructed, noticing with curiosity that she spoke without the trace of an Asian accent, as he'd expected her to. She showed Krieger a small smile of greeting. "Hello, Yoshiko," he said. Then he introduced her to Bennett. She shook Bennett's hand, showing him her small smile once more.

"I apologize if we're disturbing you," Bennett said.

She'd dropped to the floor and was sitting Indian-style, her legs crossed. "Why do you want to talk about my son?"

Bennett looked from Yoshiko to her husband. Ed McWilliams had taken a seat in the wing-backed chair, turning it so that he could face the others in the room. McWilliams was watching him intently.

Bennett spoke carefully, measuring his words. "Five weeks ago, on the morning of May twenty-fifth, I was driving into San Patricio along Highway Nine. I was just outside the city limits when I had a kind of vision. I wasn't behind the wheel of a car anymore. All of a sudden I was a little boy."

He paused momentarily. "I don't mean to say that I was watching myself as a boy. What I'm saying is that I *was* that boy. Seeing everything through his eyes." He took a deep breath. "Please understand. It wasn't like I was dreaming, nothing like that. Nor that I was floating and detached and observing any of this. It was happening *to me*. It was raining, and I was running through some kind of construction site. Somebody was chasing me, a grown man. He kept coming closer, till at last I felt him grabbing me from behind."

Bennett drew another careful breath. "At that instant I snapped back into my own body and mind. I was myself again. It happened a moment before I wrecked the car I was driving. I knocked myself cold, and ended up in the hospital."

Yoshiko said, "I'm not sure I understand what you're telling us."

"That boy," said Bennett, looking from Yoshiko to her husband. "The boy I 'became.' It was your son. For a few seconds I was Craig. Your son. Right before he died."

Bennett could feel the eyes of the people in the room fixed upon him. "In the hospital," he continued. "When I came to, I was able to tell the police where your son's . . . where they could find him. I knew just where he was."

A pall of silence descended. Then Ed McWilliams said in a challenging tone of voice, "Mr. Bennett, who in the hell are you?"

Bennett looked from McWilliams to Yoshiko, then back to McWilliams again. *Do it*, he thought.

"I'm a criminalist," he said.

CHAPTER TWELVE

Once Bennett had concluded his narration, both Yoshiko and her husband turned to Wil Krieger, their expressions querying. Krieger said sincerely, "Ken is exactly what he purports to be. One of my oldest and dearest friends is a colleague of his at Wash U. I've known Ken personally for many years. I've known about him for a lot longer than that."

Yoshiko turned to Bennett. "Do you really believe you can find whoever killed my son?"

Bennett nodded. "I do."

She frowned thoughtfully. "How can I help you?"

McWilliams blurted incredulously, "Yoshiko, are you crazy?"

He was pushing himself out of the chair when she spun around and froze him with an icy glare. He caught himself, then eased back down in his seat. There was an expression of surprise on his face, as if his wife's chilly stare was the last reaction he'd expected from her.

She turned back to Bennett. "I'd like to examine some of your son's things, if I can," he said. "Sometimes I can get impressions if I handle someone's clothes or something they owned that was valuable to them."

She nodded. "Craig's things are in his room. I'll show you."

Yoshiko rose from the floor. Bennett came to his feet, pausing to look at Krieger for a moment before following her out down the dark hallway.

She stopped outside a closed door at the end of the hall, waiting for Bennett to catch up with her. As he came up from behind, she pushed open the door. She reached for a switch, turning on a light.

Bennett moved into the doorway, looking into the room over Yoshiko's shoulder. *So ordinary*, he thought bitterly. *So normal. So sad.*

It was the bedroom of a vivacious twelve-year-old boy. On the walls were posters: Liam Neeson as Qui-Gon Jinn; Green Day; others. A bookcase stacked full with comic books stood in one corner, beside a small desk. On the desk was an iMac computer, and above that, on the wall, hung a bulletin board on which were displayed three blue ribbons and one yellow: science-fair awards. An all-in-one boom box CD player and radio rested atop the desk, a pile of compact discs beside it.

On the nightstand next to the bed was a small framed photograph of Craig and his parents. In the picture they were standing on a stone bridge that crossed a small stream in the middle of deep woods. In the background Bennett could see the corner of a pagoda. *Japan*, he realized. The three of them— Craig, his mother, and his father—all smiling at the camera. The bed was made. The room was clean and free of dust. Everything was in place, as if waiting for the boy who belonged here, but who would never return.

Bennett laid a hand on Yoshiko's shoulder. She turned to him, her eyes filling with tears. "I don't have all his things," she said, her voice breaking. "The clothes he was wearing when he . . . The police still have those. . . ."

Registering her anguish, Bennett said, "Dr. McWilliams, if you don't want me to be in here . . ."

She shook her head. "I'll just leave you by yourself. All right?"

Before he could reply, she was pushing past him, moving back into the hallway. He watched her go to another closed door and pull it open. She vanished behind the door, shutting herself in.

Bennett stared at the door for a moment, then stepped all the way into Craig's bedroom. He took his time examining the boy's things, opening the closet and several drawers, touching the clothes and shoes. A baseball bat and glove. A radio-operated model plane. A set of boy-sized Alpine skis.

He had been in the room for forty-five minutes, and he sensed nothing at all.

Dejected, Bennett sat on the edge of the bed. He reached to pick up the photograph of Craig and his parents. He held the picture, turning it over in his hands. *C'mon*, he urged himself, frustrated. *Something happen, dammit.*

He studied the faces in the photo. Craig. Edward McWilliams. Yoshiko.

He thought, *Yoshiko.*

It's a shrine, Bennett decided as he looked around the room. A shrine to someone who had died, constructed by someone else who had loved him very much.

He was startled by Wil Krieger's voice, quiet from the doorway. "Ken?"

Bennett looked up. Krieger was with Ed Mc-Williams, both of them regarding him curiously. "You okay?" Krieger asked.

"I'm fine," Bennett lied as he replaced the photograph on the nightstand.

"It's almost midnight," said Krieger.

Bennett nodded. "I guess it's time we left these people alone."

"I think that's a good idea," said Krieger.

On their way out, Bennett thanked Ed McWilliams for allowing him and Krieger to visit. Yoshiko hadn't returned from the room into which Bennett had watched her go, hadn't bothered to say good-night. McWilliams saw the two men off by himself.

CHAPTER THIRTEEN

Krieger and Bennett rode home in silence. When they arrived at Krieger's house, both of them went straight to their rooms, exhausted.

At one A.M., Bennett was lying in bed, eyes open, staring into the darkness. At that moment he realized—with no small amazement—for the first time in a long while he was thinking about a woman who was someone other than his dead wife. He tried to make Yoshiko's face disappear from his mind's eye, tried to conjure Christina's instead. He tried for some time. But he could not make Yoshiko's image go away.

JULY

CHAPTER ONE

The celebratory air that customarily swirled around San Patricio on an Independence Day weekend was nonexistent this year. Instead there was tangible evidence that something about the city had changed, and not for the better.

On Friday, July first, a story by Jeffrey Webber in the San Jose *Press-Telegram* disclosed that area merchants whose primary source of income came from tourism were showing a 25 percent drop in business compared to that of the previous summer. Webber had conducted an informal poll of several seaside motels and discovered that all had suffered cancellations for the Fourth of July weekend. At a time when they were usually filled to overflowing, every motel in the county had vacancies.

There were also other manifestations of the shroud of fear that had descended upon the area. Many of the local store owners interviewed by Webber reported that sales of such items as handguns, Chemical Mace, dead-bolt locks, baseball bats, Maglites, and home burglar alarm systems had risen dramatically. Attendance at summer camps and day-care centers diminished to a trickle.

William Relling Jr.

By the end of June, because of the degree to which their business had fallen off, the managers of the amusement park along the boardwalk considered laying off dozens of summertime employees and changing their hours of operation to those that were followed during winter months. Webber's story quoted Mayor Barbara Underwood, who stated unequivocally that the Pied Piper was to blame.

Then came the Fourth of July.

CHAPTER TWO

On Sunday, July third, San Patricio County Deputy Sheriff Glen Noreen reported for duty at two-forty-five P.M. Following roll call, he paused on his way to the department garage to examine the roster schedule for the next day. Noreen was pleased to discover that the shift commander had granted his request to have the holiday off.

While on solo patrol that evening, he drove to visit his girlfriend, Dee Ferguson. Dee worked as a claims adjuster for an insurance company, and she owned a duplex in the Aptos, south of San Patricio. One half of the duplex she rented to a pair of UC San Patricio students, and she lived in the other half herself. Noreen had been spending most of his nights at Dee's since the two of them began dating, six weeks before.

Dee was a short, slim-waisted, round-hipped, big-breasted blonde, a twenty-four-year-old divorcée. Her ex-husband, Gary, was, like Noreen, a San Patricio deputy sheriff. Though Noreen and Gary Ferguson weren't friends, they were amiable acquaintances, having in common not only their jobs but an intimate knowledge of the same woman.

As he was driving to Aptos, Noreen was thinking about two things. The first was the Fourth of July barbecue that his surfing buddies were planning, a party that he and Dee could now attend, since he was going to be off duty. The second was how he intended to use the party as an opportunity to ask Dee to marry him, as soon as he could afford the down payment on an engagement ring.

Noreen was unaware, however, that Dee's sexual relationship with her ex-husband—supposedly over since their divorce in February—had resumed a week before. Earlier that afternoon Dee had called Gary, inviting him to her apartment so that he could sign over to her a life-insurance policy to which he was the beneficiary. She wanted to cash out the policy, intending to use the money to buy a new car. Noreen knew about the meeting, and also that Dee planned to prepare a home-cooked meal for her ex-husband as a way of expressing her thanks for Ferguson's signing over the policy without making a fuss. What Noreen didn't know, though, was that after Dee and her ex-husband had finished dessert, they retired to her bedroom. Where, for the next three hours, they fucked to the brink of sweaty exhaustion. Gary Ferguson left his ex-wife's apartment at ten-thirty that night, a half hour before Noreen's shift ended, giving Dee just enough time to shower and douche. By the time Noreen arrived at eleven-thirty, looking for a little tender loving care of his own, the only evidence that Dee's ex-husband had been there at all was his signature on her insurance policy.

Since that night, the Fergusons had continued their surreptitious assignation. Neither of them had any interest in reestablishing a relationship that was not purely sexual. Dee, in particular, had no desire to be tied to Gary, and she certainly did not want to be married to him again. She promised Noreen truthfully that she'd fallen out of love with her ex-husband long ago. She explained carefully, so as not to wound Noreen's masculine pride, that she would always feel that Gary Ferguson was the sexiest man alive. *No reflection on you at all, baby,* she assured her new beau. *I swear, I love screwing you more than anybody else in the world, including my ex-husband. But Gary is catnip to women. He knows it, too. That's why I divorced him. They couldn't keep their hands off him, and he can't keep his hands off them, either.*

Tonight, July third, the sun had set an hour before Noreen pulled his patrol car to the curb across the street from the duplex. One half of the single-story structure—the apartment rented by Dee's tenants—was dark. A light was on in the living room of her apartment, shining behind sheer curtains that covered the picture window facing the street. A shadow was moving on the other side of the curtain.

Noreen was smiling to himself, glad that he'd decided to share in person the news about his having the holiday off tomorrow. He got out of the car and closed the door quietly, not wanting to arouse Dee's attention so she would pull the curtains aside to see who was visiting. He crossed the street and walked up the lawn, avoiding the concrete driveway so that his footsteps wouldn't be heard.

There were two vehicles parked in the drive: Dee's 1997 Mustang and a new GMC Jimmy. The truck registered on Noreen. Like most police officers, he automatically and unconsciously noted the details of any setting in which he found himself. But he gave the truck no more than a moment's thought, assuming that it belonged to one of Dee's tenants or their friends.

As he stepped onto the front porch, the lights in the living room went out. The room was still illuminated from within by a dim, flickering, bluish glow—Dee's television set, Noreen told himself. She liked to watch TV in the dark.

Noreen was reaching for the doorbell when he paused, frowning. He was hearing peculiar sounds from the other side of the door: a man grunting, low and guttural, and a woman letting out small *eeks* of pleasure. He recognized the latter sound immediately, and his frown became a scowl of rage. He could feel his cheeks becoming hot.

Noreen moved off the porch, edging his way to the picture window. Pressing his face to the glass, he squinted so that he could peer through the diaphanous curtains that hung on the other side of the glass. The only light in the living room came from the TV set. A *Murder, She Wrote* rerun was playing.

The two people in the room—Dee and her ex-husband Gary—were oblivious to the television show. They were naked on the floor in front of the TV, bathed in its flickering glow. Dee was on all fours, bucking in time with her ex-husband. He knelt behind her, doggy-style, his hands on either side of her waist, pressing her buttocks to his groin. Her breasts swayed rhythmically. She was squealing with passion.

Noreen watched for a time, waiting for the murderous urge to kick down the front door and confront the two lovers. Finally he turned away and went back to his patrol car. He sat in the car for some time, trying to make up his mind what to do. At last he started the engine, pulled away from the curb, and resumed his patrol.

Fortunately, the rest of Noreen's shift was uneventful. Had he encountered a lawbreaker—especially one who resisted being arrested—Noreen's foul mood might have gotten the better of him. As it was, by the time he went off duty, the hot rage he'd felt while peeping through the curtains at his girlfriend and her ex-husband had been dampened somewhat by the passing of time.

Arriving back at headquarters, Noreen telephoned Dee and canceled their "date" for that night. As he spoke to her, he had to control the tightness in his voice. He lied to her that a buddy on the San Jose PD had called unexpectedly and was on his way down to spend the night so the two of them could go surfing in the morning. Dee accepted the excuse without question, as Noreen hoped she would. She knew that next to spending time with her, surfing was Noreen's favorite avocation.

On his way out of headquarters, Noreen stopped again to check the duty-roster schedule. He found Gary Ferguson's name, and he noted that on July fourth Gary was scheduled to work the day shift: seven A.M. to three P.M. As Noreen stood at the roster board, his expression darkened as if a thundercloud were passing over his face.

Noreen drove back to Aptos in his own car and parked across the street from Dee's duplex, in the same spot where he had parked earlier that evening. The lights were on in Dee's living room. Her Mustang was the only vehicle in the driveway.

Noreen waited.

A few minutes past midnight, Gary Ferguson's

Jimmy came rumbling up the street and pulled into the driveway behind the Mustang. Ferguson climbed out of the cab and trotted to Dee's front porch. The front door opened, and he stepped inside. Moments later, the living room lights went out.

For the next several hours, Noreen sat in his car, maintaining a surveillance of the duplex. As he watched, he ran through his mind ugly, vengeful fantasies. He conjured the worst kind of coitus interruptus he could think of: imagining himself bursting in upon Dee and her ex-husband, his nine-millimeter Colt automatic in hand, opening fire, blowing the two of them away. Easy, straightforward, direct.

By four-thirty A.M., however, Noreen had made up his mind that revenge was a sucker's game. Killing the two of them would only create a world of shit for himself. Two counts of first-degree murder would mean a long term in prison, if not the death penalty. Besides, Noreen really didn't have anything against Gary, and he could understand the man's attraction to Dee. Noreen had no doubt that she was the instigator. Sometimes she seemed to like sex as much as she liked breathing.

But if Noreen took out his anger on her alone— regardless of how badly he may have wanted to— there was no way to tell how Gary Ferguson might respond. On the few occasions he and Noreen had run into each other, Gary seemed to be an easygoing guy. Still, you never knew how another man would react when he found out that a woman he cared about had been knocked around, whether she deserved it or not. Noreen decided that, in the end, Dee simply wasn't worth the risk.

He stayed put for another hour. The eastern sky was

just beginning to turn gray when Gary Ferguson emerged from the duplex, climbed into his truck, and drove away. Noreen waited five minutes more, then got out of his car and made his way to Dee's front door. He pressed the doorbell.

Within moments Noreen heard quick footsteps approaching the door from inside. The porch light went on. The door opened, and Dee stood before him wearing a thin kimono and a broad smile.

The smile vanished the instant she recognized who had rung her bell. Her jaw dropped, her eyes widened with shock, and she whispered in disbelief, "Oh, my God . . ."

Noreen regarded her stonily. She stammered, "Glen . . . oh, God . . ."

"You slut," he said in a voice like dry ice. "You fucking cunt."

"Glen, please, let me explain—"

He turned away. As he stalked to his car, she shouted his name, begging him to come back, pleading with him to give her another chance. For the entire drive back to his apartment, he could hear her voice echoing inside his mind.

Noreen arrived home at daybreak. Waiting for him was a message from Dee on his answering machine. The message implored him to call her back right away. As he listened to her voice his face twisted into an expression of bitter vindication. He erased the message, switched off the machine, and unplugged the phone.

He went into the kitchen to retrieve a half-full quart of Jack Daniel's from a cupboard above the sink. He took the whiskey with him to his bed. He sat up for a time, pulling straight from the bottle until he emptied it. As he drank, he thought black thoughts about women in general and Dee Ferguson in particular. Exhausted by having gone more than twenty-four hours without sleep, inebriated by the booze, he passed out around seven A.M.

Noreen was awakened at two-thirty that afternoon by an insistent pounding at his front door. He was badly hung over. A nagging headache pressed against his temples. It felt as if his mouth were stuffed with a wad of sticky, sour-tasting cotton. He staggered into the living room just as a loud, cheerful male voice was calling from outside the front door, "Hey, Glen? You home, or what?"

Noreen eased open the door. Bright afternoon sunlight streamed in. He had to reach up with a hand to shade his eyes. He blinked, trying to focus.

The young man on the porch was dressed in cutoffs, flip-flops, and a Billabong T-shirt. A pair of Vuarnet sunglasses hung on a fluorescent-pink cord around the man's neck. Noreen grunted hoarsely, "Langdon?"

John Langdon was a friend with whom Noreen surfed regularly, a real estate agent who worked in downtown San Patricio. "I stopped by to see if you were still coming to the barbecue," Langdon said. "I tried calling, but nobody answered the phone. I was on my way to the beach when I thought I'd check and see if maybe your car was here." Langdon's nose crinkled, and he waved a hand in front of his face as if to clear the air. "Jesus. I was about to say we got six cases of Corona waiting for us, but it smells like you already got the jump on everybody."

Noreen stared blankly at the other man. "Huh?"

Langdon's eyes narrowed with concern. "Hey, Glen, you okay?"

Noreen shook his head.

"What's the matter?" Langdon asked.

Noreen coughed. "I had a fight with Dee."

"Bad?"

Rubbing his face with a thick hand, Noreen nodded. "Bad enough. We broke up."

Langdon's look of concern deepened. "Sorry to hear it."

Noreen shrugged.

"Maybe it'd do you good to get out," said Langdon.

Noreen shook his head again. "I don't think so, John."

"C'mon," Langdon urged. "It'll beat the hell out of moping around here. I know if I was gonna drink myself into a stupor, I'd much rather do it in the company of friends than all by myself."

Noreen frowned. Langdon grinned. "That's the first symptom of alcoholism, *amigo*," he said. "Boozing alone."

Noreen was still frowning.

Langdon enticed, "C'mon . . ."

At last, Noreen relented.

CHAPTER THREE

Twelve hours later, in the custody of San Patricio County Sheriff's Department detectives, Glen Noreen admitted that he did not recall the precise order of events that culminated with his arrest and the arrest of three of his friends for murder. He remembered that it was around three-thirty in the afternoon when he arrived with John Langdon at the secluded beach cove where a dozen of their acquaintances had gathered. He remembered that by nightfall he had downed a six-pack of Corona beer by himself, and he was drunk for the second time that day. He did not recall, though, which of the friends still with him by then—Langdon, Rob McCleary, or Gene Davis—had brought up the subject of the Pied Piper.

Nor did he recall which of them had asked if it was true that he himself had found the body of one of those poor, dead kids. He recounted to his friends the story of the rainy night when he and another deputy had gone out with that lady detective, Rachel Siegel, who was in charge of the Pied Piper case. Following a tip, the three of them had hiked to the site of a housing subdivision under construction. Noreen was the first one to shine a light on the body hidden in the woods that surrounded the construction site.

According to Noreen—in his own words, taken from the transcript of his interrogation by Det. Roberto Ornelas at two-forty-five A.M. on Tuesday, July fifth—what happened after he told that story to his friends was this:

"It was Rob McCleary who started bagging on the Sheriff's Department. 'How come you guys can't catch that sick motherfucker? What the hell's wrong with you?' That sort of shit. Rob was the one who said he thought it was some fucking troll . . . you know, a transient? Gene Davis started bitching, too. Gene agreed with Rob—the Pied Piper probably was some troll who'd come up from L.A. or something. I told them the Sheriff's Department had been checking out that angle all along, that we'd brought in a whole bunch of transients and questioned them, but it was a fucking blind alley.

"Anyway, by then it was dark. It must've been an hour, hour and a half after sunset. We were watching this fireworks display from across the bay, off Monterey, and still arguing about this Pied Piper shit. That's when we ran out of beer. All four of us were pretty loaded, and we didn't really need any more, but we decided we'd get into John's van and drive to this 7-Eleven he knew of, the only place we could think of that'd be open.

"We get into the van, and Rob is still giving me shit about the Pied Piper the whole time we're driving to town. We get the beer, and we're heading back to the beach. Then we get to the top of the road that leads down to the cove, and right there on the side of the road is this long-haired guy with a backpack, hitchhiking, holding up this cardboard sign that says 'Frisco' on it. Middle of the night, and the dumb fucker's hitchhiking. There weren't any other cars around. I forget who it was, but one of us said, 'Let's get that son of a bitch.'

"Honest to God, I don't know what we were thinking of. Too drunk to know what we were doing, that's all I can say now. Plus I was already in a pissed-off mood about something else. Anyway, John pulls over, and the other three of us jump out and grab this guy. We drag him into the van, and we're going, 'What the fuck are you doing out here on the highway in the middle of the night, hair-head? You running away from something?' Of course, this guy doesn't know what the hell we're doing, just that we're trying to grab him, so he starts to put up a fight. He punches Rob in the mouth, and that's when Gene picks up this tire iron from the floor of the van and whacks the guy over the head with it.

"We drive the guy back down to the cove. We drag him out of the van and carry him to the beach. Rob's got this shovel he found someplace, and he says, 'Bury him.' So we dig a hole in the sand and bury this guy up to his neck. He's unconscious the whole time, till Gene goes over and opens a beer and pours it on the guy's head, and that wakes him up.

"Then John holds up this Coleman lantern he's brought down from the van, and he shines it in the guy's face. Rob starts saying to the guy, 'You're the Pied Piper, aren't you, motherfucker? Admit it. And right away the guy starts yelling for help. That's when I kicked him in the mouth. I said, 'Nobody's gonna hear you down here, asshole.' Then Rob says, 'We'll fix you, you hippie faggot prick.'

226

"Then he takes the lantern from John and opens up the valve on the bottom. He starts to pour the fuel on the guy's head. By now the guy's crying like a baby, begging us to let him go. Rob looks at Gene and John and me, and he says, 'Stand back.' Then he pulls a book of matches from his pocket. He squats down in front of the guy and lights a match. 'Burn, motherfucker,' he says to the guy, and then he drops the lit match on his head.

"The four of us just stood there, watching the guy's head light up like a flare. He screamed for a long time. And then he stopped. There was this awful smell, and this sound like meat sizzling on a grill. Then I think I can still hear him screaming, until I realize it's a siren, and I can see the flashers coming out from town along the highway, heading toward us. Somebody else must have heard him after all. And John and Rob and Gene and me, we're just looking at each other. And we've all got this same look on our face. Like we only just now understood what it is we'd really done . . ."

The subsequent front-page headline of the final edition of the San Jose *Press-Telegram* for Tuesday, July fifth, read, *San Patricio Deputy Sheriff Charged in Bizarre Execution Slaying*. And every resident of San Patricio who read the headline, or heard the subsequent reports on the radio, or watched the local news on television that night, knew that however bad things had been for their community for the past several months, they had just become much worse.

CHAPTER FOUR

Barbara Underwood was scowling as she said to herself, *There are days when I despise this fucking job.*

It was nine-twenty-five A.M. on Wednesday, July sixth. Mayor Underwood had called an emergency meeting of the San Patricio city council, commencing at nine-fifteen. The topic for discussion was the murder on Monday night of a twenty-year-old Stanford University student named Wayne Allen. Allen had been hitchhiking back to school following a weekend trip to Big Sur. Mistaken for the Pied Piper by a group of drunken vigilantes, one of whom turned out to be a San Patricio deputy sheriff, Allen was beaten up and burned to death.

Early yesterday morning, when Mayor Underwood had been phoned by Sheriff Pete Joyce with the news of Allen's killing, he'd said to her at the time, "Barb, I'm afraid the shit is really gonna hit the fan over this." Now, as she glanced toward the first row of the council chamber gallery where Joyce was sitting, she recalled his words. *Pete*, she thought, *what you said yesterday morning is about to become the understatement of the decade. The shit has hit the fan, all right, and then some.*

228

The entire nine-member council was present in the chamber, each in his or her customary seat on the dais at the front of the room. Mayor Underwood had called for a closed-door meeting. No private citizens were allowed to attend, and no representatives of the media. The only nonmembers of the council there were seated in the gallery's first row: Sheriff Joyce, Lt. Dan Sloane, District Attorney Robert Baggott, and CBI Special Agent Frank Killoran.

The source of Underwood's displeasure sat two seats to her right on the dais: Councilman Davis Grimes. Grimes was a tall, thin, fifty-year-old expatriated Jamaican who had been living in San Patricio for a decade and a half. He was dressed in his customary fashion: a colorfully patterned dashiki over well-worn dungarees. He had thick dreadlocks that hung to his shoulders, and he affected a Caribbean accent when he spoke.

Grimes had been recognized with reluctance by the chair moments before. Taking the floor, Grimes had launched into a tirade that had Barbara Underwood telling herself that Sheriff Joyce was absolutely correct when he suggested that the shit was going to hit the fan. Grimes was leaning forward in his seat, holding up a copy of yesterday's *Press-Telegram*. "Has everybody had a chance to see this?" he challenged. " 'San Patricio Deputy Sheriff Charged in Bizarre Execution Slaying.' " He waved the paper in Pete Joyce's direction. "One of your men, Sheriff. One of your own men."

Mayor Underwood sighed wearily. "Everybody's seen the story, Davis. Is there some particular point you wanted to make about it?"

Grimes glared at her. "First off, I want to know what

229

specific charge the district attorney intends to bring against these killers. The paper doesn't say."

Underwood nodded toward the district attorney. "That's why Bob Baggott's here, so we can help him decide what the charge should be."

"What's to decide?" Grimes demanded. "If the DA charges these men with anything less than murder in the first degree, this community will not stand for it. That I promise you."

Irritated, Bob Baggott said, "Councilman Grimes, I really don't appreciate being threatened—"

Grimes cut him off. "Let me read you something, Mr. Baggott." The councilman took a sheaf of paper from the table in front of him. "California Penal Code Section 189. 'All murder which is perpetrated by means of any kind of willful, deliberate, and premeditated killing, or which is committed in the perpetration of, or attempt to perpetrate, arson, rape, carjacking, robbery, burglary, mayhem, kidnapping . . .' " Grimes paused for dramatic effect. "That would be the criteria for first-degree murder in this state, would it not?"

Baggott responded icily, "Believe it or not, I'm familiar with the murder statutes."

The mayor said to Councilman Grimes, "Nobody's saying they won't be charged with first-degree murder, Davis. We just want Bob to consider every option before he makes a move, that's all."

"That's bullshit, and you know it," Grimes snapped. "Don't be telling me you called this meeting so we could 'consider our options.' If you want to sweep this mess under the rug, Ms. Mayor, you're welcome to try. But don't expect me to stay quiet about it, 'cause I am not about to!"

Several people in the council chamber began to speak at once, all of them angry. The mayor reached for her gavel and rapped for order. When everyone had quieted, she regarded Grimes sternly. "I don't know what gave you the idea that the purpose of this meeting was to arrange some sort of coverup, but that's not the situation at all. It's too late for that, anyway. There's no question that the DA is going to prosecute these men. But as a group we need to settle on what we think the specific charge ought to be, in order to make sure that it's something that'll stick."

District Attorney Baggott cut in. "We can't just automatically charge these guys with first-degree murder. I'm not at all certain I could make the case for premeditation against them. . . ." He paused, looking to the mayor.

She nodded to him: *Go on.*

"First of all, they were drunk," the DA continued. "When they were arrested, the lowest blood alcohol level that any of 'em had was point one-oh. What that means is the defense will likely argue diminished capacity, and it'll probably succeed. Second, they acted totally on impulse. They grabbed this kid off the highway—a total stranger—and dragged him down to the beach. Does that make it a kidnapping? I don't know."

One of the other council members asked, "Has whoever's defending them made an offer to plea-bargain to a lesser charge? Like second-degree murder?"

"I haven't had a chance to talk with any defense attorneys yet," answered Baggott. "That deputy, Noreen, is being defended by one of the Sheriff's Department's lawyers, at least for now. One of the other defendants has somebody from the public defender's office. The other two have private counsel. I intend to speak to all the attorneys before I file formal charges this afternoon."

"What we need to keep in mind," said Mayor Underwood, "is that a plea bargain isn't necessarily something we should turn up our noses at. If letting them plead guilty will avoid the negative publicity that's sure to accompany a trial like this, the better it will be for all of us. And when I say 'us,' I'm not just thinking of the Sheriff's Department. I mean the whole city."

Baggott added, "There's something else to consider, too. With a charge of first-degree murder, I can make a motion that the defendants be held without bail. That means they stay in jail until they come to trial. If I file a lesser charge, then no bail's a lot tougher to ask for. But these guys are all first-time offenders. When you consider how vicious nature this crime was, though, you can just imagine how up in arms the media and the public will be if we set them free. Even if it's just on bail."

"Obviously," said Mayor Underwood, "the most important thing we have to take into consideration is how the community's going to react—"

"I *knew* it," Davis Grimes interrupted. "The only thing anybody gives a damn about around here is public relations."

"For God's sake, Davis," argued the mayor, "I don't think there's any reason to make things worse out there than they already are."

"Let me tell you how bad 'things' are, Ms. Mayor," Grimes said testily. "Unlike my fellow council members, I *know* what it's like out there on the streets."

Underwood rolled her eyes, whispering to herself, "Spare me, Lord, please?"

"I am not exaggerating when I say this city is turning into an armed camp," Grimes went on. "Neighbor against neighbor, friend against friend. You can't trust any strangers, no matter who they are. The way everything's been going lately, what happened the other night was bound to happen sooner or later."

He paused. "You want to know the truth? If there's anybody who should be charged with murder here, it's the man who hasn't done a thing about catching whoever's killing our babies. That man *right there*." Grimes jabbed an accusatory finger in the direction of Pete Joyce.

The sheriff said in a growl, "Hold on a damn minute—"

Grimes ignored him. "Now we find out he can't even keep his own men in line—"

Sheriff Joyce bellowed, "Why, you black son of a bitch!"

The mayor cried, "Pete, no!"

But Joyce was already out of his chair and charging at Grimes like an enraged bull. Instantly the councilman was out of his seat, lunging across the table in front of him to get at the sheriff.

Both men were restrained immediately, Grimes by the councilman sitting beside him and Sheriff Joyce by Dan Sloane. The two combatants cursed at one another, their shouts rising above the voices of those who were trying to keep them apart. The mayor pounded her gavel repeatedly, pleading for order.

It was to no avail. At last Mayor Underwood slumped in her chair and covered her ears to shut out the cacophony. Thinking, *This is not worth it. This fucking job is just not worth it.*

CHAPTER FIVE

Ninety minutes later, Barbara Underwood was ushering Pete Joyce and Frank Killoran into her office. As soon as she had closed the door behind them, Killoran was saying, "Can somebody please explain to me who this prick Grimes thinks he is?"

"He's a pain-in-the-ass loudmouth son of a bitch, that's what he is," complained Sheriff Joyce.

"Pete," cautioned the mayor as she moved to sit down behind her desk. Joyce and Killoran took their places in chairs opposite the desk from her.

"I'm serious," said Killoran. "I don't understand why you both took so much shit from that guy."

The mayor sighed, then said to Killoran, "Mr. Grimes represents a certain constituency. You've been here long enough to know how large a counterculture element there is in San Patricio. Grimes is a sort of self-appointed spokesperson for that group. Blacks, Chicanos, hippies, the homeless. They're his political base."

"He's still got a big mouth," said Killoran.

The sheriff grunted. "Tell me about it."

Killoran eased back in his chair. "I was just wondering. Did it occur to either of you if maybe the reason why Mr. Grimes comes on so strong is because he's putting up a smoke screen?"

The mayor looked puzzled. "I don't know what you mean."

Killoran said, "While I was watching him this morning, I couldn't help thinking, If this guy is so mouthy, maybe it's because he's got something to hide. A lot of times that's the case with people like him. You know, like that guy in New York, what's-his-name, Sharpton? He's another bigmouth who likes to stir up shit so he can get his name in the papers and see his face on TV. Guys like them, they figure if they bitch loud enough and long enough, nobody'll ever challenge 'em over some shady business they may be pulling themselves."

The sheriff asked, "What are you trying to say, Frank?"

Killoran answered, "Only that it'd be easy enough for me to have one of my people run a thorough check on Grimes, if you'd like. Hell, I'd be surprised if he didn't at least have some kind of record, wouldn't you? Not that we'd be looking for anything in particular. Just something that he wouldn't necessarily want to have spread around." He paused. "I'm only interested in giving you and the mayor a little leverage, Sheriff, that's all. Just in case you need it."

The mayor and Sheriff Joyce were looking at each other with guarded expressions. Mayor Underwood turned to Killoran, and he showed her a thin, dangerous smile. "To tell you the truth, Mayor, considering what I've observed about your relationship with Grimes, I'm surprised you haven't done something like that already."

William Relling Jr.

Before the mayor could reply, her desk telephone tweedled. She pressed the intercom button on the phone, switching on the speaker. "Yes?"

"Chief Novak is here, Ms. Mayor," came a voice from the speaker.

"Send him in." Mayor Underwood switched off the intercom. Thoughtful, she drummed her fingers on the phone. She turned to Killoran, studying him, thinking, *Mr. Killoran, remind me never to have you for an enemy.*

Killoran was still showing her his thin smile. "It's up to you, Mayor. I could have somebody start on it today."

There came a knock at the door. "Come in," the mayor called. The door opened, and Earl Novak entered. "Hello, Earl," said the mayor. She gestured to him to close the door, then motioned him to an empty chair beside Sheriff Joyce. As Novak took his seat, he nodded a greeting to the sheriff and Killoran.

Assuming a steely demeanor, the mayor said, "Gentlemen, the reason I asked for this meeting with you three is that bullshit time is over. I wanted to let you all know I got a call yesterday afternoon from the agent in charge of the FBI field office in San Francisco."

The three men exchanged looks of consternation. "That's right," continued the mayor. "Now. Do any of you have one good reason why I shouldn't take them up on their offer to turn the Pied Piper case over to them and wash our hands of the whole damn mess?"

CHAPTER SIX

As Earl Novak drove from City Hall to Sheriff's Head-quarters, he could feel his stomach churning. It was twelve-fifteen P.M., and the chronic acid reflux from which he suffered had kicked in for the day. His gut roiled as if he'd swallowed a bucketful of red-hot coals.

The heartburn had struck him minutes into his meeting with Mayor Underwood, Sheriff Joyce, and CBI agent Killoran. The sour pain in his stomach was the reason Novak had turned down the sheriff's invitation to join him and Killoran for lunch. Sheriff Joyce loved Mexican food, and he had lunch at the same restaurant every day. Novak had no desire to try to choke down anything spicy, while at the same time having to listen to Joyce and Killoran commiserate about the mayor. Novak decided that he would rather suffer alone.

He could tell that Sheriff Joyce, in particular, was very pissed off. But it wasn't just about the mayor's threat to take the Pied Piper investigation away from him and the CBI and turn it over to the Feds. Not that that wouldn't have been enough, as it usually didn't take much to incite Pete Joyce's temper. But Joyce had taken the news about the mayor's call from the FBI with equanimity—for him, anyway. Because he was already angry about something else. What that could be, however, Novak didn't have a clue.

He supposed that it had to do with the fallout from what had happened the other night, when that drunken, dumb-ass deputy sheriff and his drunken, dumb-ass buddies roasted that poor hitchhiker to death. Thinking about the incident—and the shit storm that had deluged the whole Sheriff's Department as a consequence—caused Novak's stomach to churn again.

The incident reminded him of something that had happened nearly twenty years ago. Novak couldn't recall the exact year, but it was sometime in the 1980s. The San Patricio Five—that was the name that the local media had taken to calling five members of the city's police department—not the Sheriff's Department, thank God—who'd formed their own vigilante group. For more than two years, the Five spent their off-duty hours harassing transients who hung around the city's parks and beaches. "Troll-bashing" became the popular name for the Five's activities. When one of the officers found a stray vagrant roaming the streets or sleeping under a tree or on the strand, the officer would radio his buddies, calling in a "code blue." Blue for bruises.

After they were caught, the officers defended themselves by insisting that they'd been pressured into doing what they did by local merchants who kept bitching at the police department about all the "undesirables" floating around the city and scaring away customers. Though Novak's memory of the incident was dim, he recalled ruefully that blaming the merchants didn't do the Five a whole lot of good at their trial. He also remembered that the San Patricio chief of police had been forced to resign over the whole fucking debacle. Not that it mattered. Even if he couldn't recall the particulars at the moment, Novak had little doubt that it was only a matter of time before some punk reporter dredged up the story of the San Patricio Five and rubbed Sheriff Joyce's nose in it. Then *everybody* would remember.

Arriving at headquarters, Novak rode the elevator to the second floor. He walked down a narrow hallway and opened the door leading to the detectives' squad room. Only a handful of detectives seemed to be on duty. *Lunch hour*, Novak reminded himself, and the thought of eating caused the fiery pain in his stomach to rise in his esophagus like a solar flare.

As he made his way to his office, thinking about the bottle of Maalox that he kept in a desk drawer, Novak passed an open interrogation room. He peered into the cubicle as he walked by. What he saw inside did not register on him until he was reaching to open the door to his office. He paused, his brow furrowing with puzzled annoyance. Novak turned around and called toward the interrogation room, "Rachel?"

Rachel Siegel poked her head from the cubicle. "Did you call me, Earl?"

"Would you come here, please?"

Rachel emerged from the cubicle and walked up to Novak. The expression on her face queried him. "What's up?"

Novak nodded toward the interrogation room. "Who's that guy in there with the visitor badge?"

Rachel seemed to shrink away from him for a moment, then drew herself up. "Kenneth Bennett."

"Who?"

"I told you about him before. He's the guy who had the vision about the kid whose body we found at that construction site. Around Memorial Day?"

Novak frowned. "What the hell is he doing here? I thought you told him to get out of town."

"I did," Rachel replied. "He came back."

"That doesn't answer my question," said Novak. "I meant what's he doing here *now*?"

Rachel hesitated. "He's going through the physical evidence we took from the Pied Piper's victims. He's trying to see if there's something there that might give him an impression of the killer."

Novak could feel his face reddening. He swallowed a deep breath of air, hoping that it would dampen the furnace in his gut. He reached behind him to open the door to his office. He commanded her in a low voice, "Come in here with me, will you, please?"

Rachel stepped into the office, and Novak followed. As soon as he had closed the door, she quickly said to him, "Earl, before you blow your stack, give me a chance to explain, all right? Bennett showed up on my doorstep a week ago, completely out of the blue. He really had left town when I told him to the last time—gone home to St. Louis, where he's from. But he came back because something happened to him. He hasn't explained to me what it is, but he told me in no uncertain terms that this time he's not leaving till he helps us catch the Pied Piper."

Rachel paused. "I've run a thorough check on him, and he is a hundred percent legit. He's helped out on dozens of police investigations all over the country. I figure if he tumbles onto something, great. If he doesn't, then we're no worse off than we were before."

Novak asked, "Does Killoran know about him?"

Rachel made a face. "Ever since the day he and his bozos got here, Frank Killoran has had me sitting around twiddling my thumbs. I had to do something, make some kind of move of my own, or I was gonna go nuts."

"In other words, he doesn't know."

Rachel hesitated, then shook her head.

"Were you gonna tell him, eventually?" asked Novak.

"Eventually."

Novak winced. Rachel asked, "Are you all right?"

He glared at her. "No." He took another deep breath. "I just came from a meeting with the mayor. She told us that she got a call yesterday from the FBI They're 'offering' to take over the Pied Piper investigation."

"The FBI?"

Novak nodded. "She's seriously considering the offer." He chopped at his throat with the edge of his hand. "She's had it up to here because nothing seems to be happening with the case. She's been taking a lot of heat from the local businesspeople and citizen groups and the media—and to top it all off comes this little drama on the Fourth of July, in which one of our own deputies plays a starring role. You can understand how she's feeling, can't you?"

Rachel said nothing.

Novak continued. "I assume you can also understand how the sheriff and Killoran feel about being told that because of their incompetence, this big, splashy case is gonna be taken away from them. They're sure to look like total boobs if that happens. As will the rest of us."

Rachel asked, "So is the mayor gonna bring in the FBI, or what?"

"One month," answered Novak, holding up a finger. "We've got that long to make some tangible progress on this fucking case. That's assuming, of course, that no more dead kids turn up and no more hitchhikers get toasted."

Rachel frowned.

"Which brings us to you, specifically," Novak continued. "Already you are on very thin ice, as far as Frank Killoran is concerned. Calling him an asshole to his face last week didn't exactly endear you to him, but at least you apologized for that. But now you want to end-run him by bringing in some fucking psychic? Didn't we bury that issue months ago?"

"Earl, this time it's different, I swear—"

Novak cut her off. "I don't want to hear about it. That's between you and Killoran. I have to tell you, though, he's just itching for an excuse to ream you. If you piss him off, and he goes to the sheriff and demands your suspension for insubordination or failure to follow the chain of command or not saying, 'Pardon me all to hell,' when you bump into him in the hallway, there isn't a damn thing I can do about it. You're screwed. End of story."

Rachel fell into a sullen silence.

"Play it however you like," Novak said finally. "You need to be aware, though, that you are running a very big risk if you push Killoran too far."

Rachel nodded glumly. "Anything else?"

Novak shook his head. "Just get out of here. I gotta take something for my stomach."

Rachel nodded again. She turned and went out the door, closing it behind her.

Novak watched her through the glass until she disappeared into the interrogation cubicle. The volcanic pain in his stomach was worse than it had ever been before. Trying to remember in which drawer he'd put the bottle of antacid, he was hoping to God that the pain didn't mean he was getting an ulcer. That would be the last thing he needed, Novak told himself, today or ever.

CHAPTER SEVEN

At one o'clock that afternoon, Rachel Siegel and Ken Bennett were in her Sienna, traveling west, heading out of downtown San Patricio. They'd said little to each other since they had gotten into the minivan at headquarters, after Rachel had outlined their itinerary for the day. She was driving Bennett to the last three sites where the Pied Piper's victims had been found.

Rachel suspected that Bennett was aware that she was preoccupied and not willing to engage in make-shift conversation. *He's an unusual man*, she told herself, glancing over to study Bennett surreptitiously. Not "unusual" in any pejorative sense, she decided. Rather it was that, unlike most human beings, Ken Bennett seemed keenly tuned in to his surroundings. Especially the *people* who surrounded him. *What's the term I'm looking for?* Rachel asked herself. She flipped through the pages of a mental dictionary until she found the word. *Empathic*, she thought. *That's it. He's empathic.*

As they passed beyond the city limits and turned onto U.S. Highway 1, Bennett said dryly, "You know, this is the most unusual police car I've ever been in."

Rachel smiled. "It's pretty convenient. The department gives me an allowance for gas and oil, and they take care of all the maintenance. The only difference is that I'm the one who actually owns the van."

"How do you keep in touch with headquarters?"

"Cell phone." She indicated the dashboard in front of him. "There's also a two-way radio in the glove compartment. Plus I've got flares, a first-aid kit, and an extra handgun tucked away in the back, with the spare tire. And a portable flasher underneath my seat."

Bennett appeared impressed. "How 'bout that?"

"How 'bout that," acknowledged Rachel.

Neither of them spoke for a few moments. Bennett was looking through the windshield at Monterey Bay, which lay to their left. It was a clear, sunny afternoon. The water sparkled.

"This place we're going to first," he said at last. "What's it again?"

"It's a state park," Rachel answered.

"You seem to have quite a few of those around here, don't you? State parks, I mean?"

"I suppose."

"That's where most of the bodies have been turning up, haven't they? In the woods?"

Rachel nodded. "Most of them."

"But not all?"

"Not all. Two of the victims were found buried at beach locations. Then there's the one you helped us find at that housing site. The rest were in the woods."

Bennett's forehead furrowed with concern. Rachel asked, "What's the matter?"

"I was just trying to figure out if there might be some kind of pattern."

245

"There isn't," she said. "Not really. That's been our problem. Based on the usual kinds of stuff that serial killers do, there isn't any obvious design to the way he's behaving. He's consistent with his choice of victims, except for their gender, and he dispatches them all the same way, but that's it. The kids disappear from places all over the county at all hours of the day and night. It doesn't happen at a specific time of the month, like during a full moon, or on the same date or anything like that. Some months he's done only one kid. Last month he did three. If there's some kind of occult or numerological significance to the way he works, it's beyond me."

Bennett asked, "So the only thing that's consistent with him is that the victims are always kids?"

"Even that hasn't been much help," Rachel answered. "No victim's been younger than eight years old or older than thirteen. He's killed more boys than girls, but that seems to be another random arrangement rather than a calculated choice. Also race doesn't seem to matter to him. Black, white, Hispanic, Asian—we've had at least one of each. Which is another reason developing an accurate profile of him has been so hard to do. Most serial killers only go after victims who are the same race as they are."

"I didn't know that."

Rachel nodded. "Not always, but most of the time." She looked toward Bennett once again and noticed that he was frowning. "Ken," she said, "if you're trying to make yourself think like a real detective, don't bother. Between the CBI and the Sheriff's Department, we've run all that stuff by one another a thousand and one times in the past six months."

Rachel could see the muscles in his jaw working.

She smiled again. "We'll get him," she said. "All we need is a break, and we'll get one sooner or later. Hopefully sooner."

"That wasn't what I was thinking about," said Bennett.

Rachel noticed that there was a vaguely anguished quality to his voice that hadn't been there before. Her eyes questioned him. "What, then?" she asked.

He said, "I was just wondering about how much trouble you were making for yourself. By taking me with you."

Rachel returned her attention to the road, hoping that her face did not show the degree to which she was marveling at him. She hadn't mentioned a word to Bennett about the conversation she'd had with Earl Novak, which was why Bennett had caught her by surprise. She said, "Have you been reading my mind?"

"I didn't have to," Bennett said.

Rachel considered for a moment. "While I was in my boss's office—not more than an hour ago, mind you—his exact words regarding whether or not I should accept your assistance were, 'Play it however you like.' "

Bennett eyed her skeptically. "Really?"

Rachel crossed her heart. "Scout's honor."

Bennett hesitated for a moment, then said, "Tell me what makes you so certain there's going to be a break in the case."

Rachel shrugged. "Because that's what always happens. The Pied Piper isn't the first serial killer we've had around here. Back in the seventies there were a couple of famous ones. Kessler and McNeal."

Bennett shook his head. "I never heard of them."

"Very charming individuals," Rachel replied mordantly. "Between them they murdered something like two dozen people, completely independent of each other. They were operating at the exact same time, but they didn't actually meet each other until they were locked up side by side in adjoining cells in the county jail, after they'd been caught." She chuckled humorlessly. "When I went away to college, whenever somebody found out I was from San Patricio, all they'd want to talk to me about was Kessler and McNeal and what a panic they'd caused."

Rachel paused, reminiscing. "Herb McNeal was this dope-addled burnout, a real acid casualty. To him, his victims were all sacrifices, part of some ritual he'd made up that was supposed to keep earthquakes from hitting San Patricio. He was a real loon."

"What about the other one? Kessler?"

"Right," she said. "Ray Kessler. He was even nuttier than McNeal, and a lot more dangerous. He shot his grandparents to death when he was fifteen. Then, years later, after a psychiatrist decided he was 'cured' and it was okay to let him out of the booby hatch, he mutilated six coeds from the university and, finally, his own mother. He probably could have kept going indefinitely, except he turned himself in because after he killed Mom, what he called his 'task' was completed. McNeal just plain got himself caught." She paused again. "Eventually the same thing'll happen with the Pied Piper. Either he'll make a mistake, or we'll finally get lucky."

They'd come to the entrance to the park. Rachel made a right turn and slowed the minivan to a halt beside a kiosk from which a ranger emerged. Rachel showed her badge and ID to the ranger and was waved though. She parked the Sienna, and she and

Bennett got out. Rachel led the way along a hiking trail that wound deep into the woods.

Checking a map that she had brought along, she guided Bennett through dense underbrush to a tiny clearing two hundred yards from the main trail. The clearing was shaded by tall, overhanging trees. A shallow pit had been dug at the far side of the clearing. Sunlight shone down on the pit through a break in the trees.

"That's it," Rachel said, motioning to the pit. "The body probably wouldn't have been found at all if a raccoon hadn't dug it up and exposed enough of it so a couple of park rangers could smell it once it started to decompose."

Bennett moved to the side of the pit and crouched. He hung his head and closed his eyes. Rachel stood nearby, trying to remain as silent and unobtrusive as she could.

After several moments Bennett opened his eyes. He reached down to scoop up a handful of earth, then let the dirt dribble back into the pit, sifting it between his fingers. He turned around to look at her, but said nothing. She could read the disappointment on his face.

They stayed there for half an hour, then drove north along Highway 9 to another state park. An hour later they were driving north again, to a piece of private property near a place that, according to Rachel, was called Pine Mountain. The terrain at each location where the bodies of the Pied Piper's last three victims were found was similar: heavily wooded, close to a marked trail, but far enough away to remain undiscovered by casual passersby. At each location she was pressed to disguise her disappointment that Bennett appeared to receive no impressions, no sensations, no clues.

By four o'clock they were heading back to San Patricio. They traveled in a mutually imposed silence, until she pulled the Sienna into Wil Krieger's driveway. Bennett thanked her for the ride. Rachel offered to pick him the next day at ten A.M. He nodded, agreeing, and got out of the minivan. Rachel waited until he'd disappeared into the house before rolling back out of the driveway and starting for home.

CHAPTER EIGHT

Bennett let himself into the house with a key that Krieger had made for him the day before. Closing the door behind him, he moved through the foyer and into the kitchen. He went to a cupboard and found a heavy stone mug and a box of Lemon Lift teabags. He filled the mug with water from the tap, then placed it in the portable microwave oven next to the stove.

As he was setting the timer on the microwave to boil the water, the phone in Krieger's living room began to ring. Aware that Krieger had a message machine attached to the phone, Bennett debated with himself whether he should answer the call. *I seriously doubt it's for me*, he thought with glum sarcasm.

After five rings, Bennett wondered if the answering machine had been turned on. He hurried from the kitchen into the living room and picked up the receiver just as the phone was concluding its sixth ring. He had to catch his breath before he could speak. "Hello?"

For a moment there was no reply. Just as Bennett was about to repeat his greeting, a soft female voice spoke hesitantly. "Is this Mr. Bennett?"

He felt an odd, anticipatory shiver along his spine. "Who's calling, please?"

Another momentary hesitation, then: "Yoshiko. Yoshiko McWilliams."

Surprised, Bennett wondered, *Yoshiko?*

She was saying, "I hope I'm not disturbing you."

"Not at all." He moistened his lips with the tip of his tongue. "I just wasn't expecting you to be calling me, that's all. Not that I was expecting anybody else, for that matter."

"I've been trying to get hold of you since this morning," she said. "But nobody's answered the phone there."

"Nobody's been home," Bennett explained. "Wil drove up to Berkeley for a meeting with somebody he's working on a grant proposal with. I guess he forgot to turn on the answering machine. He's spending the night up there, and he told me not to expect him back till sometime tomorrow afternoon. I've been out all day myself, on business. I only just walked in the door a few minutes ago."

"Wil's not there?"

Bennett thought he detected a peculiar tone in her voice. "Just me," he said. "Did you want to leave him a message?"

"No, no," she said quickly. "You're really the one I . . . I thought if he was there that I could . . ." A heavy sigh. "I didn't actually want him to know."

"About what?"

"That I wanted to see you again."

"I beg your pardon?"

"I wanted to see you again. To talk to you. About Craig. My son. Would that be all right?"

"When did you want to see me?" Bennett asked.

"Are you busy tonight? I thought, if perhaps you were free, and you didn't have plans for dinner . . . ?"

"I'm wide-open," Bennett said. "I don't have a car, though. You and your husband will have to come pick me up."

"Not Edward," she said sharply. "He's teaching tonight. His class doesn't let out until ten. It would be just the two of us. You and me. If that's all right?"

The odd shiver was playing along Bennett's spine once again. "Of course it's all right," he answered. "What time would you like to come get me?"

"How's six o'clock?"

"That sounds fine."

"Is it all right if I pick you up there? At Wil's?"

"That fine, too," Bennett said.

CHAPTER NINE

Yoshiko arrived a few minutes before six. They rode in her car, a Volvo station wagon, to a European-style café in the mountains above San Patricio. The place was small and dark and quiet. They were seated by the maître d' at a table in the rear. As the maître d' handed them their menus, Yoshiko asked him to bring two glasses of the house's sauvignon blanc. Catching herself, she looked to Bennett. "I'm sorry," she apologized. "That was presumptuous of me. You would like some wine, wouldn't you?"

He nodded. "Thank you. I would."

After the maître d' departed, Yoshiko asked Bennett what he'd been doing to keep himself busy for the past week, since the night they'd met. Very little until today, he told her. He'd just begun to describe what happened while he was out with Rachel Siegel that afternoon, when a waiter appeared with the wine Yoshiko had ordered. Serving them, the waiter asked if they were ready to order. Yoshiko answered that they would like to take their time with the meal and asked him to come back in a little while.

Once the waiter was out of earshot, Yoshiko said

to Bennett, "I should probably tell you the reason I wanted to see you again."

"I'm curious about that," he said. "You said something about your son?"

She nodded. "It was because of something you talked about the other night. If what you said happened really did happen, then I think, in a way, you were the last person to see Craig alive."

Bennett sipped his wine. "I wasn't sure if you believed me."

"I didn't, at first," Yoshiko said frankly. "Being a scientist, there's a part of me that was very skeptical about what you do." She paused. "I didn't know if you knew that about me. That I'm a scientist."

Bennett nodded. "Wil told me about you and your husband. Before we came over."

Yoshiko's face clouded. "What did he say?"

"Only that you were both Ph.Ds, and that Edward's an English teacher and you're a biologist. And that both of you took your son's death very hard."

A flicker of agony lit her eyes. "I'm sorry," Bennett said quickly, with sympathy. Without thinking, he reached across the table to take her hand. He laced his fingers with hers and squeezed tenderly.

She hesitated for a moment, then pulled her hand away to reach for the napkin in her lap. She dabbed at a tear that was trickling down her cheek. Composing herself, Yoshiko replaced the napkin. "There's something I wanted to ask you. . . ." She paused.

"What is it?" Bennett urged.

She seemed to have difficulty finding the words. "Can you tell me what . . . what did it feel like? To be with Craig?"

"I'm not sure what you mean."

William Relling Jr.

"As I said, I can't begin to understand how you do what it is you do. I'm still not even sure that I believe it's possible." Yoshiko shook her head, frowning. "Maybe I'm asking this completely the wrong way, but I'd like to know what was it like when . . . ?"

Another pause. Bennett allowed the words to hang in the air for a time, then said, "When I tuned in to Craig?"

She nodded gratefully.

Bennett frowned uncertainly. "It might be better if I didn't talk about this."

Her eyes flashed with displeasure. "Why not?"

"Because it's not something that's easy to explain. Even if I wanted to try."

"Why wouldn't you want to try?"

He regarded her seriously. "Because I don't want to cause you any more pain than you've already had."

Yoshiko looked at him with a strange expression. To Bennett it was as if she were seeing him in a way that she had never seen him before. There was an enigmatic, provocative light in her eyes. The realization caused something that he'd believed dormant for months to stir inside him. The sensation surprised him. *What's going on?* he wondered uncomfortably.

Before either of them could say anything more, their waiter reappeared. Both Bennett and Yoshiko had to fumble open their menus and peruse hurriedly before they could place their dinner orders. The waiter refilled their wineglasses, then moved off again.

Bennett was studying Yoshiko, watching her watching him. He'd clenched both hands into fists. His fingertips were cold. "There's something you don't know about me," he said. "Five months ago I got married

256

for the first time. It all happened very fast—we'd only met each other last fall, not even a year ago. Then last April—this past April—my wife was killed in an accident. We hadn't been husband and wife for two months." He paused. "I loved her very much."

"What was her name?" Yoshiko asked.

It surprised Bennett that, for a moment, he seemed to forget. Then: "Christina."

Yoshiko waited.

"Part of why I'm here in San Patricio," he continued, "why I'm helping the police, is because of her. To try to get my mind off her and onto something else."

This time Yoshiko reached across the table to take his hand. She wrapped her fingers around his and smiled at him.

Her smile caused his heart to ache. "Your fingers are cold," she said.

She squeezed his hand, then eased the pressure slightly but did not let go. She glanced at their entwined fingers resting atop the table, then tilted her head to gaze into his eyes.

Bennett could feel his heart pounding. "Please," she said. Her voice was hushed. "Please tell me about Craig. I promise, you don't have to worry about hurting me."

It was as though he could hear her voice in his mind, whispering to him, assuring him: *You could never hurt me. I'm certain of that.* The touch of her hand became magnetic, and he could not let go of her. He took a deep breath, then nodded.

"All right," he said.

CHAPTER TEN

At nine o'clock they came out of the restaurant hand in hand, walking to where the Volvo was parked. Standing beside her as she unlocked the driver's-side door, he put his hands on her shoulders and turned her around to face him. As he leaned down to kiss her, her lips parted and she closed her eyes. The kiss was long and deep.

They drove back to Wil Krieger's house. She parked the Volvo in the driveway. They got out of the car and crossed to the porch together. He unlocked the front door and held it open for her. He followed her inside, closing the door behind them and locking it. As he was reaching for the switch on the wall of the foyer, she put her hand over his. "No," she commanded. "I'd like us to stay in the dark."

He led her to the guest bedroom, allowing her to precede him into the room. He pushed the bedroom door closed, then turned around to see her standing in front of the room's only window. She became a silhouette outlined by the light of the moon and stars shining in from outside. Already she had begun to undress.

Bennett moved to the bed, pulling down the spread

and blanket and top sheet. When he turned to her once more, he could hear the whisper of her underclothing falling to the floor.

She came to him. She began to unbutton his shirt, and when she had exposed his bare chest, she laid her cheek against his flesh. He could feel the warm exhalation of her breath on his skin. He reached up to caress her face. He tilted her chin and kissed her again.

By the time he'd undressed, she lay on the bed waiting for him. He settled himself beside her and pulled her close, feeling her smoothness, pressing his firmness into her. He was aware of the chilliness of the air surrounding them and also the scalding warmth within; holding closely, the contours of their bodies melding together, filling the hollow spaces. He could feel his loneliness exploding; the chest-aching, happy-making burst of rapture; the giving and taking; the shuddering and release. Bennett listened to her groans of agony-ecstasy as she clung to him with desperation.

Afterward they lay beside one another in the darkness. She held herself tight against him, her lips searching for his. Then she drew back for a moment, and he heard her whisper, "It's been a long time since I've made love with anyone."

He pulled her to him again.

She stayed until midnight. He lay in bed, watching her as she dressed in the dark. Then he got up and put on a bathrobe so that he could walk her to the front door. She refused his offer to accompany her to her car, pressing a finger to his lips to quiet his protestations. Then she kissed him good-bye, but not before promising that nothing could prevent her from seeing him again. Nothing in the world.

CHAPTER ELEVEN

Yoshiko was saying to Bennett, "I think I'd like for the two of us to go away for a while."

It was late afternoon, Saturday, July thirtieth. They lay in each other's arms, in bed, in the motel cottage where, for the past two and a half weeks, they had been meeting whenever both of them could spare a few free hours. The motel was on the beach overlooking the San Patricio harbor, east of downtown. Bennett had taken a month's lease on the cottage on Monday the eleventh, five days after the first evening he and Yoshiko had made love. They had yet to spend an entire night together. All of their meetings had been like this one today, on afternoons when she was not teaching or attending to other obligations, or was not expected to be someplace with her husband. For Bennett the arrangement was simpler. He still spent his nights at Wil Krieger's house, but during the day, except for the hours he worked with Rachel Siegel, his time was his own.

Lately the amount of time he spent with Rachel had been decreasing. Over the past three weeks he had visited all of the sites where the Pied Piper's victims had been discovered, several times each. He'd devoted countless hours to examining pieces of physical evidence, studying autopsy reports, interviewing distraught family members—all to no avail. The last time he'd been with Rachel—on Thursday the twenty-eighth, two days before—he could sense that her impatience with him was nearing a breaking point.

The negative feeling was palpable, but it wasn't unexpected. Bennett was aware of the pressure that the mayor was putting on the Sheriff's Department and the CBI, and he knew that Rachel was doing her best not to transfer the pressure to him. Still, although she assured him that she understood that his power wasn't something he could simply turn on and off at will, it was obvious she was near the limits of her forbearance. And Bennett was as frustrated as she was about his inability to come up with anything.

All of this was running through his mind as he lay in bed, holding Yoshiko. Lost in thought, at first he didn't hear her speaking to him. She pulled herself up to study his face. His eyes were open and focused someplace far away. His expression was a dreamy frown.

"What's the matter?" she asked, concern edging her voice.

He turned to her. "I was just thinking about something."

"What?"

He shook his head. "It's not important."

"Did you hear what I said to you just now?"

"No, I didn't. I'm sorry."

"I said, I'd like the two of us to go away for a while."

He smiled. "Go away where?"

"Anywhere. Away from here. From San Patricio."

"How come?"

She touched his cheek with her fingertips. "Because I'd like to know how it feels to wake up beside you in the morning. I'd like to not have to worry about how many minutes I've got before I have to leave you because somebody might get suspicious about where I've been."

He laid his hand atop hers, pressing it lightly to his face. "You're serious, aren't you?" he said.

She nodded.

"When would you like to go?"

"As soon as we can."

"For how long?"

She shrugged. "I don't know. A while."

He showed her a wistful, acquiescent smile. "Are you sure?"

She nodded again. "I'm sure."

CHAPTER TWELVE

Shortly after five-thirty P.M. she dropped him off at Krieger's. The green SAAB was parked in the driveway. Before she kissed Bennett good-bye, Yoshiko promised to call him later that evening, to let him know how soon they would be leaving San Patricio and for how long.

Bennett stood on the porch, watching as she drove away. Turning to go into the house, he took scant notice of the white Jeep Cherokee parked at the curb two doors down, in front of the house of one of Krieger's neighbors. Nor did Bennett take much notice of the figure behind the wheel.

He was pushing open the front door and stepping into the foyer as the Jeep made a U-turn and rolled away in the direction Yoshiko's Volvo had gone. Krieger was in the living room, watching the news on television. He turned toward the doorway at the sound of Bennett's entrance and gave a wave of hello.

Bennett nodded, acknowledging the greeting. Then he went upstairs to the bedroom that Krieger's lover used for an office. In the room was a phone extension. Bennett picked up the receiver and punched Rachel Siegel's number.

After two rings Aaron Rodgers answered. "Can I speak to your mother, please?" Bennett asked. "It's Mr. Bennett."

He could hear the boy set down the phone, then Aaron's voice, faintly: "Mom! It's Mr. Bennett!"

Seconds later Rachel came on the line. "Ken?"

"Hi. Listen, something's come up, and I'm going out of town for a couple of days. I know we talked about getting together again on Monday, but since it wasn't anything definite, and we've been kind of butting our heads against the wall anyway lately, I thought it would be all right. I just wanted to let you know."

"How long will you be gone?" she asked.

"No more than a week, I imagine."

"Is it something I should know about?"

"Not really," Bennett said. "It's personal."

There was a brief silence from the other end of the line. Then: "Whatever you say," she told him. "We have been butting our heads, I suppose. Maybe a week away from each other would do us both some good."

"You're making it sound like I'm abandoning you."

"Don't be silly," Rachel said too quickly. "Our arrangement was on a strictly voluntary basis from the beginning. You're not abandoning me. What the hell, the investigation's no worse off than it was a month ago, is it? It's no better, but it isn't any worse."

"You're sure it's all right with you? That I go?"

"I'm sure. Just call me when you get back."

"I will."

Bennett hung up. He frowned, aware of a vague, sour feeling of dissatisfaction. He was startled by the sound of Krieger's voice from behind him. "You're leaving?"

Bennett turned. Krieger was standing in the doorway of the office, wearing an expression of reproach. "I apologize for eavesdropping," he continued. "But did I just hear you say you were going out of town?"

"For just a few days," answered Bennett.

"With Yoshiko?"

"That's right." Bennett had informed Krieger about the affair a week ago, after Yoshiko's almost-daily telephone calls and her frequent afternoon visits to pick up Bennett and take him who-knew-where had made it obvious to Krieger that something was going on.

Krieger looked away for a moment, pressing his lips together. When he turned back to Bennett he spoke with conviction. "It may not be my place to bring this up, but I think it's something that needs to be said. Do you two have any idea what you're doing? You and Yoshiko, I mean?"

Bennett was puzzled. "What we're doing?"

Krieger gestured absently. "This . . . relationship." He scowled. "You know I like you both very much, and I can certainly understand the attraction you've got for one another. You're two lonely people who happened to find each other under rather difficult circumstances. I couldn't care less that she's married to somebody else, especially since Ed is such a bastard anyway. You're adults; you can do whatever you please. If the situation were different I'd think it was great. It's just that . . ."

Krieger paused, scowling again. "It's just that what?" urged Bennett.

Krieger said, "I don't think it's Yoshiko that you're really seeing. And I don't think it's you she's really seeing."

"You're not making sense, Wil."

Krieger said, "It's just . . . I'm trying to say this in a way that won't make you angry."

"I don't get angry with my friends," Bennett replied. "Regardless of what I might hear from them."

"Except you don't know what I'm trying to say," Krieger countered.

Bennett could feel his jaw tightening. "I think it'd be best if you just came right out and said it."

Krieger took a deep breath. "I don't think you're interested in Yoshiko because she's Yoshiko. I think it's for another reason."

"What reason is that?"

"I think it's because she reminds you of your wife."

Before Bennett could respond, Krieger was saying, "You're not the only one who's doing it. I also don't think it's you—Ken Bennett—that Yoshiko's really interested in, either. It's that you remind her of Craig. I think she believes that you have some sort of psychic connection to her son, or whatever you want to call it. She wants to be with you because it makes her feel like she's with him."

Bennett's face had clouded over. "You're coming dangerously close to saying something very ugly about someone I'm starting to care a great deal about."

"For God's sake, don't you think I know that? I've been going crazy running this back and forth through my mind ever since that day you told me you two were involved. But I can't help how I feel about this, Ken. Frankly, I'm worried about both of you. You're using each other, and in a way that I just don't believe is very healthy—"

Krieger was interrupted by the phone's ringing. Bennett looked at the phone, then looked a question to Krieger. "Be my guest," Krieger said. "You're closer."

Bennett lifted the receiver to his ear. "Hello?"

Yoshiko's voice came to him with breathless urgency. "Ken, Edward . . . he's on his way over there right now—"

"Yoshiko, slow down—"

"He's on his way there *now*," she repeated. "Don't you understand? He knows."

"Yoshiko—"

"He followed us. He came home right after I did, and he confronted me. He forced me to tell him—"

Krieger's front doorbell rang.

Bennett felt electric fingers playing along his spine. He stared at Krieger, who, he could tell, was able to read the expression of apprehension on his face. Krieger was looking at him with bewilderment and concern.

The bell rang again, followed immediately by the sound of a heavy fist pounding on the front door. Krieger turned away hurriedly to answer the summons.

Over the patter of Krieger's footsteps descending the stairs, Bennett could hear Yoshiko calling his name faintly. His hand holding the phone receiver had dropped to his side. He lifted the receiver to his ear. "Edward's here," he uttered.

Yoshiko whispered, "Oh, my God."

Bennett could hear angry, quarreling voices from the floor below. The voices were shouting, but he could not discern their words. "Are you all right?" he asked Yoshiko. "Did he do anything to you?"

"I'm fine," she said. "I'm just worried about what he might do to you."

The shouting downstairs had become louder. "I have to go," Bennett said, controlling a tremor in his voice. "I'll call you later."

"Ken, don't," she implored. "Just put him on and let me talk to him—"

Bennett replaced the receiver in its cradle. He hesitated for a moment, listening to the voices downstairs. Then he strode from the room.

Bennett descended the stairs slowly. When he reached the landing between the first and second floors, he could hear the voices clearly, could finally distinguish between Krieger's and McWilliams's.

Krieger was yelling, "I told you, I'm not letting you in unless you calm down!"

McWilliams snarled. "And I told *you* to get the fuck out of my way!"

Bennett had reached the first floor. He turned into the foyer. The front door was open. Krieger stood in the doorway, arms spread, his back to Bennett, blocking McWilliams, who was outside on the porch. McWilliams was craning his head to peer around Krieger into the house. His face was flushed, the veins in his neck and forehead bulging. Beyond McWilliams, Bennett glimpsed the white Jeep parked behind the SAAB in the driveway.

McWilliams saw Bennett standing at the end of the foyer and took a menacing step forward. Krieger stiffened, and McWilliams had to restrain himself from taking another step. He showed Krieger a terse nod in Bennett's direction.

Krieger turned around, looking over his shoulder at Bennett. "It's okay, Wil," Bennett said. "Let him in."

Krieger hesitated, turning from Bennett back to McWilliams. Then he stepped aside reluctantly, leaning against the wall of the foyer, leaving the two men to face each other.

As soon as Krieger had moved out of the way, Bennett could see McWilliams clearly. Bennett thought he detected a brief flicker of uncertainty in the other man's eyes. Almost immediately, however, McWilliams's rage rekindled itself, and he was stalking past Krieger. He came toward Bennett, who stood, almost relaxed, at the other end of the foyer, arms folded across his chest.

When McWilliams was just a few paces from him, Bennett let his arms drop to his sides. He said calmly, "I don't know what you thought you'd accomplish by coming over here like this, but—"

Before Bennett could finish speaking, McWilliams's right fist was a blur arcing toward his face. Reflexively, Bennett tried to bob away, but the fist caught him high on the left cheekbone.

Fireworks exploded inside Bennett's skull. His legs wobbled, then refused to support him. He slumped to the floor, swallowing blood and choking on fragments of broken teeth. He could feel the side of his face beginning to swell, as if it were filling with air. There was a high-pitched roaring in his ears, like the whine of a jet engine. Above the keening whine swirled other sounds, disjointed words:

"... teach him to stay the fuck away ..."
"... Jesus *Christ*, Ed ..."
"... from my wife ..."
"... are you some kind of fucking Neanderthal ..."
"... keep an eye on your faggot friends ..."
"... get out before I call the police ..."
"... my *wife*, dammit ..."
"... just get out ..."

William Relling Jr.

Then the words were dissolving in a sweet, soothing blackness that wrapped itself around Bennett like a lover's embrace. He was thinking, *This is a totally new experience for me. I have just been punched in the face by a jealous husband. Isn't that the damnedest thing?* And smiling stupidly to himself. And then passing out.

CHAPTER THIRTEEN

In the ambulance, Bennett was awakened by the sound of voices speaking in hushed tones. One of the voices was familiar. He tried to say, "Wil," but the effort sent a bolt of agony coruscating across the left side of his face. He groaned, closing his eyes.

He heard Krieger speaking his name softly, opened his eyes again, and saw his friend's face floating above him. "It's all right, Ken," Krieger said gently. "Don't try to talk. Just relax. We'll be at the hospital in a few minutes."

Bennett nodded gratefully. The motion of his head caused the explosive pain to return. He closed his eyes, and within moments he'd passed out again.

CHAPTER FOURTEEN

The oral surgeon on call at Community Hospital found Wil Krieger in the waiting area of the emergency room at ten-thirty P.M. Krieger was sitting with a San Patricio deputy sheriff named Doyle, recounting the story of Edward McWilliams's assault upon Ken Bennett, when the surgeon came out to inform him that Bennett would be released presently, as soon as his prescription for liquid codeine had been filled. The doctor then told Krieger that Bennett had suffered a fracture of his left maxilla. His jaw had been wired. He'd also lost three teeth and bitten through a tiny piece of his tongue. The injuries were not severe enough to keep him hospitalized. But, according to the doctor, he was going to be in some pain for the next several days. Talking would be difficult for him, and he would be unable to eat solid food for a few weeks.

The doctor departed, and Bennett appeared. He was sitting glumly in a wheelchair transported by an orderly. Krieger introduced Bennett to the deputy. They helped Bennett out of the chair, walking him outside to where the deputy's patrol car waited. Still woozy from the pain medication he'd been given, Bennett had to be steadied by the two men as they guided him into the backseat of the cruiser. Krieger climbed into the passenger side of the front seat, and Deputy Doyle took his place behind the steering wheel.

As they rolled out of the hospital's parking lot, Krieger turned to Bennett. "Do you feel up to talking to Deputy Doyle when we get home?"

"About what?" Bennett responded. In order to speak he had to skin back his lips over clenched teeth.

"Edward."

"What's there to talk about?"

"Aren't you're going to press charges against him?" Puzzled, Bennett said, "Should I?"

Krieger shrugged. "It isn't up to me."

"But if it were?"

Krieger nodded. "If it were me, I'd do it."

Bennett frowned. "Have you spoken to Yoshiko?"

Krieger shook his head. Bennett said, "You didn't call her, or she didn't call you?"

"Neither one."

Bennett grimaced. "So as far as we know, he could've gone back home and beat her up, too, right?"

"We've got Mr. McWilliams in custody, Mr. Bennett," the deputy said over his shoulder.

Bennett looked to Krieger, who nodded, confirming. "After he hit you and you collapsed, all the anger seemed to deflate out of him. He just turned around and went home. After I called nine-one-one for an ambulance, I called the Sheriff's Department."

"We found him in his living room," Doyle said to

Bennett. "He was just sitting there. Like he was waiting for us."

"But you have to sign a complaint if you want him formally charged," Krieger said.

Bennett turned to look out the side window, thinking. Krieger directed the deputy off the freeway, then said to Bennett. "Ken?"

The blackness outside the car made the window glass like a mirror. Bennett was staring at his reflection, studying his swollen face. He grunted, acknowledging Krieger. "There's something else I need to tell you," said Krieger.

"What?"

"I talked to your sister."

Bennett's injured cheek began to throb.

"Why didn't you tell her you were back in California?" Krieger continued.

Bennett spoke to his own reflection. "Because I didn't want her to know."

"Why not?"

Bennett shrugged.

Krieger said, "If I'd known that, I wouldn't have called her. Actually, I called Tom Hanson first. He gave me Denise's number." Krieger paused briefly. "She sounded awfully upset when I talked to her. Not just about what happened with Edward, but because she didn't even know you were in San Patricio. I had to talk her out of driving down here. I told her to wait until you'd had a chance to talk to her yourself."

Krieger paused again, awaiting a response. There was none. Bennett continued to study his reflection.

"I'm sorry if I did something that's going to make trouble for you," Krieger said at last. "Calling your sister, I mean."

"It's all right," Bennett grunted.

"What about that complaint against McWilliams, Mr. Bennett?" asked the deputy. "Are you going to sign one, or what?"

Bennett sighed.

The deputy prompted: "Mr. Bennett . . . ?"

"I'll sign," Bennett uttered, grimacing.

CHAPTER FIFTEEN

"Denise?"

"Oh, my God, Kenny, are you all right?"

"I'm fine."

"You sound horrible."

"It's hard to talk, that's all."

"Your friend, the one you're staying with—"

"Wil. Wil Krieger."

"Wil. When he called me, I . . . I just . . ."

"I'm sorry I didn't let you know I was in San Patricio again. I didn't want you to get upset about it. Anyway, what's done is done. I've been here for a month. I apologize for not letting you know. Can we please just leave it at that?"

Silence.

"Denise?"

"How long do you plan on staying there?"

"I don't know."

"Do you want me to come down?"

"No. Not right away, anyway. Maybe later."

Silence.

"Denise?"

"Are you sure you're all right?"

"My face hurts."

"But otherwise you're all right?"

"I'm fine," he lied.

"Will you call me tomorrow? Just to let me know how you're doing?"

"Sure. I have to go now. I'll call you tomorrow. All right?"

"All right."

"I'm sorry, Denise. Really."

"I said it's all right."

A pause. "Good night, Denise."

"Night, Kenny."

CHAPTER SIXTEEN

Though the codeine dulled the pain in Bennett's cheek and jaw, it was not enough of a soporific to help him sleep. He tossed fitfully, unable to stop thinking about Denise, about Yoshiko, about Rachel Siegel, about Christina.

He finally dozed off at dawn.

The nightmare of the monstrous black shape and the silver angel awakened him a short time later. When he awoke he could hear the screams of children resounding in his mind. Wearily he climbed out of bed. Dressing himself in bathrobe and slippers, he went into the guest bathroom, urinated, then went to the sink beside which he'd left the bottle holding his prescription. After washing his hands, he reached for the bottle. He unscrewed the cap, raised the bottle to his lips, and sucked the bitter liquid through his teeth.

He went downstairs to make tea. He tried to ignore the rumbling in his stomach, having had nothing to eat since lunch the day before. But the thought of preparing something that he could ingest only through a drinking straw did not appeal to him. *Later*, he told himself. *After Wil gets up. I'll eat something then.*

At eight-thirty A.M. he went to the phone in the living room and pressed Yoshiko's number. He let the number ring a dozen times, then depressed the hook. Lifting his finger, he pressed Rachel Siegel's number. Her husband answered, "Hello?"

"Roy? It's Ken Bennett."

"Ken? You sound funny."

"I know. It's a long story. Is Rachel there?"

When Roy didn't answer immediately, Bennett said, "Is something the matter?"

"Rachel got an emergency call about an hour ago," Roy said. "She's downtown."

"What's the emergency?"

Roy hesitated once more. "They found some more bodies last night."

"Bodies?"

"Two of them," Roy said grimly. "Two more kids."

CHAPTER SEVENTEEN

Rachel had been awakened at seven-fifteen A.M. by her son Aaron. He shook her gently, then spoke in a whisper when she opened her eyes. "Mom? There's somebody on the phone for you."

She blinked sleepily. "Who?"

"Somebody named Seelig."

Rachel was bewildered for a moment until she remembered who Seelig was. She got out of bed carefully so as not to disturb Roy, who was sleeping soundly beside her. "Did he say what he wanted to talk to me about?" she whispered to her son.

Aaron shook his head. "Huh-uh."

Rachel padded out of the bedroom and went downstairs, passing through the family room. The TV was on, the sound turned low, a SpongeBob SquarePants cartoon flickering on the screen. Aaron followed her into the kitchen. She lifted the receiver from the counter where he'd set it down. "Seelig?"

"That you, Rachel?" Seelig said. "Killoran wanted me to call and tell you to haul ass downtown."

"What for?"

"We just got two more dead kids."

"*Two?*"

"Yeah. Frank wants the whole team to assemble at the office ASAP. He's convening a press conference at nine-thirty. We made an arrest, and he wants to be sure everybody's been fully briefed before we confront the media."

Rachel blinked, utterly confused. "There's been an arrest?"

"That's what I said," answered Seelig.

"I'm on my way," she told him.

CHAPTER EIGHTEEN

At three A.M. that morning, a security officer named Fletcher Deboe had been patrolling the UC San Patricio campus on foot. As he strolled along the footpath that wound through the quiet, tree-lined campus, he'd felt an irresistible urge to relieve his bladder. Deciding that he was too far from any building to make it in time to a rest room, and since it was the middle of the night anyway and nary a soul—except for himself—seemed to be about, he stepped from the path and headed into the woods. Shining his flashlight ahead of him, he made his way toward a grove of redwood trees. He never got there.

Halfway to the trees Deboe tripped over something bulky that had been buried under a pile of leaves. He stumbled to the ground, losing his grip on the flashlight. It fell from his hand and rolled several yards away from him, its light spreading a cone of brightness on the forest floor. As he lifted himself to his hands and knees and began to crawl after the flashlight, Deboe's fingers closed on something that felt damp and rubbery. Whatever it was had fingers of its own. It took a moment for Deboe to realize that he was clutching the hand of a dead human child. At which point his bladder let go, and he wet his pants.

A trio of deputy sheriffs arrived at the scene twenty minutes after receiving a call at three-thirty A.M. from Deboe's supervisor. Det. Bobby Ornelas, who was working the graveyard shift, arrived at four-fifteen, the same time as the coroner. By then the bodies—a boy and a girl—had been uncovered. They appeared to be close to the same age, and they bore a resemblance to each other. Both of them were fully dressed, and neither seemed to have been sexually molested. They had both been strangled to death.

By six A.M. the bodies were identified as Dean and Laura Larson, eleven-year-old twins who'd disappeared Friday afternoon from a church picnic. Because it had been announced publicly a month before that the forty-eight hour waiting period before missing persons could be reported no longer applied to children aged fourteen or younger, the dead children were identified quickly. On Saturday morning Dean and Laura's father, a Presbyterian minister from the church in Half Moon Bay that had sponsored the picnic, had notified both the San Mateo and San Patricio County Sheriff's Departments of his children's disappearance.

Rachel was apprised of all this by CBI agents Seelig, Santos, and McEvilly when she arrived at headquarters shortly after eight A.M. Seated at her desk in the Pied Piper task force's suite, with Moe, Larry, and Curly surrounding her, she was just about to inquire as to the details of the arrest that Seelig had mentioned to her on the phone. At that moment Frank Killoran strode in, grinning triumphantly. *He looks like a shit-eating baboon,* Rachel thought.

Killoran greeted her sarcastically. "Nice to see you, Detective Siegel. Glad you could make it."

She indicated the other CBI agents. "They were just about to tell me that you arrested somebody . . . ?"

Still grinning, Killoran looked to his underlings. "Should we tell her, guys, or just let her wait till the rest of the world finds out?"

The three agents chuckled. *Spare me*, Rachel thought.

"I guess we can't very well keep it a secret from you," Killoran continued to Rachel. "At seven-thirty this morning we booked Davis Grimes on suspicion of murder."

Rachel's jaw dropped. "Davis *Grimes*?"

Killoran spread open his hands, a gesture of *What can I say? Am I brilliant, or am I brilliant?* Rachel uttered incredulously, "You've got to be shitting me."

Killoran's grin faded. "Why do you say that?"

"Because he's a fucking city councilman, that's why! He's been a major political figure in this city for years!"

"He's also got a police record," McEvilly cut in.

"Jesus Christ," Rachel snapped. "Everybody knows that. He got busted for pot twenty years ago. It was some stupid misdemeanor possession charge—"

"What about his divorce?" Killoran cut in.

Rachel frowned. "What divorce?"

Killoran eyed her disdainfully. He pointed his chin toward Seelig. "Tell her."

Seelig said to Rachel, "While we were checking Grimes out, we came across a copy of his divorce proceedings. From Florida, in 1990. His wife was granted the divorce on grounds of physical and mental cruelty. He was also denied the right to visit their

284

three kids because he liked to smack them around, too—"

Rachel held up a hand to quiet Seelig. "Wait a minute. There are two things I'd like to ask. First off, what the hell were you doing checking out Grimes in the first place? And second, how come I didn't know you were doing it?"

"I'll be happy to answer that, Rachel," Killoran said smugly. "Grimes happens to be a suspect. One of several, in fact. If you'd been spending more time around here doing the work you should be doing and behaving like a real member of this team, instead of farting around with some mind reader, you'd be a lot more up on who's being investigated and who isn't."

"That doesn't answer my question," said Rachel. "Why is Davis Grimes a suspect at all? And whose idea was it to investigate him?"

"What difference does it make?" said Killoran. "He's a suspect. He's got a history of child abuse. He's got no alibi for his whereabouts last Friday, when those last two kids disappeared. Besides, for now he's only booked on suspicion. All we want to do is ask him some questions. . . ."

He paused. Rachel had pushed herself from the desk abruptly, come to her feet, and started for the door. "Where do you think you're going?" Killoran called to her. "We've got a press conference in forty-five minutes."

Rachel spun around. "I assume you've got Grimes in the holdover?"

"So?"

"Then that's where I'm going."

Rachel stalked toward the door. Killoran cried out her name, but she ignored him. As she was pulling open the door, Killoran bellowed, "Dammit, Detective, you *stop right there*, or I swear to Christ, I'm going to fall on you like a fucking wall!"

She halted. Taking a deep breath, she turned around. Killoran was glaring at her, red-faced, his jaw clenched. He was quivering with rage. She fixed him with a firm stare, but said nothing.

Gradually his rage seemed to subside, though he did not take his eyes off Rachel as he spoke. "My dear Detective Siegel, like it or not, as long as I'm in charge of this investigation you are under my command. That means you'll do whatever I tell you to do. I am now giving you a direct order. Disobey it, and your ass is grass. Do you understand me?"

Killoran waited for a response, received none, then continued. "I don't want you speaking to Davis Grimes—or anybody in the media—without my permission." He turned to Moe, Larry, and Curly. "That goes for you guys, too."

Rachel challenged, "Why not?"

Killoran turned back to her. "Excuse me?"

"I said, 'Why not?' Why can't any of us talk to Grimes or the media unless you say it's all right?"

Killoran regarded her stonily. "Because I said so, that's why not."

Rachel fought an urge to shout back at the man facing her down. She blinked, then locked her eyes onto Killoran's. "And that's it? Those are your orders?"

Killoran nodded. "That's it."

Rachel was thinking, *You rotten, arrogant, ratfucking bastard.*

"Whatever you say, Frank," she told him.

CHAPTER NINETEEN

The press conference was held in the headquarters' media room and was conducted by Special Agent Killoran and Sheriff Joyce, in tandem. Joyce read from a prepared statement that recounted the grim discovery of the twelfth and thirteenth victims of the Pied Piper. After that Frank Killoran stepped forward and read a second statement describing Councilman Davis Grimes's "detention for questioning" in connection with the case.

The bombshell burst almost instantaneously. The room was filled with a cacophony of shouting voices, each trying to raise itself above the next. All the while Rachel stood in the back of the room, behind a line of video camera operators and other technicians. She was leaning against the rear wall, arms folded across her chest, regarding the tableau before her. *I don't think I can take much more of this fucking dog-and-pony show*, she thought, ill-concealing her disgust.

Rachel was seriously questioning whether she should go to Earl Novak and ask to be let off the case entirely. She'd been tracking the Pied Piper for seven months, the last two of which had been under the supervision of a man whom she despised. She believed as fiercely as ever in the necessity of capturing the Pied Piper. But she was also coming to realize that as long as Frank Killoran was in charge of the investigation, whatever satisfaction she might derive from the killer's eventual arrest would be undercut by her having to endure Killoran's reveling in self-glory. She felt beaten-down, drained, exhausted.

Rachel was debating with herself whether to attempt a surreptitious escape, when the door to the media room opened and a uniformed deputy entered. The deputy was a young woman named Julie Johnson, whom Rachel knew well. Johnson had been on the department for a year. Last September, not long after Johnson had become a deputy, she'd invited Rachel out for lunch. There she pumped Rachel for information as to what exactly a woman had to do to become a detective, how much harder she had to work than her male counterparts, how much shit she would have to endure from paternalistic—and, generally, sexist—colleagues and superiors. Their lunch date that day became the first of several. Rachel liked the young woman quite a bit, recognizing in Johnson much of the same drive and ambition she had possessed herself, long ago.

She saw Johnson motioning for her to come to the door. Rachel pointed to herself and mouthed, *Me?* Johnson nodded.

As Rachel eased her way toward the door, Johnson stepped out of the media room. Closing the door behind her, Rachel followed the deputy into the corridor. The circus of voices from behind the door was still audible.

Rachel smiled gratefully at the deputy. "You have

no idea how happy I am that you got me out of there."

Johnson replied in a conspiratorial tone, "That man's here to see you. The one who's been working with you on your case. Mr. Bennett."

Rachel frowned, puzzled. "Bennett?"

Johnson nodded. "He's out at the front desk. I didn't think it would be wise to bring him back here, so I told him I'd just go and find you."

Rachel's frown deepened. She recalled her phone conversation with Bennett the day before, that he'd told her he was going out of town for a few days. A part of her had been relieved, since Bennett had come up with absolutely bupkis on the Pied Piper, and she could feel her patience wearing thin. But another part of her was annoyed with him because it seemed as if he were running out on her. It was irrational to feel that way, she knew, but there it was. *If he's supposed to've left town*, she thought, *what's he doing here now?*

Deputy Johnson was saying, "Rachel?"

Johnson's voice brought Rachel out of her brief reverie. "I'm sorry, Julie. What were you just saying?"

"What I did was all right, wasn't it? Leaving him out there at the desk, instead of bringing him back here?"

Rachel nodded. "That was the right thing to do. I guess I ought to go find out what he wants."

CHAPTER TWENTY

Rachel found Bennett sitting on a wooden bench near the headquarters' front doors. She started when she emerged from the corridor and saw him. His face looked nearly as bad as it had the day she'd met him in the hospital, two months before. The left side was puffy and discolored, the flesh blue and brown. The skin over his swollen cheek was tight and shiny. He rose from the bench as she approached, shifting the top coat he was carrying from his right forearm to the left so he could shake her hand.

"What happened to you?" she asked, keeping any hint of alarm out of her voice.

He shook his head stubbornly, dismissing the inquiry. "I'll tell you later," he said through clenched teeth. "I took a cab straight here after I got off the phone with Roy. He said two more kids were found last night."

Rachel motioned tersely in the direction of the corridor from which she'd come. "They're alerting the media even as we speak."

Bennett looked away for a moment. Conflicting emotions played across his face: anger, frustration, pain, helplessness. Finally he turned back to Rachel. "Where'd they find them?"

"Out in the woods, on the UC campus."

Rachel gave Bennett an encapsulated version of what had happened in the past six hours. She concluded by informing him of Davis Grimes's arrest. At her mention of Grimes, a spark glowed in Bennett's eyes. "I have to see him," he said resolutely.

"I really don't think that's a good idea," said Rachel.

Bennett was adamant. "If I can talk to him, there's a chance I can tell you if he's the one we've been after."

Rachel regarded him skeptically. He looked back at her with stubborn determination. She pressed her lips together in a stern line. *If this doesn't work*, she told herself dourly, *there's going to be hell to pay.*

Then: "Okay," she said. "Let's go see if we can't find out where Mr. Grimes is being stashed."

CHAPTER TWENTY-ONE

The interrogation room was a dingy, ten-by-ten windowless cubicle. The room smelled of stale cigarette smoke and body odor, tinged by the vague aroma of a cheap, pine-scented cleaning solution. To Rachel, the room's unique redolence had always struck her as the smell of fear.

Davis Grimes, however, seem not the least bit afraid of anything. He sat at the scarred, Formica-topped table in the center of the room, opposite Rachel and Bennett, and spoke with haughty contempt. "You know why I'm in here, don't you? It's that power-hungry bitch of a mayor and that racist motherfucker of a sheriff. This is their doing, make no mistake about it. They're trying to get rid of me. I'm too much of a political threat."

Rachel said, "You'll pardon me if I say that doesn't make a lick of sense, Mr. Grimes. I'm afraid I don't buy it."

Grimes sneered. "No? Shit, all they have to do is

hold me for forty-eight hours. They don't have to say anything to anybody. The word goes out I'm being investigated. Not charged, not accused, nothing like that. But what's the first thing the public thinks of when they hear somebody's in jail? 'Maybe you aren't guilty of whatever it is they're investigating you for this time, but you sure as hell must be guilty of something, or else they wouldn't have brought you in.' Politically I'm finished. There goes my reputation, and there goes my career."

Rachel shook her head. "I can't believe they'd run the risk of your suing them for false arrest, and in the process make a martyr out of you."

"It's no false arrest," Grimes said. "I'm only being held on suspicion. I know how the law works. They're allowed to keep me here a couple of days, and they don't have to prove a damn thing. Then they let me go with an apology. 'We're sorry we inconvenienced you, Mr. Grimes. But you understand how important this Pied Piper thing is. We have to check out everybody.' And soon as I walk through that front door, the reporters will be waiting for me. 'How come they had you under arrest, Mr. Grimes?' And I say, 'Ask the sheriff.' So they'll ask him, and he'll say, 'No comment.' I can defend myself till I'm blue in the face. I'm not guilty of anything, but he never said that I was. I was only being held on suspicion."

Rachel was shaking her head again in disbelief. Grimes smiled at her condescendingly. "You're a nice lady," he said. "Too nice to be a cop. That's why you don't recognize it when somebody's playing hardball."

She fixed him with a hard stare. "You swear you

didn't have anything to do with the death of these kids last night? Or any of the other ones?"

Grimes's eyes became flat and cold. "I'm not even going to dignify that question with an answer."

CHAPTER
TWENTY-TWO

After returning Grimes to his cell, Rachel took Bennett to a second-floor lunchroom. Except for the two of them, the lunchroom was deserted. While he waited at a table, she retrieved two Styrofoam cups of black coffee from a coin-operated dispenser. As she was setting Bennett's coffee on the table in front of him, he said, "Could somebody actually be that stupid and vindictive?"

"Who are we talking about?" Rachel asked, sitting opposite him.

"The mayor and the sheriff?"

Rachel asked cynically, "They're politicians, aren't they?" She took a sip of her coffee. "Still, regardless of what Grimes says is the reason he was arrested, it's possible he's a legitimate suspect."

Bennett blew steam from his coffee, sipped it, made a face. "Ugh."

"I know," she said. "Tastes like lighter fluid."

"Worse."

Rachel smiled. "So tell me, Ken. What's your impression of him?"

"You mean Grimes?"

"Wasn't that who we've been talking about?"

Bennett lowered his eyes, looking down at the Styrofoam cup in his hands. Rachel thought, *Why do I have the feeling he's trying to hide something?* She wondered why she found the notion unsettling.

Bennett brought his eyes up slowly, looking away from her. His expression was dreamy, as if in his mind he were someplace far from there.

Then he winced. He set the cup on the table and reached up to touch his injured cheek. He pressed the bruised flesh gingerly and winced again. He looked to Rachel, the corners of his mouth turning up into a forced smile. "I haven't been in an actual fistfight since grade school," he said, running his fingertips along his cheek.

Rachel watched him, not speaking. She lifted her cup and swallowed the last of her coffee.

Bennett went on. "I didn't tell you that I'd gotten romantically involved with someone. Someone who's married. Yesterday her husband found out about it." Bennett touched his cheek again.

Rachel had placed her empty cup on the table in front of her and was turning it around in her hands. She looked down at the cup, then brought her eyes back to Bennett's face. She thought, *How come you're stalling me?* She could feel a cold fire building inside her. "Ken," she said at last, restraining the emotion in her voice. "What about Grimes?"

Bennett nodded absently. "Grimes," he acknowledged. "I don't think he's the one."

"You don't 'think' he's the one?"

Bennett took a deep breath. "I don't know. He might be. But I doubt it."

Rachel said, "You *doubt* it—"

The sound of the lunchroom door opening cut her off. They turned, and Rachel saw CBI agent Seelig poke his head around the edge of the door. He peered at her and smiled an evil smile. "I've been looking all over for you, Rachel. You're wanted in the sheriff's office right away."

The cold fire inside her flared briefly. Rachel looked from Seelig to Bennett. "I'll wait here for you," Bennett said to her. "If you like."

She nodded, then got up from her chair, crumpled the empty cup in her hand, and walked to the door that Seelig held open for her. Just inside the door was a trash receptacle on which she noticed a sign: *Good Guys Don't Wait for Others to Clean up Their Mess. No shit*, Rachel thought. She tossed the cup into the trash, and moved past Seelig, who closed the door behind her.

CHAPTER
TWENTY-THREE

Sheriff Peter Joyce:

"Detective Siegel, can you tell me what in the name of heaven was going through your mind when you decided to take it upon yourself to question Davis Grimes? And to do it without even suggesting to him that he could have his lawyer with him while you talked? You're not that stupid—at least Earl Novak says you're not. In any case, you've been a law-enforcement officer way too many years not to know there's no such thing as an 'informal' interrogation of a suspect. Grimes's lawyer is at the county courthouse this very moment screaming blue murder about how his client's constitutional rights to counsel have been blatantly violated. By noon he'll be back here pounding on our doors with a writ of habeas corpus, if not a whole fucking lawsuit, and there won't be a damn thing we can do except turn that son of a bitch loose.

"But now we come to the real issue. What the hell am I supposed to think when Frank Killoran comes to me and says, 'Sheriff, when she went down to talk to Grimes, Detective Siegel flagrantly disobeyed a direct command I gave her not one hour before. I've got three witnesses who heard me order her not to see him. It's a clear case of insubordination, and I'd like to know what you propose to do about it?'

"Well, I'll tell you what I propose to do. Detective Siegel, you are hereby suspended from duty for fourteen days, without pay, pending an official investigation into Agent Killoran's charges. You are to turn over your badge and your gun to Chief Novak. And I think it would behoove you to get in touch with legal services, 'cause you're going to need them. It appears to me that there is a very good chance of your being dismissed from this department."

CHAPTER TWENTY-FOUR

For the entire drive back to Wil Krieger's house, Rachel and Bennett rode in an oppressive silence. When she pulled the Sienna into Krieger's driveway, coming to a stop behind the green SAAB, she shifted into park, but left the motor running. Resting her hands on the steering wheel, she looked straight ahead through the windshield. *Don't say a word*, she willed Bennett. *Just go inside, and don't say a word.*

He reached for the handle of the passenger-side door, then paused. "Rachel?"

She spoke without looking at him. "Please don't tell me you're sorry. I really don't need to hear that right now."

Bennett sucked a breath of air between his teeth. "That wasn't what I was going to say."

She swung her head around and regarded him coldly. "What, then?"

"Turn off the car, will you?"

She reached for the ignition key. The minivan's engine stopped. She looked to Bennett. Waiting.

He spoke with great effort, as if measuring the words. "There's something you should know about people who have the power that I have, who do what I do. There's a . . . personality trait, I guess you'd call it. Something we all seem to have in common. Kind of a compulsion just to use the power. To help people whenever we can. I've known psychics who get so wrapped up in it, they drive themselves nuts. They burn themselves out, and then they're totally useless. Some have even committed suicide when that happens. But in spite of the risks, they can't not do it."

He paused. "Do you understand what I'm saying? It's like we have to use this gift. We've got to help whenever we can, regardless of what it might cost us."

"Didn't we have this conversation a month ago?" Rachel asked wearily.

"This is different," said Bennett. "I'm trying to tell you something that's very difficult for me to say. When I talk about being compelled to use the gift I've got, I'm just like everybody else who's like me. I'm compelled to help. I *have* to help."

"You just said that, didn't you?"

He whistled another breath between his teeth. "I know you know about the accident I had when I was a kid, the one that changed me. It was a head injury. That's what triggered whatever power I got in the first place." He shook his head. "What's happened to me . . . what I *think* happened, last May, when I had that other accident, right before you and I met, when I cracked my head and got knocked unconscious . . ."

He turned away from her briefly. When he turned back, his eyes were damp with tears. "It's gone," he said.

"What's gone?"

301

Bennett tapped his forehead with a fingertip. "My power. My gift. It's been gone from the moment I woke up in the hospital. That flash I had when I was driving, where I saw Craig McWilliams, right before I wrecked the car, that was the last time. Ever since then, all these times you and I were out together, I've been faking it."

She stared at him with wide eyes. "*Faking* it?"

He said shamefully, "Remember what you told me the first day we went out together? 'Don't try to play detective, Ken.' That's exactly what I've been doing. I've been racking my brain, trying to figure out who this killer is, and pretending that I was tuning in to him psychically. But that's all I've been doing, just pretending. . . ."

Rachel had turned away and was looking through the windshield again. "This morning," she said to the glass, "when you told me you might be able to get a read on Grimes if I could get you in to see him. You were lying to me?"

"I didn't mean to. I was hoping . . . I thought it might be possible that I'd feel something. A vibe . . . something."

Rachel's head sagged. She closed her eyes, feeling as if she were being crushed by a tremendous weight.

"Please go away," she uttered, barely loud enough for him to hear.

"Rachel, I—"

"Please," she repeated emphatically. "Just go away."

After a moment, her eyes still closed, Rachel heard Bennett opening the door. She felt the weight of the Sienna shifting as he climbed out. He shut the door. She could hear his footsteps on the concrete drive.

She could hear him opening and closing Krieger's front door.

When she finally lifted her head and opened her eyes, she was alone.

She had to command herself to reach for the ignition key and start the Sienna. She sat there for a time, listening to the running engine, her face a stoic mask that disguised her awareness of the heavy shroud of despair and defeat enveloping her. Then she shifted the minivan into gear, backed out of the driveway, and started for home.

AUGUST

CHAPTER ONE

Ken Bennett was standing at the window of the guest bedroom in his sister's house, sipping a cup of tea. It was four in the afternoon on Wednesday, the third of August. Outside, the sky was overcast and gray, the air chilly. The weather in San Francisco had not changed since Monday, and Bennett was asking himself, *How's that saying go? "The coldest winter I ever spent was a summer in San Francisco"?*

He was alone in the house. Denise had left an hour ago to meet with the woman who was publishing the book of photographs she'd taken on her trip down the California coast with her brother last May. Clem was at the pet groomer's; Denise would pick up the dog on her way home. The only sound in the house came from the stereo downstairs. Bennett had found a cache of classical music compact discs in the living room. Up here, in the guest room, the Scarlatti concerto he'd put on sounded distant and faint.

Bennett took a sip of tea, and he felt a twinge of pain beneath his left eye. He reached up to touch the side of his face. The swelling had gone down over the last couple of days and his color was better. But sometimes the slightest involuntary twitch could cause him to feel as if someone were jabbing a hot needle into his cheek.

Turning, he glanced in the direction of his bed. Atop the bedspread lay a copy of the San Jose *Press-Telegram*, its sections separated and strewn about. Bennett had bought the paper that morning from a newsstand on Union Street, while taking a solitary walk after breakfast. He'd kept the newspaper hidden from Denise, waiting until she left for her meeting before opening it.

Bennett found the story he was looking for on page three of the front-page section. The headline read, *San Patricio City Councilman Released from Jail.*

AUG 2: San Patricio city council member Davis Grimes was released early Tuesday afternoon from San Patricio county jail, after being held for forty-eight hours on suspicion of involvement in the so-called Pied Piper serial murders that have been plaguing the area for the last several months.

Grimes, 50, a member of the San Patricio city council for the past two and a half years, was arrested Sunday morning at his home by Sheriff's Department deputies.

According to a Sheriff's Department spokesperson, Lt. Daniel Sloane, while Grimes was in fact detained, "He was never formally charged with any crime. As far as the Sheriff's Department is aware, Mr. Grimes is not guilty of any criminal wrongdoing."

Grimes's arrest and subsequent release are the latest in a series of events connected to what has become known locally as the Pied Piper murders that began last January, with the discovery of the body of eight-year-old Emma Lyons.

Since then the bodies of twelve more children have been discovered in and around the San Patricio area, all of them apparently murdered by the same elusive individual. The two most recent victims were discovered last Saturday night in the woods on the campus of the University of California San Patricio.

Lieutenant Sloane also announced that, as of Thursday, August 4, agents from the Federal Bureau of Investigation field office in San Francisco would be officially taking over the Pied Piper investigation. Sloane stated that the FBI would be working in conjunction with the current investigation team, which includes members from the San Patricio Sheriff's Department and the California Bureau of Investigation.

In the op-ed section of the paper Bennett found a long editorial regarding the release of Davis Grimes. The editorial took San Patricio's municipal powers-that-be to task for two things: that Grimes's arrest had been obviously motivated by political opportunism, and that it had taken so long for the FBI to be brought in on the case. Two names, besides Grimes's, were prominent in the scathing piece: Barbara Underwood and Peter Joyce. The mayor and the sheriff were all but accused of complicity, the editorial suggesting that their self-serving incompetence was the reason why no one had been able to prevent the most recent Pied Piper murders.

As Bennett stared out the window now, he was wondering just how awful things really were in San Patricio right now. He'd participated in other investigations where politicians and police officers had become territorial and self-centered, especially when substantial prestige and publicity were at stake, but in San Patricio it had been worse than he'd ever seen.

That was why a part of him was relieved to be away from there. He'd left on Sunday evening, having phoned his sister a few minutes after watching Rachel Siegel pull away from Wil Krieger's house. Denise arrived at Krieger's later that same afternoon. They returned to San Francisco in her Alfa Romeo, making it back to the city just after nightfall.

From the moment Denise greeted him, Bennett sensed that she was walking on eggshells. She'd made only small talk for the past three days, never once asking him directly why he'd gone back to San Patricio without telling her, nor prodding into what had happened to him while he was there. He had no doubt that her careful behavior was partly a consequence of her concern over the physical and emotional trauma he'd suffered. Still, Bennett told himself, she must be burning with curiosity. But it was as if a wall had been erected between them. He knew that he'd delivered a blow to their relationship, and that she'd been hurt badly. Not telling her that he was back in California was a breach of the trust and affection they held for each other. So far Denise had managed to disguise the hurt almost as well as she'd buried her inquisitiveness.

She doesn't know I've lost my power, Bennett thought. *She doesn't know about that, and she also doesn't know about Yoshiko.*

Yoshiko.

Bennett had tried calling Yoshiko's number several times on Sunday afternoon, but no one answered the phone. He supposed that she was somewhere downtown, posting her husband's bond, perhaps awaiting his release. Bennett tried calling her one final time, at five o'clock. At last there was an answer. But as soon as Edward McWilliams grunted a cheerless hello at his end, Bennett hung up. Minutes later the phone rang in Krieger's house. Krieger answered, then handed the phone to Bennett.

That was you who just called, wasn't it, Ken? I thought it might've been. I'm sorry I haven't tried to reach you, but I haven't been home very much. I talked to someone at the hospital this morning, and they told me you were all right. Of course, I don't blame you for signing a complaint against Edward. I probably would have done the same thing. You understand that I had to bail him out of jail, don't you? That's all I'm doing for him, though. I've made up my mind to leave him. You know that I care for you very much, but I think it'll be better if I don't tell you where I'm going. We probably shouldn't see each other again. I really do think that's for the best.

Bennett could still hear her voice echoing in his mind. *I really do think that's for the best.*

Not that what she said had been unexpected. But since the moment he'd put down the phone after speaking with her, he'd felt empty and cold. Their conversation had been three days ago, and the feelings of emptiness and coldness had not ebbed.

311

You've really made a mess of things this time, Ken, he chastised himself. *It's probably a good thing for everyone concerned that you won't be around here much longer.* Yesterday he'd bought a ticket to fly back to St. Louis. He would be leaving in four days, on Sunday. This time, he told himself, there would be no return trip to California. Not for a long, long while.

Bennett swallowed the last of the tea in his cup, then walked out of the bedroom and made his way downstairs. In the kitchen he prepared another cup of tea. He carried it with him as he wandered aimlessly through the house. There was nothing that he wanted to do, no place he wanted to be. He was simply killing time.

He moved through the kitchen and into the living room, pausing for a time to listen to the music before going back upstairs. He paused in the second floor hallway and looked into his bedroom. *I was just in there*, he thought, not wanting to return.

He looked toward Denise's bedroom, then to the open door of her workroom. Denise had partitioned the room into two sections. The smaller section was a homemade darkroom, a cubicle in the far corner made of plasterboard walls with a separate door of its own. The rest of the space was a studio cluttered with furniture and photographic equipment: a steel-case desk, two chairs, several file cabinets, boxes of film, light tables, umbrella reflectors, cameras, flash rigs. Bennett smiled ruefully to himself. There was something ironic about this being the only room in the house that wasn't fastidiously tidy.

He entered the workroom. Absently he moved to Denise's desk. On top of it, scattered among other detritus, lay a stack of proof copies of black-and-white prints she'd made that morning. Though Bennett hadn't seen the photographs before, he knew what they were: samples to show Denise's publisher. She'd taken a portfolio stuffed with pictures along with her to her meeting.

Bennett set down his cup on the desk and lifted the pile of photographs. He thumbed through the sheaf of pictures. Turning over the top one, he saw that she'd scribbled the date and location where and when the shot was taken.

As he worked his way through the stack, he noted that many of the pictures were variations of the same image, each altered somewhat in terms of the contrast between light and shadow. Darkroom experiments, Bennett decided. Denise had been playing with the developing and printing of each photograph, attempting to achieve precisely the effect that she wanted. *These must be the rejects*, he thought, riffling through the stack. To his eye they were still quite striking. He recognized several of the places and structures from their trip: a cabin in Big Sur, the outdoor swimming pool at San Simeon, a waterfront seafood restaurant in Malibu, and . . .

Holy Mother of God . . .

. . . the photograph he'd brought to the top of the stack.

This is it. Bennett thought, *It can't be . . . this is my nightmare*

But it was.

This shape like a big black hill, I can hear it, the clacking and rattling and the screaming, the children screaming. . . .

Bennett's fingers trembled as he turned the photograph over. On the back Denise had written in pencil,

313

William Relling Jr.

San Patricio Boardwalk. Roller coaster. Thursday, May 26.

Bennett thought, *But I've seen this. Rachel drove me past the boardwalk at least a dozen times.* He turned the picture over again to study the image, and immediately a fireball of pure white light seemed to explode in his brain. A frisson ran along his spine. He could feel the hairs rising on the back of his neck.

Because it didn't look like this.

In broad daylight, live and in color, the shape was nothing that had caught his attention. Nothing more than an ordinary amusement park ride. But in Denise's photograph, the structure lay in stark relief against a gray sky. Lines and shadows, and shadows within shadows. And the silver figures dwarfed by the behemoth, milling about at its base. Waiting to ride. Waiting to die.

Rattling and clacking and screaming . . .

The silver angel. The angel of death.

Bennett stood beside the desk, recalling his nightmare with clarity, culling the image from his memory. Looking down at the photograph in his hands, he thought once more: *This is it.*

He wondered, for a moment, how he could be so sure. It wasn't that his power had suddenly returned; of that he was certain. The power was gone. No, this was something else, an indubitable knowledge. He simply *knew*.

This is it.

Bennett separated the photograph from the others and carried it with him downstairs. He hurried into the kitchen and laid the photo on the countertop next to the sink while he went to the cupboard where Denise kept her telephone directories. He pulled out the

Yellow Pages and carried the book back to the counter, laying it down beside the picture. Opening the directory, he leafed through the pages until he came to the one he was looking for. He ran his finger down the page, stopping at the number he wanted. He crossed to the telephone that rested on the end of the counter, beneath a row of cabinets. He lifted the receiver and dialed the number he'd found.

CHAPTER TWO

In the note he left for Denise, Bennett told her that he was going out to an afternoon movie and that afterward he would eat dinner someplace alone. He apologized for wanting to be by himself tonight. He then telephoned for a taxi that took him to the Transbay bus terminal downtown. The Greyhound bus to San Patricio departed at six-forty-five P.M.

The ride was interminable, the bus making stops in Scotts Valley and San Jose and Santa Cruz before pulling into the San Patricio depot at five minutes after nine. Bennett climbed off the bus and hurried into the depot. He went up to the ticket counter, rudely elbowing his way in front of another customer to face a service representative. "What's the fastest way to get to the boardwalk from here?" he demanded.

"On foot," the representative, a black man, answered irritably. He pointed south, in the direction of the beach. "Eight blocks, that way."

Bennett emerged from the depot into cool evening air, the sun having set over an hour before. He turned in the direction the ticket agent had indicated, walked quickly for a block, then began to run. Presently, ahead of him lay the boardwalk. He forced himself to slow down and catch his breath.

Pausing, he studied the scene before him. Directly across the street was an ugly, garishly lit, block-long, two-story casino. The center of the structure was a semicircular dome flanked by twin obelisks. At either end of the casino were hipped-roof pavilions housing pinball and video-game arcades.

Bennett crossed the street, weaving his way between slow-moving cars that were searching, mostly in vain, for parking spaces. He joined a throng of people moving along the boardwalk. As he walked, he recalled several news stories he'd read over the last month about the drop in attendance at the various boardwalk attractions. *You sure couldn't tell by this crowd tonight*, he thought. There were hordes of happy revelers—most of them teenagers or tourists or young children and their parents. The scene was an assault on Bennett's senses: the flashing lights; the air filled with a cacophony of overlapping sounds, the piercing *boop-boop-boop* of merry-go-round calliope music, the thumping *boom-chuck* of a ghetto blaster, shouts and laughter; the seaweed- and fish-scented air of the nearby bay, undercut by the aroma of hot-dog grease, popcorn, and saltwater taffy.

Bennett continued east along the boardwalk, until he came to the rides beyond the end of the casino. He halted. There, less than a hundred yards ahead of him, was the roller coaster. He told himself once more, with absolute certainty, *This is it*.

The ride was a huge, old-fashioned structure, three stories high, made of wood. Its frame was intricately latticed, beam upon beam. Its name, Big Dipper, was spelled out in electric bulbs on the side of the structure. A queue was lined up, waiting excitedly for the current riders to finish their trip. To Bennett, the impatient riders-to-be seemed as if they were lined up before the maw of some great leviathan that had beached itself, its dead flesh rotted away.

He looked up and saw a line of roller-coaster cars poised at the final summit, just beginning its last downward swoop. The cars rattled and clacked, and the riders screamed in happy terror. Bennett turned away to walk to a ticket booth a short distance from the line of people waiting to get on the Big Dipper. He purchased a ticket and made his way to join the people climbing aboard the now-emptied cars.

As he reached the head of the line, Bennett was studying the roller coaster, not paying attention to the man who took his ticket. "Enjoy the ride," the man said to him cheerfully. Bennett turned, looking the man in the eye, for the first time really *seeing* him.

It's you.

The man was wearing dungarees, work boots, and a knit golf shirt. He was not quite as tall as Bennett, but he was broader in the chest and stomach and arms. He had thick, dark hair that was shot through with gray, heavy eyebrows, and a bushy beard. His complexion was ruddy. He had twinkling green eyes and a wide smile that showed small, sharp teeth. He looked like nothing so much as a friendly teddy bear.

Then the man read the accusation and awareness in Bennett's expression, and his smile metamorphosed into a look of shock. Then recognition. And then fear.

Several people who had lined up behind Bennett began pushing him forward, toward the cars. Bennett climbed into an empty seat and pulled the restraining bar down across his lap. He turned to look back at the man who had taken his ticket.

The last of the riders had gotten aboard, and the man had moved over to the shift lever-and-clutch mechanism that operated the roller coaster. He depressed the clutch and pushed the lever, all the while keeping his eyes locked onto Bennett's as the cars rolled away.

CHAPTER THREE

The ride lasted for only 120 seconds, though to Bennett it seemed nearly as long as his bus trip from San Francisco earlier that evening. When at last the cars braked to a stop, he threw open the bar and scrambled from his seat. Pushing his way past his fellow riders, he craned his neck, searching for the ride operator.

The man was gone.

Someone else was operating the ride now, a rail-thin young man with acne scars and a blond ponytail that hung to the middle of his back. The young man was taking tickets as Bennett came up to him and asked, "That other fellow? The one who was just here? Where did he go?"

"You mean Josh?" asked the young man.

Bennett nodded. "Josh. Do you know where he went?"

"He said he wasn't feelin' too good all of a sudden," the young man replied.

"Which way did he go? Did you see?"

The young man motioned toward the casino. Bennett nodded thanks, started off, then turned back. "You said his name's Josh . . . ?"

"Yeah. Short for Joshua. Joshua Wright. As in Orville and Wilbur."

Bennett nodded thanks again and trotted off.

A few minutes later he'd found a pay telephone in a bar across the street from the amusement park. The place was decorated in pseudo-Polynesian style— bamboo walls and palm fronds and tiki lamps. A Don Ho record was playing on the jukebox. Bennett stopped at the bar to order a glass of club soda from a waitress clad in a muumuu, then crossed to the phone, which was hung on the wall between the doors to the rest rooms.

Bennett easily remembered Rachel Siegel's home number. She answered the phone herself, after the second ring. "Hello?"

"Rachel, it's Ken Bennett."

Silence.

"Rachel?"

"Where are you?"

"Back in San Patricio. At a bar down at the boardwalk. Across from the amusement park."

"You're back in town? What for?"

"I know who the Pied Piper is. I just found him."

Silence.

"Did you hear me?" Bennett asked. "I said I know who the Pied Piper is. His name's Joshua Wright. He works at the amusement park, next to the casino on the boardwalk. He runs the roller-coaster ride."

Bennett quickly explained all that he'd done over the last six hours: his discovery of Denise's photograph and his moment of satori, the bus trip from San Francisco, his brief encounter with Joshua Wright, and Wright's subsequent disappearance. "I went over to the park office," Bennett concluded. "They told me he all of a sudden went home sick, right after I saw him. Right after he and I looked each other in the eye. I found out he lives in Davenport Landing. Do you know where that is?"

"It's between here and Half Moon Bay, up the coast," Rachel said. "On the way to San Francisco."

"He's the killer,' Bennett insisted. "I *know* he's the one."

Rachel's voice took on a noticeable chill. "And so I'm just supposed to accept that on faith? Run out and arrest this guy because Ken Bennett is sure he's the Pied Piper?" She paused. "Assuming for a moment I even believe you, you're still forgetting something. I'm under suspension. As far as the Sheriff's Department is concerned, I have zero authority. If I go out and try to bring this guy in, or even just go over and question him, I'm liable to end up in jail myself. Do you understand that?"

It was Bennett's turn to be silent.

"Ken," Rachel said finally, "I don't want you to take this the wrong way, but I'd really appreciate it if you didn't call me again."

"Rachel—"

"Take care of yourself, all right? I mean that."

"Rachel—"

She hung up.

CHAPTER FOUR

Joshua Wright was sitting on the sofa in his living room. None of the lights in the house was on.

Sitting in the dark was something he did whenever he wanted to retreat deep inside himself. At those times he found the darkness comforting, like a blanket that he could pull close and wrap around him. Too many people were afraid of darkness and solitude, but they did not understand. Wright knew that it wasn't the darkness or the solitude that made people afraid. It was the *not understanding*.

Be not afraid, he told himself.

Because before, earlier tonight, he *had* been afraid—when he'd seen the man, looked into the man's face, read the dark knowledge in the man's eyes. *He knows*, thought Wright. *He knows about the children*.

Wright understood now why the man had frightened him, had caused him to panic, to hurry to his supervisor and feign illness and beg to be excused from work for the rest of the night. Wright made himself picture the man's face floating before him in the darkness, the man's eyes boring into him, piercing him to his soul.

323

He knows.

Wright wondered, *But how? How could he know? Unless . . .*

He is the Tempter.

"Get behind me, Satan," Wright whispered aloud. "You are a hindrance to me."

At that moment, in the darkness, his telephone rang.

Wright looked over from the sofa. The phone was on an end table, next to a floor lamp. Beside the phone was an electric clock. He switched on the lamp, and he had to blink his eyes to accustom them to the sudden brightness. He looked at the clock and saw that it was ten minutes past eleven. The phone continued to ring. At last he picked up the receiver and held it to his ear.

"Joshua Wright?"

He knew who was calling him, though he'd never heard the voice before. "Speaking."

"I know who you are," said the Tempter. "I know what you've done."

"I know who you are, too," Wright said.

The Tempter said, "I want you to meet me. So we can go to the police. Together."

"Meet you?"

"At the park. By the roller coaster."

"When?"

"They've just closed the rides and the casino, but they're still cleaning up and locking things down. You'd know better than I how long that might take, how long it'll be before everyone's gone home."

"Less than an hour," said Wright. "No one should be there past midnight."

"Are there any guards?" the Tempter asked. "Security?"

"No."

"I don't know how far away you live. Could you make it back here by twelve-thirty?"

"Yes."

"I'll be waiting for you. Don't try to run away. If you do, I'll go straight to the police and tell them who you are. Do you understand?"

"I'll be there."

Wright lowered the receiver from his ear and replaced it in the cradle. He stood for a moment, thinking. Then he reached under the table and opened the drawer there. He looked down. In the drawer, atop stacks of bills and other papers, lay a gun.

Daddy's gun, he thought. Jud Wright's Smith & Wesson K-22 Masterpiece, bought shortly after Jud and his son moved to Davenport.

This ain't no Promised Land, Joshua. It's just California. You know what they say about California, don't you? It's just like cereal. Take away the fruits and the nuts and all you got left is the flakes. We need just as much protection here as anyplace else.

Except now it was *Joshua's* gun, and he treated it lovingly, as Daddy had taught him a gun should always be treated. *You might never need it, Joshua. But it'll be a comfort to you, 'cause it's always better to have and not need than to need and not have.*

Wright lifted the gun from the drawer. He cradled it in his hand, running his fingers along the gun's gleaming, chrome-plated barrel. He was so startled by a knock at the front door that he nearly dropped the weapon. He spun around to gape at the door, feeling

William Relling Jr.

the same flush of panic he'd felt when he looked into the Tempter's eyes a short time before.

There came another knock.

Wright had to force himself to stay calm. *It can't be him*, Wright told himself. The Tempter had just phoned him from near the boardwalk. That was obvious from what the man had said. There was no reason to be afraid.

Replacing the gun, Wright closed the drawer. Crossing to the front door, he paused to switch on the porch light, then pulled open the door.

Standing on the porch was a woman whom Wright had never seen before. She was short, a few inches over five feet tall, and she had dark hair and dark eyes. She was pretty, in her way, but there was nonetheless something about her that Wright found unappealing. *Jewish*, he decided, judging by the shape of her nose. She was dressed casually, in jeans, a flannel shirt, a down vest, a shoulder bag, and boots. The expression on her face was stern but not suspicious.

"Mr. Wright?" she asked.

He nodded.

"I'm Det. Rachel Siegel," the woman said, "from the San Patricio Sheriff's Department. Is it okay if I come in?"

CHAPTER FIVE

Next door to the bar from which Ken Bennett had phoned Rachel Siegel and Joshua Wright was a motel. After he'd gotten off the phone with Wright, Bennett left the bar and walked over to the motel office. He asked the desk clerk there if he could have a few sheets of blank paper and an envelope. The clerk handed over a sheaf of stationery with the motel's logo and address, and an envelope imprinted in the upper left corner with the same information.

Bennett thanked the clerk and took the paper with him back to the bar. Resuming the booth seat he'd found before, he ordered another club soda from his waitress. When she returned with his drink, he asked her if she might have a pen that he could use for a while. She did.

By the time he finished writing, it was twenty minutes after twelve. He folded the sheets of paper and inserted them into the envelope. He sealed the envelope, wrote something on the outside, then slipped it into an inside pocket of his jacket. Taking out his wallet, he dropped a twenty-dollar bill on the table in front of him. He assumed that it was sufficient to pay for the three club sodas he'd nursed in the time he was there. He hoped the change would be a generous enough tip.

Bennett walked out of the bar. He paused out front for a moment to look across the way. The boardwalk was lit by a few street lamps, spaced at intervals. The street lamps threw down narrow circles of illumination. The casino and all of the park rides were dark and deserted. Beyond the casino and the rides lay the strand, and beyond that lay the black waters of the bay. The street was quiet enough so that Bennett could hear the waves lapping. A chilly breeze blew in from across the water. Shivering, Bennett pulled up the collar of his jacket.

Crossing the street, he walked to the ticket booth near the roller coaster. A metal-shaded lightbulb that hung from the eaves of the structure was burned out, leaving him cloaked in darkness.

Leaning against the wall of the booth, hugging himself to keep away the chill, Bennett waited. Studying the infrequent cars that rolled along the street in front of the boardwalk, he listened to the waves and the low whistle of the breeze blowing through the supports of the roller coaster.

At twenty-five minutes to one, a many-years-old Pontiac station wagon came into view. The station wagon moved slowly, as if its driver were searching for an address. The vehicle paused in the middle of the street for a moment, then pulled to the curb beside the boardwalk. The driver switched off the wagon's headlights and engine, then got out of the car. Bennett watched as the driver's burly shadow figure stepped around the front of the station wagon, walking toward the roller coaster. The figure approached apprehensively.

Bennett called out, "Over here."

He stepped away from the ticket booth, separating himself from the structure so that he could be seen. The shadow figure started at the sound of Bennett's voice. Turning, the figure hesitated.

"We're alone," Bennett assured him. "There's just you and me."

The figure started toward him.

CHAPTER SIX

A half hour earlier, at twelve-oh-five A.M., Rachel Siegel had been sitting in her minivan. The Sienna was parked under a tree two hundred yards from the end of the cul-de-sac where Joshua Wright's house was situated. The minivan faced away from the property. Rachel was asking herself unhappily, *What in God's name am I doing here?*

It had all started with Ken Bennett's phone call two hours before. Bennett was the last person in the world she'd expected to be on the other end of the line when she picked up the phone. Since Monday, when she had called Wil Krieger's house to apologize to Bennett for her treatment of him during their last encounter, and Krieger told her that he'd gone back to San Francisco with his sister, Rachel assumed that Bennett was out of her life for good.

She felt bad about that, because in the twenty-four hours between his "confession" and her call to him on Monday afternoon, her anger had dissipated. It wasn't his fault that she'd been suspended. It had been a deliberate choice on her part to flout Frank Killoran's orders. Bennett just happened to be a convenient excuse.

Not that she wasn't upset by the revelation that Bennett had been faking it all along, that his psychic ability no longer existed. Her residual ill feeling over that had flared during their conversation tonight. It was why she'd treated him so curtly on the phone.

I'd really appreciate it if you didn't call me again.

Rachel frowned, feeling guilty. It was an impulsive and rude thing to do, dismissing him that way. But what the hell did he expect? Calling her like that, out of the blue, telling her that he'd found the Pied Piper, wanting her to do something about it. What did he expect?

After she'd hung up on Bennett, she sat at the kitchen table for a time, stewing. She was so lost in thought that she didn't hear Roy's footsteps approaching from the family room. She was unaware of his presence until she heard his voice. "Honey?"

She looked up. Roy was leaning in the doorway, arms folded, looking at her with concern. "Who was on the phone just now?" he asked.

"Ken Bennett."

Roy's eyebrows went up. "Oh?"

Rachel nodded.

"What did he want?" Roy asked.

She frowned again. Then she told him what Bennett's call had been about. When she finished, Roy took a moment to digest the information. Then he asked, "Do you believe him?"

Rachel shook her head. "I don't know."

"What about maybe checking out this guy Wright? How much effort would that take? That seems to me the least you could do."

Rachel regarded her husband strangely, and her

look seemed to unsettle him. "What?" he asked. "What's the matter?"

"What you just said," she replied. "About how even if I don't believe what Ken told me, checking it out is the least I can do."

"So?"

"It's the same thing he said to me the night I met him. When he was in the hospital. When he told me where I could find the McWilliams boy."

Roy smiled thinly. "I guess Ken Bennett isn't the only one around these parts who's psychic."

"There's only one problem," said Rachel. "I'm still persona non grata at headquarters, remember? I can't just waltz down there and run a record check on this guy."

"You still have connections, don't you? Maybe you could get somebody else to do it for you."

It wasn't Roy's suggestion so much that surprised her, but her own instantaneous realization: *I could do that.* And the concurrent awareness: *I have to do that.*

Without replying to Roy, Rachel got up from the table and went to the phone. Glancing at the list of numbers taped to the wall, she lifted the receiver and punched a number. A gruff, familiar voice greeted her with, "Siefert residence."

She said, "Harold, it's Rachel. I know it's late, and I apologize, but I need a big favor."

After bitching about having to drive to headquarters in the middle of the night when he was off duty, Harold Siefert acceded to Rachel's request. He called her back from headquarters thirty-five minutes later. "Joshua David Wright," he announced. "White male, just turned fifty-three. Six-one, two hundred fifteen pounds. That's just the data from his driver's license. You want his address?"

"Shoot," said Rachel.

She scribbled the information Siefert gave her on a notepad. "He owns an old Pontiac station wagon," concluded Siefert; then he read off Wright's license-plate number.

"Does he have a record?" Rachel asked.

Siefert snorted. "He doesn't have so much as a speeding ticket. It looks like he's never even been fingerprinted. He's so clean he squeaks."

"Are you sure?"

"I'll run him through the national crime computer, if you insist, but I honestly don't think I'm gonna find anything. The guy's a citizen, Rachel. Why the hell are you so interested in him, anyway?"

Playing a hunch, she asked Siefert to go ahead and run a full check on Joshua Wright. She apologized once more for putting him out. He promised to call her as soon as the full report came through.

Before she could hang up, Siefert was adding, "Guess what? Your pal Killoran? Him and his prick underlings? Scuttlebutt has it the mayor's running their asses out of town as soon as the FBI shows up to take over the Pied Piper case. Apparently he's taking the heat for the Davis Grimes fiasco. How 'bout that, kiddo? I also heard that once your fourteen days are up, you're going to be fully reinstated with just a reprimand. Score one for the good guys, eh?"

Rachel was feeling a warm glow of vindication as she got off the phone with Siefert. *Score one for the good guys indeed*, she thought as she looked over at the kitchen clock. It was ten minutes to eleven.

Roy had gone back into the family room to watch

TV. She went in to tell him that she was going out for a while and that he shouldn't wait up. If Harold Siefert called, she said, Roy should forward him to Rachel's cell phone. After Roy kissed her farewell, he said, "I don't have to warn you to be careful, do I?"

She gave him a kiss in return. "No. You don't."

Before getting into her minivan, Rachel opened the rear hatch and lifted the sheet of fiberboard covering the Sienna's spare tire. She opened a metal box bolted next to the tire and pulled out the short-barreled .38 Special she kept as an extra weapon. Having turned in to Earl Novak the nine-millimeter Browning automatic she usually carried, along with her badge and ID, she felt comforted knowing that the .38 was still in her possession. Closing the box and replacing the fiberboard, she slipped the .38 into her shoulder bag.

She got in the van and headed for Davenport. When she arrived at Joshua Wright's house at eleven-fifteen, she realized that the reason she had gotten there so quickly was that she'd driven much more rapidly than she thought she'd been. She debated with herself a few moments whether she should go in before deciding, *What the hell?*

Not quite an hour later, Rachel was back in her van, trying to sort through her impressions of the man with whom she'd just spoken. That Wright was an oddball, hard-core Christian was obvious. He must have quoted the "Good Book" to her a dozen times, if he did it once. She knew she had to be circumspect in her judgment, though, telling herself, *Just because you don't have much use for flaky, fundamentalist types, that doesn't make the guy a serial murderer, does it?* Or that he seemed so pathologically fixated on the memory of his late father? Or that he seemed to possess a creepy sort of sympathy for the Pied Piper, because of something he'd mentioned when she asked him if he knew anything about the killings? *Only what I heard on the news*, Wright had said. *But at least we can be sure the little ones are up in heaven now, can't we? At least that much good has come out of these terrible crimes, hasn't it?*

Or that he'd seemed awfully anxious for Rachel to leave?

The vague suspicion was still nagging at her when she heard a faint noise in the distance: the closing of a car door. She looked up at her rearview mirror. She was parked near enough to see the front of Wright's house. In the mirror she watched him cross his lawn and disappear around the corner of his house.

A moment later he was in his station wagon, backing out of the driveway. As the Pontiac rolled past her, Rachel ducked out of sight. She waited until the sound of Wright's engine had diminished, then sat up and started her vehicle. *Where do you suppose he's going?* she asked herself as she wheeled away from the side of the road, following him.

She stayed behind him, turning, as he did, onto U.S. 1 and heading south, in the direction of San Patricio. There was little traffic. Rachel allowed Wright to get a ways ahead of her before she increased her speed to pace him. He did better than sixty-five miles per hour until he reached the San Patricio city limits, slowing only when he exited the freeway.

Gradually Rachel closed the gap between their vehicles. When he turned right, heading for the San Patricio boardwalk, she was certain she knew his destination. She wondered why he might be going there, hoping none of the reasons that occurred to her was correct.

She followed the Pontiac till the street dead-ended and Wright made a left turn. Below them, at the bottom of the hill down which the wagon was descending, lay the boardwalk. The casino and amusement park were on the bay side of the street. Rachel watched Wright's station wagon brake as it neared the casino and then pull to the curb beside the boardwalk. Wright was getting out of his car as the Sienna rolled past him.

Rachel drove to the end of the block, another dead end. She swung the minivan into a U-turn and turned back, heading in the opposite direction from which she'd come. She pulled to a stop at the curb across the street from Wright's station wagon and switched off her headlights. She hesitated a moment before shutting off the Sienna. In the silence she thought that she could hear her heart pounding.

She thought, *Now what do I do?*

CHAPTER SEVEN

Wright was saying to Ken Bennett, "What is it you want from me?"

Bennett studied the other man. "You think I'm trying to blackmail you or something? Is that what you think this is about?"

"What do you *want* from me?" Wright repeated stubbornly.

"I want you to give yourself up," said Bennett. "I want you to come with me and turn yourself in to the authorities."

Wright shook his head. "That isn't what you want."

Bennett had begun to say, "Yes, it is—"

The last word caught in his throat. Wright had lifted up his shirt to reach into the waistband of his trousers. Before Bennett could react, a gun was in Wright's hand, pointed at Bennett.

"No, it isn't," Wright asserted. "Don't keep saying it is. That isn't what you want at all."

CHAPTER EIGHT

Rachel was holding her long-barreled Maglite in her left hand, and the .38 Special in her right. She carried the flashlight high, close to her shoulder, gripping the upper part of the casing just below the lens fitting. The light was off, her thumb resting on the switch.

As she crept up to the two figures by the ticket booth, Wright's back was to her. He was standing several feet in front of Bennett. Wright's right arm was raised slightly, as though he were holding something in his hand. Rachel drew near enough to them to recognize Bennett's voice. She thought grimly, *I was afraid of this.*

She snapped on the flashlight, leveled the gun at the center of Wright's back, and called out to him, "Sheriff's Department, Mr. Wright. Raise your hands where I can see them and turn around. Slowly."

Wright spoke over his shoulder. "I have a gun." He spoke calmly, without inflection. He nodded toward Bennett. "It's pointed at his heart."

"Drop it," Rachel commanded.

Wright shook his head. "You drop yours. Or else I'll shoot him."

Wright's body was still blocking her view of his hand. Rachel thought desperately, *Is he really armed, or isn't he?* She raised the flashlight, bringing it up to shine on Bennett's face.

"He's not lying, Rachel," said Bennett. "He really does have a gun."

"Shit," she hissed under her breath. Then: "Put it down, Mr. Wright!" she ordered. "Now!"

Wright shook his head.

A thought flashed through Rachel's mind: *Just shoot him.*

Then a second thought: *Damn it, I can't risk it. He might shoot Ken.*

She lowered her hand, letting the gun slip from her fingers. The .38 clattered to the ground. Bennett blurted, "Rachel, no!"

Wright turned around. At last she could see the .22 Smith & Wesson in his hand. He gestured with the gun for her to come forward.

Taking a deep breath, Rachel moved past Wright to stand beside Bennett. "Raise your hands," Wright said as soon as they were facing him. "Both of you." They did as they were told. "Your flashlight," he continued to Rachel. "Bend down and roll it over to me."

Rachel crouched, taking care not to move suddenly. She laid the Maglite on the ground and pushed it toward him. Wright stopped the flashlight with his foot, then bent down to pick it up with his left hand. All the while he kept his gun trained upon Rachel and Bennett. He straightened, shining the light on his prisoners.

"I don't know what you intend to do with us," Rachel said to Wright, "but you should realize that I'd never try to arrest you all by myself. I called for backup before I got out of my van. They'll be here any minute."

Wright said, "I don't believe you." He gestured to her shoulder bag. "What else do you have in there?"

"Nothing."

"Then you don't need to keep holding on to it, do you? Put it down."

Rachel eased the bag from her shoulder and rested it on the ground at her feet. Wright motioned with the .22 once more, directing them toward the roller coaster. "Come this way."

Bennett and Rachel preceded Wright. He shone the flashlight ahead to guide them. None of them spoke until they reached the platform from which riders loaded and unloaded themselves from the roller-coaster cars. Then Wright called out, "Stop there."

Rachel glanced down at the empty cars in front of her. A heavy length of chain snaked through their restraining bars. The chain was secured by a large padlock. The light in Wright's hand swept past her and Bennett, beyond the cars, shining up the tracks toward the roller coaster's initial incline. The tracks rose steeply to an apex sixty feet above the ground.

"Go on," said Wright. "Start climbing."

Rachel's jaw dropped. "Up *there*?"

"You heard me," snapped Wright.

Bennett whispered to Rachel, "Do it."

They moved toward the tracks. "It's not as hard to do as you think," Wright was saying as he trailed them. "Whoever operates the ride on the early shift has to come out here every day, before we open for business, and walk the tracks, beginning to end. Just to make sure they're okay and nobody's fooled around with them. Sometimes people like to play jokes, tie a hobo or a dog to the tracks. That's why they have to get checked out every day. After a while you get used to it. Pretty soon you find out it's no harder than walking down the street."

He stayed behind them, stepping as nimbly as a cat. A quarter of the way up the incline Rachel's foot slipped and she pitched forward, losing her balance. She fell to her knees, one hand clutching the outside rail, the other a wooden tie.

Bennett dropped beside her instantly, reaching to hold on to her shoulders and support her. "You okay?" he whispered.

She nodded. Coming to her feet, she slipped and fell again, barking a shin. "God*dammit*," she spat.

"Don't say that," Wright ordered her coldly. "You're blaspheming."

Rachel was about to rebuke him when she felt Bennett's hand squeezing her shoulder. "Don't," Bennett said. "Don't make him mad."

Dampening her temper, Rachel drew a deep breath and started to her feet again. When she slipped once more, she whirled around and said to Wright, "I can't do this."

Wright's figure was a silhouette behind the harsh glare of the flashlight. He was silent, as if thinking hard about something. At last he said, "Maybe you should just crawl up on your hands and knees. That's probably better. You'll be able to keep your balance."

"I think that's a good idea," said Bennett. He turned to Rachel. "Okay?"

She grumbled, "Fine."

Bennett released her. He looked at her for a moment, his expression unreadable. "You go ahead of me," he said. "That way I can catch you if you slip again."

She nodded, and they started up the tracks once more.

As they climbed, Rachel had to will herself not to look anywhere other than straight ahead. She had no particular fear of heights, but out here in the open, clinging to the roller-coaster tracks, there were few people who would not be courting acrophobia. She ascended single-mindedly, focused on the task of reaching the top of the incline. She could hear Bennett behind her, his breaths coming short and fast. By the time she reached the apex she was out of breath herself.

She heard Wright say, "Both of you turn around."

Rachel moved slowly, feeling her way, clutching for hand- and toeholds. She managed to bring herself to a sitting position, hands clinging to the tie she was perched upon. Bennett had brought himself to a like position a few feet below her. The two of them were now facing Wright, who was standing straight up, straddling the rails. He held the flashlight in one hand, the gun in his other.

What had been a chilly breeze on the ground was up here a stiff wind that cut through Rachel like slivers of frozen glass. The stinging wind brought tears to her eyes. She had to lower her head, trying to blink the tears away.

"Look!" shouted Wright, his voice cutting above the keening whine of the wind in her ears. "Look around you!"

Rachel brought her head up. Below them, encircling the black water that lay to their right, was a horseshoe of lights that sparkled like flaming gems—

white and green and red and yellow. The city of San Patricio was spread out before them spectacularly. Around the bend of the horseshoe, stretching to a point more than thirty miles to the south and west, the lights glimmered all the way to Monterey.

Wright opened his arms munificently. "Then the Tempter took him to the holy city," he shouted into the wind, "and set him on the pinnacle of a high place! And he showed him all the kingdoms of the world and the glory of them! And the Tempter said to him, 'All these I will give you if you fall down and worship me!' " He glared madly at Bennett. "*This* is what you wanted! To tempt me!"

Bennett cried, "No!"

Wright pointed the gun at Bennett's face. "Yes! You are the Tempter! But I am . . ." He paused, turning his head slightly as if listening to the voice of the wind. "I am Azrael," he whispered. "The angel of death . . ."

He regarded Bennett again, and Rachel could see Wright's finger tightening on the trigger just as she heard, in the distance, the wail of approaching sirens.

She brought her eyes around toward the sound. A rapidly moving ribbon of whirling red and blue lights was approaching from mere blocks away. The sirens' wail grew steadily louder.

Rachel turned back to Wright. He was watching the oncoming patrol cars, the gun lowered to his side. "You should have believed me, Mr. Wright!" she cried, raising her voice above the wind. "You should have believed me!"

He glared at her. Then, in a single, swift motion, he was bringing up the gun, pointing it at her. His face was a mask of maniacal rage. Before Rachel could react, however, Bennett was leaping at Wright. Immediately the two men were grappling with each other, teetering atop the tracks, each trying to keep his balance while pushing the other away.

Rachel barely heard the gunshot above the sound of the wind and the wailing sirens of the gaggle of patrol cars that had spun onto the street below. Then both the gun and her flashlight were dropping away, rattling off the roller coaster's wooden supports. For a moment, in the sudden darkness, it seemed to Rachel that Bennett and Wright were locked in a kind of macabre embrace. *They look like they're dancing*, she thought crazily. Then their precarious balance shifted, and Joshua Wright toppled over the edge.

As if by reflex, Bennett lunged after him. Rachel shrieked, "Ken!"

The top of the incline was suddenly floodlit with spotlights from the patrol cars below. Wright dangled in the center of a cone of dazzling brightness. Bennett was lying across the tracks, clutching Wright's arms.

The stockier man's weight was pulling Bennett to the edge, until Rachel shot forward to wrap her arms around Bennett's legs, pinning him. "Ken, I got you!" she shouted.

"I can't . . . hold him." Bennett grunted. "Can't hold . . . too slippery . . ."

He let go.

The abrupt shift in weight caused Rachel to jerk backward. For a moment she felt as if she and Bennett were going to tumble over the other side of the tracks, before they settled. She heard an awful sound: something thick and heavy and wet landing very hard on the ground, five stories below.

Then she heard Bennett's voice, saying: "It's okay, Rachel . . . everything's okay. . . ."

Something about the tone of his voice frightened her. She reached for his hands, but she couldn't get a grip because the blood that was smeared on his palms and fingers made them too slick. She pulled him close, turning him to her. Finally she could see the dark stain spreading out from the center of his chest. Lit by the floodlights, the blood had turned his shirt and jacket bright red.

Rachel leaned across him to shout down at the band of deputies scurrying at the base of the roller coaster, "Dammit, get us out of here! Somebody get us down from here *now!*"

"Everything's okay, Rachel . . ." Bennett repeated weakly. "Everything's okay . . ."

She was cradling his head in her lap. He showed her a feeble smile that forced up the corners of his mouth. The effort seemed to agonize him, the smile faded, and he shuddered. "Don't," she pleaded. "Please don't try to talk."

He mumbled, " 'S okay . . . really . . ." His breathing was weak and shallow. He coughed wetly, "I . . . don't mind. . . ." He smiled at her once more. His eyelids fluttered, closing.

She leaned over the edge of the tracks to shout down again. "I need help, dammit!" But by the time the deputies had scrambled to the top of the tracks to carry him down, Kenneth Bennett had died in Rachel's arms.

345

CHAPTER NINE

The sun was peeking from behind wispy clouds that marked the tail end of a thunderstorm that had passed through St. Louis shortly after dawn. The storm brought an end to a heat wave that had gripped the city for a week. The passing storm not only cooled temperatures, but it scrubbed clean the stagnant, hot air, leaving behind a gorgeous, unseasonably pleasant Midwestern summer morning that presaged the coming autumn.

While it was likely that none of them would have said so out loud, the mourners gathered at Ken Bennett's funeral were grateful for the cooler weather. The air at the cemetery was brisk and fresh smelling, tinged with the aroma of damp earth and recently mown grass. In fact, the only people at the grave site not secretly pleased about the storm were Rachel Siegel and Roy Rodgers. Their flight from San Jose the night before had been jostled by turbulence almost the entire way. And Rachel was not a good flier under the best of circumstances.

The burial service having concluded, the mourners were filing away, returning to their waiting cars. Bennett's casket rested on a hoist above an open grave, next to the grave of his late wife, Christina. As soon as the mourners had departed, the casket would be lowered into the ground and covered with the earth and sod that lay in a pile under a tarpaulin near the canvas tent where Bennett's relatives and friends had sat during the ceremony.

Finally just three mourners were left: Rachel and Roy, and Denise Bennett.

Rachel had been waiting for an opportunity to speak to Denise alone for some time. This was the first chance she'd had. Last night, by the time she and Roy had landed, gathered their luggage, picked up their rental car, and checked into their hotel, it was after ten P.M., too late for them to attend Bennett's wake. Earlier this morning, at the mortuary, Denise was never without some other person at her side, and Rachel hadn't been able to do more than say hello. There were too many people wanting to offer their condolences, to express sympathy over the loss of the last remaining member of Denise's immediate family.

Rachel had spoken to Denise several times over the past five days, starting last Thursday, when she took it upon herself to call with the news of her brother's death. When Denise drove to San Patricio that afternoon to make arrangements to have Bennett's body sent back to St. Louis, she ended up staying overnight with Rachel and Roy. On Friday Denise accompanied Bennett's body on the flight east. Rachel had telephoned her on Sunday at her brother's house. Their conversation had been brief, just long enough for Rachel to pass on the information that she and Roy would be arriving Monday evening, in time for Bennett's funeral on Tuesday.

Now Denise stood alongside her brother's casket, her head bowed. While Roy waited a few yards away, Rachel came up beside the other woman. Denise lifted her head to see Rachel, who hesitated for a moment before reaching out. They embraced each other. Then Denise pulled away to dab at the corners of her eyes with a handkerchief she had balled in her fist. She looked at Rachel gratefully. "I think it was really terrific of you and Roy to fly all the way back here," Denise said. "It means a lot to me."

"It's the least we could do," said Rachel.

Denise nodded. She looked away from Rachel to take in their surroundings: the sun and sky, the pastoral green of the cemetery park. "The weather's really nice today."

"It really is," agreed Rachel.

"Pretty atypical for August. Usually it's muggy and miserable, like it was over the weekend. That's one reason why I moved to California, 'cause I always hated the summers here. Winters, too, for that matter." She sighed. "Kenny always liked it, though. He always said he preferred to have the change of seasons. Personally, I think he was full of shit."

Denise looked to Rachel once more, her eyes misting over. "Do you mind walking me to my car?" She indicated the two workmen who were standing impatiently beside the canvas tent. "I think we're getting a hint that it's time to go."

Rachel and Roy accompanied Denise through rows of neatly spaced headstones to the asphalt drive where their vehicles were parked. The Ford Taurus that Roy and Rachel had rented was several hundred yards behind the limousine that had brought Denise. The limousine's driver saw them approaching and climbed out of the car, coming around the side to open the passenger door.

As they reached the limousine Rachel was saying to Denise, "I've got something for you. It must've been misplaced somehow, or else you'd have gotten it with the rest of Ken's things. They gave it to me yesterday morning to give to you, before we left for the airport."

. Rachel opened her purse and pulled out a buff-colored envelope. In the upper left corner was the logo of a San Patricio seaside motel. Denise's name had been scribbled on the front. There was a rust-colored smear marring the otherwise smooth, clean surface. The top of the envelope had been slit open. Rachel handed the envelope to Denise, who thumbed the slit and looked a question at Rachel.

"Somebody else did that," Rachel said. "One of the other investigators. Don't be mad. For all they knew, it could have been evidence."

Denise nodded, accepting the explanation. She opened the envelope and pulled out the sheaves of paper folded inside. She began to read.

As Denise scanned the pages, tears began to well in her eyes again. When she finished with the last page, she looked up at Rachel. "Have you read this?"

Rachel shook her head. "It wasn't addressed to me."

Denise handed over the letter. Rachel looked uncertain until Denise said, "It's all right. Go 'head."

Rachel read:

Dear Denise,
If you're reading this, then it's probably the case that something bad has happened to me. I've either been badly hurt or something worse.

349

Maybe the worst that can happen. That's a funny phrase, isn't it? "The worst that can happen." I don't think I really know what "the worst that can happen" is. Things haven't been going well for me these past few months, and every time something would happen, I'd think, "Well, that's the worst that could happen." But I'd end up being wrong, because then something else would happen that seemed worse than what happened before. It's been a tough year, let me tell you.

I'm back in San Patricio. That note I left you earlier tonight was a lie, but I wrote it so you wouldn't worry about where I was if I happened to be out too late. It's a moot point now, I suppose. The reason I'm here is because while I was going through some of your pictures, one of them gave me the clue I'd been looking for all along. No doubt you remember that whole escapade we had on our first time through San Patricio, and how I wanted to stay and help find whoever killed that little boy I tuned in to. No doubt you've also guessed that's why I came back here without telling you, because you were so dead-set against my helping out the first time. I came back the end of June, and I've spent the last five weeks trying to find this Pied Piper. I hadn't had any success (for a reason that I'll get to in a little bit), but when I saw your picture, it all of a sudden came to me who he was.

The killer's name is Joshua Wright, and he runs the roller-coaster ride at the San Patricio boardwalk. If something has happened to me and Wright hasn't been captured yet, you need to get this information to the San Patricio Sheriff's Department right away. If possible, you should give it to Rachel Siegel, the detective we met after I had my accident last May. She's the one who's worked hardest on this case, and she should be the one to get the credit for catching this guy. She's shown a lot of patience with me over the past month, and I owe her for that. Maybe this'll repay her a little. Hopefully, anyway.

The reason why I mention Rachel is because of what I did to her. You're not the only one I've lied to recently. The whole time Rachel and I were working together I led her on, letting her believe I still had my clairvoyant power. (I'm sure this is a shock to you, too.) The day that I wrecked the car, when I had the vision of that little boy, the concussion I got when I cracked my head must have reversed whatever it was that happened to me when I was a kid. That vision I had in the car was the last one I've had. My power's gone. I know it, because there's a hollowness inside me that I can feel. I wish I could describe it better, but I can't. All I know is, whatever it was that I had, it's gone. I am now, and probably will be for the rest of my life, a perfectly ordinary human being. You can't imagine how disappointing a thought that is. (Ha-ha!)

I'm joking, and I probably shouldn't be, I guess, since this is really pretty serious. I've spent the last month trying to play Sherlock Holmes and doing a lousy job of it. That's why I got so excited when I finally figured out who the Pied Piper was. It was just dumb luck. But then, what in my life hasn't been a matter of dumb luck, one way or another? Or anybody's life, for that matter?

Although another part of me sees something else at work here. Maybe some of us really are meant to do something. Maybe there really is some force running things, keeping everything in balance, keeping it all straight. Sometimes I wonder about that; I really do. I'll find out in a while, I suppose, since Joshua Wright is on his way to meet me right now. I'm writing this note to you for a couple of reasons. One is just to kill a little time before Wright gets here. The other is to tell you that I'm sorry I didn't trust you more, and I'm sorry that I hurt you by being that way. Now that I think about it, you've always been my favorite person in the world. I couldn't have asked for a better baby sister. I love you very, very much.

Be sure to give Clem a scratch behind the ears for me.

> Your big brother,
> Kenny

Rachel had to brush away a tear of her own before she handed the letter back to Denise. As Denise was putting the pages back into the envelope, Rachel said, "He really was a special person, wasn't he?"

Denise nodded. She slipped the letter into her purse, took a look around, then turned to Rachel. "How . . . ?" She paused, swallowing. "How long are you and Roy going to be in St. Louis?"

"Through the weekend," Rachel answered. "Neither one of us has ever been here before. We thought we might play tourist. You know—the Arch, the zoo, all that stuff. This is the second vacation we've had without our kids this year. I'm starting to enjoy the novelty of it."

Denise said, "I'll be around till Friday. If you want to get together and have dinner or something, call me."

"We will," promised Rachel.

The women embraced once more. Denise climbed into the limousine. The driver closed her door, gave a farewell salute to Rachel and Roy, then trotted around to take his place behind the wheel.

As Denise's limousine rolled away, Roy came up behind Rachel, slipped an arm around her, and pulled her close to him. "You okay?" he asked.

She nodded. "Did you want to know what was in Ken's letter?"

"I figure you'll tell me sooner or later."

She looked at him with mock disdain. "You must think you know me pretty well."

As Roy guided her toward their car, he was saying, "Nice day, isn't it? Here I kept thinking about how hot and humid it was supposed to be in this part of the country, when it's really not like that at all. It's nice."

"Don't get any ideas," Rachel cautioned. "Denise says this weather's just a fluke."

"In other words, it may be nice today, but I wouldn't want to live here?"

"Exactly."

They'd reached their car. Roy opened the passenger-side door for Rachel and said, "Weren't you the one who spent the whole flight cross-country bitching about leaving the Sheriff's Department and maybe getting out of San Patricio altogether? We could make a lot of money selling the house back there, you know. Property values are way lower here.

I checked. Imagine what we could buy with that much money."

"Just because I'm thinking about leaving San Patricio," Rachel said, "doesn't mean I want to move to St. Louis. I'm not exactly the Midwestern type."

Roy shrugged and closed her door. He crossed around the front of the car, opened the driver side door, and climbed in. As he was pulling the door closed, he said to Rachel, "So tell me what was in Ken's letter." Then he started the car and drove away.

EAST

OF THE

ARCH

ROBERT J. RANDISI

Joe Keough's new job as "Top Cop" for the mayor of St. Louis has him involved in more political functions than investigations. But all that changes when the bodies of pregnant women are discovered on the Illinois side of the Mississippi. Suddenly Keough finds himself on the trail of a serial killer more grotesque than anything he's seen before.

When the offer to join a special statewide serial killer squad comes his way, Keough has to make a decision that could change his personal and professional life forever. But through it all he continues to work frantically, battling the clock to find the perpetrator of these crimes before another young woman and her unborn baby are killed.

CHINA CARD

THOMAS BLOOD

With the Russian economy in a shambles, and the hard-line leaders in power, renegade KGB operatives an ultra-secret document detailing the exact location of over one hundred tactical nuclear weapons secretly placed in the U.S. during the height of the Cold War. Thousands of miles away, in Washington, D. C., a young prostitute is found brutally murdered in a luxury hotel. The only clue—a single cufflink bearing the seal of the President. These seemingly unrelated events will soon reveal a twisting trail of conspiracy and espionage, power-brokers and assassins. It's a trail that leads from mainland China to the seamy underbelly of the Washington power-structure . . . to the Oval Office itself.

__4782-9 $5.99 US/$6.99 CAN

An Execution of Honor
Thomas L. Muldoon

They were a Marine Force Recon unit under the CIA's control, directed to maintain the power of a Latin American dictator, despite his involvement in the drug trade and a partnership with Fidel Castro. When rebel forces drove the dictator into the jungles, the unit led the holding action while his army was evacuated. But before he left, he tortured and killed two of the Marines. Now the unit wants justice—but Washington wants to return the dictator to power. So the surviving Force Recon unit members set out on their own to make the dictator pay. Both the United States and Cuba want the surviving unit members stopped at all costs. But who will be able to stop an elite group of Marines trained to be the most effective warriors alive?

- -

CRISIS POINT
KEN CURRIE

It doesn't look good. The last message Washington receives from the U.S. ship *Regulus* reports an unidentified aircraft approaching with unclear intentions. Then nothing. Another ship is sent to investigate, but all the crew finds is wreckage floating in the Persian Gulf. Suspicions immediately turn to a terrorist attack. The military and the intelligence community scramble for answers, but they find only more questions. From the Middle East to Europe, from Washington conference rooms to the Oval Office, global tensions are quickly rising, and all hell will break out when they reach the crisis point.

JIM DeFELICE
COYOTE BIRD

The president is worried—with good cause. Two of America's spy planes have disappeared. Soon he—and the nation—will face a threat more dangerous than any since the height of the Cold War. A secretly remilitarized Japan is plotting to bring the most powerful country on Earth to its knees, aided by a computer-assisted aircraft with terrifying capabilities. But the U.S. has a weapon of its own in the air—the Coyote, a combat super-plane so advanced its creators believe it's invincible. Air Force top gun Lt. Colonel Tom Wright is prepared to fly the Coyote into battle for his country—and his life—against all that Japan can throw at him. And the result will prove to be the turning point in the war of the skies.

__4831-0 $5.99 US/$6.99 CAN